'TIS THE SEASON TO MURDER

I headed for the door, hoping to call Robert back, or at least ask him why he was leaving. I get that he was upset about Santa hitting on his newest girlfriend, but was it worth throwing away his role in the play? I had no doubts Lawrence would fire him on the spot the moment he realized what was happening.

I pushed open the door and flinched against the blast of cold air that rushed inside. A car—Robert's I imagined—fishtailed as it sped out of the lot and down the street. I was already too late.

A scream tore through the building behind me then, causing me to jump. I spun and saw the flood of people heading to the back, toward where the scream had originated. Not to be left behind, I hurried to catch up with Prudence.

"What happened?" I asked her.

"I don't know."

Just as we reached the dressing rooms, one of the female crew members staggered out of the men's side, hand over her mouth. She was only able to point back into the room, before she rushed away, tears streaming down her face.

Prudence and I looked at each other, and then started forward as one, most of the rest of the cast following at our heels . . .

Books by Alex Erickson

DEATH BY COFFEE

DEATH BY TEA

DEATH BY PUMPKIN SPICE

DEATH BY VANILLA LATTE

DEATH BY EGGNOG

Published by Kensington Publishing Corporation

Death by Eggnog

Alex Erickson

KENSINGTON PUBLISHING CORP.
http://www.kensingtonbooks.com

KENSINGTON BOOKS are published by

Kensington Publishing Corp.
119 West 40th Street
New York, NY 10018

Copyright © 2017 by Eric S. Moore

All Kensington Titles, Imprints, and Distributed Lines are available at special quantity discounts for bulk purchases for sales promotions, premiums, fund-raising, and educational or institutional use. Special book excerpts or customized printings can also be created to fit specific needs. For details, write or phone the office of the Kensington special sales manager: Kensington Publishing Corp., 119 West 40th Street, New York, NY 10018, attn: Special Sales Department, Phone: 1-800-221-2647.

Kensington and the K logo Reg. U.S. Pat & TM Off.

ISBN-13: 978-1-4967-0887-8
ISBN-10: 1-4967-0887-3
First Kensington Mass Market Edition: October 2017

eISBN-13: 978-1-4967-0888-5
eISBN-10: 1-4967-0888-1
First Kensington Electronic Edition: October 2017

10 9 8 7 6 5 4 3 2 1

Printed in the United States of America

1

It lurked beneath the rectangle of brightly colored paper. A tail swished back and forth, causing a faint crinkling sound. Though I couldn't see them, I knew there to be two wide, yellow eyes peering out at me from beneath the nearest edge. The hairs on the back of my neck rose as the entire paper vibrated.

"Don't you even think about it," I said, hiding the ribbon behind my back. It was to be the finishing touch on my gift for Dad, though a part of me knew it was already a loss. "I knew I should have locked you up."

Misfit's tail swished once more, and then went still.

I held my breath, nervous anticipation causing my stomach to flip uneasily.

And then he attacked.

I screamed as the orange ball of fur tore from beneath the wrapping paper, eyes intent on the edge of ribbon he could just barely see from around me. Self-preservation caused me to reflexively toss the ribbon across the room, knowing if I didn't, I might lose a hand or two.

Misfit veered off course, eyes completely black, and snagged it from the air. He rolled once with it, slammed into the couch, and then tore out of the living room, toward the bedroom, ears pinned back, ribbon clamped firmly between his teeth. I'd have to retrieve it from him before he swallowed it, but for now, he could have it.

I rose and took a trembling breath before breaking into a smile. As any cat owner knows, there's nothing more terrifying than a kitty in full-on psycho play mode—as well as nothing cuter. My admittedly soft flesh was no match for his needlelike claws and pointy teeth, which accounted for the fear. If I hadn't been so focused on wrapping, I might have spent a few minutes playing with him. Perhaps I would once I finished.

My phone rang as I was about to start cleaning up, causing me to jump. I snatched the phone off the floor where it sat beside a pair of gifts I'd wrapped for Misfit before he realized what I was doing. Dad's gift was the only one that remained, but at least it was wrapped. I planned on doing the rest of my shopping later, before my flight back home to Pine Hills from California.

A quick glance at the screen told me it was my dad, James Hancock, calling. I grinned and answered with a chirpy, "Hello!"

"Hi, Buttercup."

There was a hesitation to his voice, which I ignored as I picked up the extra wrapping paper bits I'd cut away. "I'm just finishing up with my gift wrapping and then I'll be all packed. Misfit is making it harder than it should be." I laughed. "I can't wait to see you."

There was a long pause as he cleared his throat.

"So, about that . . ." This time he coughed. "I was thinking that maybe you could spend this Christmas with Will. In Pine Hills."

I blinked, confused. "But we always do Christmas at your house."

"I know, but, well . . ." He sucked in a deep breath and let it out. "Something has come up."

"Is everything okay? You're not sick, are you?" I felt faint. If Dad was sick, I needed to get out there! "I can fly out tonight," I said, determined. "I'm sure I can change my flight."

"No, no, it's nothing like that." Dad chuckled, though it didn't set my mind at ease. He was all alone in California, Mom having died years ago. And since I moved away, he had no remaining family to spend the holidays with. "It's just . . ."

I waited, but he didn't continue. My mind conjured all sorts of horrible images better suited to Halloween than Christmas. Could he be calling me from a hospital bed? Or did the house burn down thanks to a freak electrical accident when he'd plugged in the tree? There might be nothing left to go home to!

I couldn't take his silence any longer. "What's going on?" I asked, voice pitched a few octaves higher than normal in my worry.

Dad sighed. "Remember when I told you I was thinking of dating again?"

I frowned. That wasn't what I'd expected him to say. "Yeah?"

"Well, there's this woman. Laura." He sounded a lot like I did every time I mentioned Will: sort of dreamy, and a little goofy. "She asked me to spend Christmas with her this year. She's going to the Swiss Alps, and well . . . I'd like to go."

My mind was still trying to catch up with the fact Dad had started seeing someone, so it took me a few long seconds to respond. I mean, I knew he was looking to date again, but some part of me never thought he'd actually do it.

"Laura?" was all I could think of to say.

"She's great." I could hear the smile in his voice. "She likes to travel, hence the Alps. She says it's perfectly safe. We'll be staying in a cabin, not climbing the mountains or adventure seeking. No camping in the cold for these old bones." He laughed, though he still sounded nervous.

"You want to go to the Alps?" I asked, still a few beats behind.

"If you think it's a bad idea, Buttercup, I can cancel." He didn't sound like he wanted to, but he'd always been willing to do anything I asked to make me happy. This was no exception.

Which, of course, made me feel like a royal jerk for sounding as if I might disapprove of his date, even a little. "I think it's a great idea," I said. I might have forced the cheer a bit, but that didn't mean I wasn't happy for him. I was thrilled he was finally moving on with his life. I was just bummed I wouldn't get to see him this holiday season. "You caught me off guard, is all."

"I just started seeing her recently," he said. "I know it's short notice. We leave late tonight, if you can believe it. I think she waited because she didn't think I'd want to go." A pause before, "If you want, I could ask her if it would be all right to invite you along. I'm sure Laura would be okay with it."

"No, that's not necessary. You two should have fun together. I can stay here and spend Christmas with

Will. Besides, I think he was a little upset I'd planned on leaving, so it works out."

"Are you sure?" Dad sounded both pleased and a little heartbroken, which made me feel better about my own feelings. I wasn't the only one who was going to have to get used to things being different this year.

"I'm sure." A thump in my bedroom reminded me Misfit had a piece of ribbon. "I'd better go. Cat's causing some trouble. Need to rein him in before I head in to work."

"I'll talk to you later, Buttercup. And . . . thanks."

"Have fun," I said and hung up, feeling a smidge melancholy. I liked the idea of spending Christmas with Will, but I'd miss Dad something fierce. I was afraid it just wouldn't be the same without him.

I hurried into the bedroom to find Misfit in the corner, ribbon wrapped around him like he was a fuzzy, wiggly gift. He'd somehow gotten tangled in it to the point where he couldn't get out. He glared at me as if it was all my fault.

"That's what you get," I told him as I untangled him. He made a swat at the ribbon as I pulled him free. I yanked it back and stuffed it into my pocket where he couldn't reach. "Looks like we're going to spend Christmas together this year." Normally, Vicki watched him while I was gone. He'd stay with her and his littermate, Trouble. From what Vicki tells me, they both manage to live up to their namesakes.

I returned to the living room and cleaned up before Misfit found something else to run off with. I put all three gifts into the spare bedroom, closing the door behind me so Misfit wouldn't get in and unwrap them early. I'd have to mail Dad's gift to him at some point, but that could wait.

Once everything was packed up, I pulled on my coat, grabbed my purse and keys, and then headed out the door, to my car.

Winter was here, but had yet to dump snow on us. There'd been a light dusting a few days ago, but it was already long gone. I hadn't paid any attention to the weather reports to know if a storm was coming since I hadn't planned on being in town to see it. As I got into my car, I mentally reminded myself to check the weather at the same time I canceled my flight.

My Focus coughed a few times before starting. I gently stroked the dash, murmuring thanks as it started to warm. I so didn't need to be car shopping this time of the year, not with all the gifts I still needed to buy. I'd planned on shopping for Vicki, Will, and the rest of my friends while in California. I could get things there I wouldn't be able to find here. I added a shopping trip to my list of things I needed to do as I fished out my phone and called Will.

"Hi, Krissy," he said by way of answer. "You caught me just in time. I'm about to head back in to work."

I glanced at the dashboard clock and noted it was a lot closer to noon than expected. I wasn't going to be late to work, but I'd be cutting it close.

"I won't keep you," I said. I didn't like driving and talking, but wanted to call him now before he made plans. "I wanted to let you know that it looks like I'll be in town this year for Christmas."

"I thought you were flying back home?"

"Dad's got a date," I said, still not quite believing it. "I'm staying here. If you have time, I would love to get together for Christmas. I know you might have already made plans, but if you could slip me in . . ."

There was a pause and the rising sound of voices in the background. "I didn't really think much about it," Will said. "I'd love to have you over. We can solidify our plans later. I really need to go."

"Okay, that's fine. I'll talk to you later."

I hung up, feeling only a little better. He had sounded distracted, but I chalked it up to the time of year. People did dumb things in the cold, and since Will Foster was a doctor, it was his job to fix the results. His waiting room was probably full of people who'd decided to take a dip in an icy pond, or slipped on some ice while walking to their car. Hopefully, his job wouldn't get in the way of our Christmas together. I was hoping we could make it special this year, now that I was going to get to spend time with him.

I parked a few blocks from Death by Coffee, the bookstore café I co-owned with my best friend Vicki Patterson. I made sure I was suitably bundled, and then hurried down the sidewalk to the store. The air temperature wasn't horrible, but the wind was bitingly cold. It stung my eyes and my nose and ears were already throbbing. It would be a great day for coffee—if you were willing to brave the cold to pick some up.

Warm, coffee-scented air blasted into me as soon as I opened the door. I all but floated behind the counter, shedding my coat along the way, to the pots. Half the seats were taken by customers whose hands were wrapped tightly around their hot drinks. A few more were browsing the bookshelves upstairs. I poured myself a cup of eggnog flavored coffee, and instead of adding my usual chocolate chip cookie, I used the house made eggnog creamer instead. I took a sip, and just about melted into the floor.

"How's business today?" I asked as Vicki came out of the back room, a freshly made batch of eggnog in hand.

"Good," she said, cheerily. "Both the eggnog and flavored coffees are a hit." We'd just started selling them that very day. "I can hardly keep up with the demand."

I beamed in pleasure. It had been my idea to go the eggnog route this year, including regular old eggnog to our menu for the holiday season. Last year, we'd tried spiced coffees and teas. While they sold okay, they weren't as popular as we'd hoped they'd be.

"How does it feel to be on your last day of work for the year?" she asked, leaning against the counter. She didn't mean to make it look seductive, but somehow, it did. Vicki was just one of those people who brightened up any room, no matter the circumstances.

"About that," I said, glancing up the stairs to where Jeff Braun, one of our employees, was ringing up a book sale. "I'm not going."

"Did something happen?"

"No. Well, yeah, kind of." I shrugged. "Dad has a date. I'm staying here."

"Oh!" Vicki's eyes lit up like I'd just told her she'd won the lottery. "What do you know about his date?"

Another shrug. "Her name is Laura and she likes to travel. They're going to the Swiss Alps."

"Really?" Vicki got a far-off look in her eye. "That sounds awesome."

"I'm sure it will be," I said, some of the melancholy slipping back into my voice. "But it does mean

I'm going to be in Pine Hills this year, so if you want to rework the schedule to fit me in, I'm willing."

Vicki came back to the here and now with a shake of her head. "No, you should take the time off. Even though you aren't leaving town, you could use the break."

"It's going to be weeks!" I normally spent a little over two weeks in California. It was like a mini vacation, one I desperately needed at the end of a long year. "I'll just be sitting around my house, so it would be no big deal," I said, though I was hoping I'd be doing a lot more than that. It all depended on Will's work schedule and how much time he'd be able to wiggle me in for. Owning his own practice took a lot of him, more than I was sometimes comfortable with.

I sighed and wondered how best to spend our newfound time together. Maybe next year Will and I could take a trip, see the world. I'd seen a few of the fifty states, but had yet to travel anywhere outside them.

But this year . . . I was already envisioning candlelight dinners and hot bubble baths.

Vicki was looking at me with a huge smile on her face as I came back to the present.

"What?" I asked.

"That look on your face." She laughed a goodnatured laugh. "You were practically swooning where you stood."

"I was not!" I blushed, covering it up by gulping some coffee. "I was just thinking."

"It's okay. I have some pretty steamy plans this year, too." She winked at me and then floated to the register to take an order.

Thoroughly embarrassed, I carried my coat and

coffee into the back room. I flung on an apron, fanned myself off (what can I say? It was a pretty steamy fantasy), and then headed out front to begin the long day at work.

Or at least I would have, but I was verbally assaulted the moment I stepped behind the counter.

"It's terrible!" Rita Jablonski wailed, hurrying over to me. "It's a travesty!"

Used to her overstating pretty much everything, I didn't drop into an immediate panic. The town gossip had a tendency to overreact. I've done a good job of late taking it in stride and not getting annoyed with her like I used to. It was just one of Rita's quirks.

"What happened?" I asked as I checked the cookie case to find it looking a little spare.

"Mandy is sick and I don't know what we're going to do! There's only two weeks until the big day and now with her out of commission, we're one short!"

I tried to follow, but she was being so vague, I could only ask, "Mandy?"

"Mandy Ortega. It's her diet, I tell you. She eats all the wrong things and it's impacted her immune system to the point that any bit of stress and she comes down sick. I knew when she was cast it was a bad idea."

A lightbulb went off in my head. "She's in a play?"

"Of course she is," Rita said with a dismissive wave of her hand. "We have it every year, dear." She stepped back and looked me up and down. "You know, you could probably fit into her costume."

This time, instead of a lightbulb, alarm bells were going off. "No, I don't think so."

But it was already too late. Rita was on a roll and there was nothing that would stop her. "She was an elf in our Christmas production," she said, speaking right over me. "Not a big role, mind you. You wouldn't have to learn many lines at all. And every time you do speak, it will be a group effort, so if you flub it, it won't be that big of a deal."

"I really don't think I . . ."

"The costume *should* fit. Your diet doesn't seem to be much better than Mandy's, so there's a risk there."

"Hey!"

"There's only two weeks until the show," she went on, oblivious. "Practices have ramped up, so there is one every night, right up until show night. That shouldn't be too much of an issue for you."

"Rita, I don't know anything about acting in a play."

"If there was someone else, you can bet I'd ask them, but since there isn't . . ." She shrugged as if saying it was out of her hands.

"What about Vicki?" I asked, grabbing hold of her as she came down the stairs. "She's done plays before. She'd know what to do."

Rita took one look at Vicki and laughed. "Weren't you listening? We only have one spare costume. There's no time to have another made and you're the perfect size! She'd practically swim in Mandy's getup."

I knew I should have taken it as an insult, especially since Rita weighed more than me, but I was too panicked to care.

"But . . ."

"You should do it, Krissy," Vicki said. "It would be a great experience."

Gee, thanks, I thought. Betrayed by my best friend.

"Practices start at six at the community theatre. I'll let Lawrence know you'll be coming."

And with that, she spun away, leaving me gaping after her.

"It'll be fun," Vicki said before she, too, left me standing there, feeling as if I'd been bull-rushed.

"Fun," I echoed. Somehow, I seriously doubted it.

2

The Pine Hills community theatre sat in the middle of downtown, not far from the church where the writers' group holds their meetings, and only a few blocks away from Death by Coffee. It's a small brick building, old, and looked a little worse for wear. I'd only ever been inside for a play once, and found the building to be showing its age then. It's only gotten worse since.

I pulled into the lot knowing full well I should have called Rita and told her I wouldn't take part in the production. I knew nothing about acting, and with so little time to prepare, it was unlikely I'd get much of a chance to learn on the job. I didn't even go to the school plays in high school: neither as an actress nor in the audience. And while I saw many of Vicki's productions back home, those were on a much larger scale than anything Pine Hills would ever produce.

But what else was I going to do this Christmas? I didn't love shopping, especially when everyone was running around, looking for that perfect gift, barreling over anyone who gets in their way. And while I love *A Christmas Story* as much as the next person, I could only watch it so many times before going mentally numb.

There were only a couple of other cars in the lot, which was expected. Since tonight was my first practice, I wanted to show up early and introduce myself. Vicki had told me to leave work early since Death by Coffee had slowed thanks to the dropping temperatures. No one wanted to be out on a night like this, yet here I was.

I hurried from my car to a side door marked "Cast Entrance." Feeling like a fraud, I slipped inside and found myself in a surprisingly tidy space. I'd figured I'd find props laying everywhere, costumes draped over boxes, and general disarray. Instead, I found a few props laying on a table, and a mostly clean and safe space. There was old paint on the floor, telling of many nights painting set pieces, but otherwise, it wasn't filthy anywhere but near the door where everyone stamped off their shoes.

"Who are you?" A round-faced elf approached. She stood five-foot at best, and was stocky, though it looked to be genetics, rather than her diet. She appeared to be in her mid-twenties, and was flanked by two other elves, one male, one female.

"Hi, I'm Krissy Hancock," I said, taking in their green outfits, pointy ears, and shoes. "Rita Jablonski asked me to fill in for Mandy."

"Of course she did," the lead elf said with a roll of her eyes. "I'm Asia. That's Greg." She jerked a thumb toward the male of the two. "And that's Prairie." This time to the female, who looked eerily similar to Greg. *Twins?*

"Prairie?" I asked.

"That's my name," the girl in question said. Like Asia, I put her age somewhere in her early to mid-twenties. She looked mildly disinterested, as if talking with me was the lowlight of her day.

Greg flashed a smile Prairie's way before rolling his eyes at me. Clearly, I didn't impress either of them.

"Does Lawrence know you're here?" Asia asked.

"Not yet. You're the first people I've seen."

She smiled. "Well, I suggest finding Lawrence as soon as possible. He'll want to see you before committing you to the part." She looked me up and down, her smile growing strained. "See you later."

Asia spun, as did her two friends, and headed for a hallway in the back.

I decided it best not to follow their lead and instead headed for the stage. A man dressed in a shirt that read CREW across the back was kneeling on the far end, looking harried. He was thirty-something and wore glasses. He looked up as I passed, gave me a quick smile, and then went back to working on whatever it was he was doing. It looked like he was putting tape on the stage, but for what reason, I couldn't guess.

The curtains were open, so I climbed the stairs and stepped through them to look out over what I thought would be an empty theatre, only to find a pair of seats occupied. It appeared as if Mrs. Claus was cheating on her jolly husband with an elf. The lip lock lasted for a good couple of seconds before the two came up for air. When they did, I just about died of shock.

"Robert?"

He jumped like I'd screamed it. Maybe I did. I was completely floored seeing my ex-boyfriend here in an actual theatre. He'd never gone with me to one of Vicki's plays, and any time I asked him to, he'd come up with some lame excuse, as if he was allergic to the very idea of going to a play. But what was most shocking now was he wasn't just visiting, but was dressed as if he had an actual part in the production.

I wasn't surprised to find him all over another woman, however. If you knew Robert Dunhill, then you knew it was pretty much his natural state. He'd cheated on me back before I'd moved to Pine Hills, and then moved here a few months later, thinking we'd get back together. Of course, when he did try to reconcile with me, he did it while he was on a date with another woman. The man couldn't seem to keep his paws to himself, and I hoped the girl he was with knew what she was getting herself into.

"Krissy?" Robert stood, looked around like he expected someone to tell him this was some sort of joke, before asking, "What are you doing here?"

"Me? I could ask you the same thing!" I was trying hard not to be angry, but Robert had a way of getting under my skin. He also had a way of popping up where I didn't want him, often appearing only to try to lure me back into his life. If he was thinking this was going to work this time, he had another think coming. "I can't believe you'd do this!"

He turned to Mrs. Claus, who was looking suitably confused and embarrassed. I didn't recognize her, so she wasn't the last random woman I'd seen him with. What was her name? Tiffany, I think. He whispered something into not-Tiffany's ear, and at her nod, he jumped up onto the stage with me. "I thought you didn't want to have anything to do with me," he said.

"I don't. You got a part in this play just so you could stalk me," I accused.

"I wouldn't do such a thing," he said, keeping his voice down so Mrs. Claus couldn't hear. "You're the one who's stalking me."

"What?" I very nearly laughed. "Rita asked me to fill in for someone. I didn't even know there was going to be a play until this afternoon. How did you find out?"

He winced. "She asked you to step in? She shouldn't have done that." He sighed. "But what's done is done, I guess. And if you must know, I tried out for my part from the beginning." He glanced back at where Mrs. Claus still sat, fixing her makeup, and pretending like she wasn't watching our every move. "Trisha thought it would be fun if we did it together."

"Trisha?" I asked, my mind trying to play catch-up. Seeing him here had really knocked me for a loop.

"Yeah." Robert grinned. "She's great. She's into all sorts of nerdy stuff like theatre, but I kind of dig it. She's the one who convinced me to try out, and, well . . ." He spread his arms to show me his outfit. "I got it."

Robert. In a play. I wasn't shocked he did it for a girl, but the simple fact he'd actually done something for someone else was stunning. Then again, Trisha, while dressed as Mrs. Claus, looked as if she had yet to see thirty, and was thin, just like Robert liked them. Her hair was hidden by a white wig, but something about her told me her real hair was likely blond. She was just the sort of girl he'd go for.

"I'm turning over a new leaf," he went on, that dopey grin still on his face. "I'm trying real hard not to screw things up this time." He looked down at his feet. "Sorry for all the, you know, stuff I've done."

"I . . ." I didn't know what to say. He'd apologized before, but it had never been genuine until this very moment. There were so many strange things happening to me today, I was beginning to wonder if I'd somehow slipped into an episode of *The Twilight Zone*.

"There you are!" I turned to find Rita hurrying over. "What are you doing out here?" she scolded. "You need to get in the back and try on the costume."

"You'd better go," Robert said. "I'll, uh . . ." He licked his lips, glanced at Trisha, before whispering, "I'll see you later."

Rita grabbed me by the arm and steered me away from the clearly flustered Robert. While I'd been talking to Robert, more cast and crew had shown and were busy getting ready. The back was buzzing with activity and laughter. I received quite a few curious looks, many accompanied by looks of sympathy since Rita was practically manhandling me on our way to the back.

We were near the hallway Asia and her crew had vanished down when a loud crash caused both of us to jump and someone else to scream. I turned to see a man in a red suit point at the crew member I'd seen kneeling on the stage earlier. Before I could see what the commotion was about, Rita urged me down the hall to a dressing room marked WOMEN. She shoved me inside.

"Here," she said, yanking a costume from a hanger. "She left it here last night when she dropped out. It should be clean enough."

"Should be?" I asked, skeptically.

"Just put it on!" She spun on her heel and hurried out of the room, leaving me alone.

I seriously considered putting the costume back and walking out. Not only had the entire thing been sprung on me at Death by Coffee, but now I had to deal with Robert. While he seemed to be into his new fling and was acting contrite, I had no illusions he wouldn't do his best to make my life unpleasant.

Or maybe he was honestly trying to turn over a new leaf, like he said. Stranger things have happened, and I supposed I owed it to him to at least give him the benefit of the doubt.

Again, I thought bitterly as I pulled on Mandy's costume. It was baggy all around, telling me Mandy wasn't a small girl. I was a little irked Rita thought the costume would fit. Sure, I could stand to lose some weight, but the elf costume looked like it would have fit Rita better than it would have me.

I grouched under my breath as I pulled on the shoes—which went over my own shoes and had bells on the front and back—and then headed out to join the rest of the cast.

People were milling around everywhere by now. And of course, Rita was nowhere in sight. A hint of panic flared through me as I looked for her, or at least, a familiar face that wasn't Robert's. I caught a few snickers when I stepped out of the dressing room, thanks to my too large outfit, but I ignored them. I shifted uncomfortably from foot to foot near the back wall, and was thinking of making a break for it, when a woman who looked more the part of Mrs. Claus than an elf—though she was dressed as the latter—came up to me.

"Are you replacing Mandy?" she asked, kindly.

"I am," I said. "Krissy Hancock." I held out a hand.

She shook. Her hands were small and bony, but held strength. "Prudence Shilling. I've been a part of the community theatre here since the place was built." She beamed with pride.

"I'm new," I admitted. "I've never actually acted on stage before, so I'm a bit terrified." Not to mention overwhelmed.

"I'm sure you'll do fine."

I wasn't so sure about that, but smiled anyway. "Do you know where Rita went? She told me to get changed, and I expected her to wait out here for me, but I can't seem to find her."

Prudence grunted a laugh. "Lawrence is here now, so she's probably out front. He doesn't like having anyone not affiliated with the production backstage during practices."

"Wait. She isn't a part of the play?"

"No, she isn't." Prudence's smile was somehow pitying. "She thinks she is and gets in the way quite often, but her heart is in the right place."

I so wanted to strangle her. The only reason I was here was because I'd thought Rita had needed me. If she wanted to be involved in the play so badly, she could have taken Mandy's place instead of wrangling me into it.

"I didn't do it!" I turned to find the crewman I'd noted earlier talking to someone I couldn't see past the stage. That someone yelled something I couldn't make out, causing the crewman's shoulders to slump in defeat.

Prudence tsked as Santa crossed the stage, grinning. "I still can't believe Lawrence hired him."

"Who? The crewman?"

"No, *him.*" She nodded toward Mr. Claus, who'd left the stage and had joined Mrs. Claus, who was currently *not* making out with my ex. Santa looked to be in his mid-fifties, which stood in stark contrast to what was supposed to be his wife. He said something to her, then leaned forward and gave her a quick smack on the butt. Her eyes just about bugged out of her head as she hurried away, rubbing at her bruised posterior. She rushed straight for Robert, who was in the process of making a beeline for Santa. She stopped him with a hand on his chest and they both turned away.

"The man is a letch if I've ever seen one," Prudence said. "Since we've started, he's made himself a menace to all the women, me included." She shuddered.

Santa chuckled and turned away from where Trisha and Robert had gone, only to find himself looking at me. He winked and shot a finger gun at me as if I was next, before he walked to the back.

"Everyone! I need everyone!" The call came from the front of the stage.

Prudence sighed. "His Lord Highness awaits," she said with a mock bow.

I followed her to the stage, making sure to bring up the rear. Robert had his arm around Trisha, who looked both embarrassed and angry. I would be too if Santa had spanked me in front of everyone. As I watched, another elf—this one a young stud of a man with a square jaw and smoldering good looks—said something to Trisha, which caused her to blush, and made Robert scowl. Before anything more could happen, a chubby man with a piercingly shrill voice raised his hands and shouted.

"Quiet down!"

Everyone stopped shuffling and whispering immediately.

"I've been informed we have a new cast member tonight," the man I took to be the director, Lawrence, said. He flashed a quick, annoyed look toward Rita, who was sitting in the back row. "Please step forward if you're here."

Prudence nudged me when I didn't move right away. Feeling all eyes on me, I slunk forward, to the front of the stage, feeling especially self-conscious in my oversized elf outfit.

Lawrence sighed, as if disappointed. "I suppose you'll have to do on such short notice. Leave your costume here tonight and I'll have someone take it in a bit." He eyed me a moment longer before barking, "Name?"

"Krissy Hancock," I replied, automatically. He had one of those commanding voices that made you jump the moment you were spoken to.

"Fine. You can step back."

I hurried back to my spot beside Prudence. She squeezed my arm in comfort and winked. It made me feel a little better to know I had at least one ally in this.

"Before we begin tonight, I'd—"

The theatre doors slammed open and a very round man with a long white beard entered. He staggered a few steps and pointed at the Santa on the stage. "You don't deserve to wear the red!" His cheeks were rosy, but I had a feeling it had more to do with drink than any sort of good, jolly nature.

"Oh, dear," Prudence said with a sad shake of her head.

"Who's that?" I asked as the man staggered forward a few more steps before leaning heavily on a chair.

"Randy Winter," she said. "He was Santa in the last dozen or so Christmas productions here, as well as all over town for as long as anyone can remember."

"I want my job back!" Randy slurred, now pointing at Lawrence. "I didn't do nothing wrong." He hiccoughed.

"He was fired for drinking on the job," Prudence added, though at this point, I think it was pretty obvious.

"Someone get him out of here," Lawrence said. "Dean!" He pointed at the crewman I'd noted earlier. "Weren't you supposed to make sure the door was locked?"

"I did, I swear!"

"Apparently, you didn't." Lawrence heaved a dramatic sigh. "You can escort Randy off the premises since you clearly can't do anything else right."

"But . . ." Dean trailed off, his entire demeanor tensing and then releasing as he slunk down the aisle toward the irate former Santa.

Someone snorted a laugh. When I looked, our current Santa was grinning ear to ear, as if watching the display was the highlight of his day. Already, I wasn't liking the man all that much. He didn't exactly fill me with holiday spirit.

In an embarrassing display, the drunken man tried to slap Dean's hands away, but kept missing, until he finally sagged in defeat. Dean took him by the arm and led him slowly out the doors, and presumably outside.

I felt bad for Randy. If he'd been Santa all these

years, only to be replaced, it had to be hard on him. I knew how dedicated actors could be. It probably felt like losing a part of himself not being up here now.

A moment later, the doors were closed and Dean double-checked the lock before hurrying back to his spot at the side of the stage. Lawrence glared at him the entire way, jaw clenched, as if he was fighting the urge not to scream at him more than he already had. He stared at him for a good thirty seconds more before turning back to the assembled cast.

"Now then." He sucked in a calming breath and let it out slowly. "Time is short and we've already had enough delays. Everyone take your places and let's get started. We'll begin from the top." He turned and looked up toward a sound booth where two people—a young man and a woman—were watching. Both were wearing crew shirts, like Dean. "Cue up the music!"

Panic flared through me then as everyone on stage started moving. "I wasn't given a script," I said, looking to Prudence for help.

She took me by the arm and gently led me to one side of the stage. Thankfully, Robert was on the far side, though he did keep looking over at me.

"Follow my lead," she said. "You ever do much dancing?"

"Dancing?" I squeaked as the music started up. Instead of it only being a lead in to a monologue, the cast started moving and singing along.

"Didn't Rita tell you?" Prudence asked as she spun in a circle. Her eyes glimmered with joy, body moving like she was fifty years younger. "This production is a musical!"

3

Muted sunlight shone in through my window, streaking across my bed and face. I threw an arm over my eyes and groaned, wishing the morning had never come.

"I think this is it," I said. "I'm a goner."

Misfit stared at me from his perch on my dresser. He'd started knocking things off it an hour ago, yet I'd made no progress in getting out of bed to feed him. I was normally up long before now, and if I didn't get up soon, he'd be on the bed, pawing at my face in an effort to rouse me from the dead.

Every part of my body ached. I was sore in places I never thought could hurt. I'd somehow made it through practice without making a complete fool out of myself. I think Prudence had more to do with that than any fortitude of my own. The twisting and gyrating had been far more than my poor out-of-shape body could handle. I didn't even want to talk about my tortured attempts at singing.

And I was supposed to do it all again that very night.

Another groan escaped me as a couple of coins hit the floor. Misfit's stare became aggressive, ears pinned back, as he swatted at my jewelry box.

"Okay, okay. I'm coming," I muttered, forcing my legs over the edge of the bed. "You're cleaning that up, you know." I gestured vaguely at the pile of loose change and other small items on the floor. He'd yet to work his way up to the big stuff, like my alarm, telling me he wasn't as hungry as he was making it seem.

I limped my way to the kitchen to feed the orange furball, though what he deserved was to be locked out of the bedroom while I stood, soaking in a hot shower. He glared at me the entire way, acting as if I hadn't fed him in a week. Sure, I might not have given him much more than a handful of dry before collapsing into bed last night, but it wasn't like he was going to starve. The cat ate better than I did most of the time.

Then again, he was a creature of routine and I was slacking in my duties. I was just as grumpy as he was before my morning coffee, so could I really blame him?

Once his royal crankiness was fed, I lumbered back into my bedroom, grabbed my clothes, and headed for the bathroom. Undressing was a chore, but I managed without too much complaint. I stood under the shower until the water ran cold, letting the heat pelt at me in the hopes it would loosen my muscles. It worked, though I still felt like someone had tried to twist me into a new shape before dropping me from a balcony. How did anyone do this sort of thing for a living?

I tried not to think about how Prudence and the

other elves might be feeling. They were used to the torture. I doubted a single one of them had so much as a tweaked muscle in their big toe. It irked me to know Robert had gone through the whole practice without so much as a grimace of pain. If anyone deserved to have their every muscle spasm, it was him.

I spent the next hour trying to get my mind and body back to where it needed to be. Coffee helped. The cookie inside helped even more. By the time I was done, I felt like I could make a go at life, even if it would only last until practice that night. Then, I'd be forced to contort myself in ways no human body should contort.

Well, at least *my* body.

I considered giving my muscles more time to rest, but decided staying in bed all day would help nothing. Not only would everything tighten up again, I'd likely find it hard to get up and leave later.

"Well," I said to Misfit, who was cleaning his whiskers while lounging on the couch, "I guess that since I'm going to be in town this year, I should get out the tree."

Kitty eyes widened as if he'd understood me. He didn't stop washing, or deign to get up, but I could tell he was interested.

It had been years since I'd put up my Christmas tree. I'd always spent the holidays with my dad, so there was no reason for me to bother. It wasn't like I ever had anyone over to my place for Christmas dinner or to watch silly holiday movies.

Speaking of which . . .

I turned on the TV and smiled when I saw that *Elf* was on. I wasn't normally a Will Ferrell fan, but I did like this movie. I turned up the volume and then headed into the laundry room where I'd stored most of my junk. Shoved into a corner with five totes of things I'd probably never unpack, was the box containing the Christmas tree. It was a little worse for wear, the box faded and torn and taped together in more places than I could count.

With what I felt was a herculean effort, I managed to drag the box from its corner, get it out of the laundry room, down the hall, and into the living room without breaking anything, myself included. I did have to sit down and rub at my back afterward, but that was a minor grievance. Maybe I should call the theatre and let them know I had to drop out due to back pain. It did make me wonder if Mandy's illness was really just a cover for her not wanting to suffer anymore.

I was about to suck it up and open the box— Misfit was already rubbing against it and purring in anticipation—when there was a knock at the door.

"Sorry," I said, rising. "You'll have to wait a few minutes more."

Misfit plopped down with a pout, tail swishing, as I headed for the door. I couldn't imagine who would be paying me a visit, especially since everyone I knew was working. A part of me was secretly hoping it was the delivery man with a box of chocolates sent straight from my favorite chocolate shop back home. Or Will. Both were just as yummy.

I opened the door and was surprised to find a woman I didn't know standing on my front stoop.

"Are you Krissy Hancock?" she asked with a smile. She was my height, of medium build. Her short hair had once been dark, but was now streaked with gray, giving her that salt and pepper look some people find attractive. She peered at me through glasses with thick black frames that were actually pretty stylish and went well with her face. Her coat had faux animal fur around the edges, and went down to mid-calf. I could just make out what looked to be a pants suit underneath.

"I am," I said, hesitantly. There was no car in my driveway, telling me she'd either been dropped off or walked.

"Hi, I'm Jane." She pulled off a glove and held out her hand to me. "Jane Winthrow."

I shook her hand, somewhat stunned. "As in, re-lated to Eleanor Winthrow?" I asked, glancing toward my neighbor's house. Sure enough, the curtain was parted just enough to let a pair of binoculars poke through. I would have been annoyed if I wasn't already used to it.

"The same," she said. "I'm her daughter." She put her glove back on. "I wanted to stop by and introduce myself. My mother has spoken about you quite a lot." By the grin that spread across her face, I knew what kind of stuff she'd been saying.

"It's not like that," I said. "Well, *I'm* not like that. She thinks I . . ." I trailed off as Jane waved my words away.

"I know how she can get. I never believe more than two words out of her mouth half the time. I prefer to make up my own mind about people, hence my visit." A frown flashed across her face, and then was gone almost before it could form. "Mom was against me coming, but I assured her you weren't going to drag me inside and tie me up."

I nudged Misfit back with my foot as he peered out

into the cold. I shivered and stepped back as a gust of wind slapped at my exposed face and hands. "Would you like to come in for a few minutes? I can make a fresh pot of coffee for us."

"No, thank you," Jane said. "I can't stay." She glanced toward her mother's house and sighed before turning back to me. "You seem like a nice person. I think it might be a good idea for you two to get together so she can see that. Maybe we can all meet for lunch sometime?"

This time, I picked Misfit up when he made a move for the door. I held him close to my chest as a shield against the cold. "You don't need to go out of your way," I said. "I don't hold any of it against her." Not really, anyway. She sometimes made my life more difficult with her constant spying, but so far, it hasn't gotten me into *too* much trouble.

Jane's smile tightened somewhat. "I think it would be good for her, honestly."

I could see some of her mom in her eyes then, a stubbornness that had to be genetic. "If you think she'd be okay with it, I'm willing." Eleanor and I had definitely gotten off on the wrong foot, and if eating lunch with her would ease some of the tension between us, it would make both our lives so much easier. We *did* live next to one another.

"Great," Jane said. "I'll check with Mom and see when she would like to do this. Do you have any preferences?"

"No," I said. "I'm on a stay at home vacation, so I'm pretty free. My evenings are booked, but otherwise, anytime should be fine."

"Okay, good. I'd better get back." She started to

walk away, and then paused to say, "Cute cat," before heading the rest of the way over to her mother's house.

I watched her go until Misfit started squirming to be let down. I backed up, closed the door, and then set him down before returning to the boxed tree.

"That was nice of her," I said. I didn't even know Eleanor had a daughter. And since she was using her maiden name, I was assuming she'd never been married, or had been and had gotten a divorce. Then again, many women weren't taking on their husband's last name these days, so really, anything was possible. She seemed nice enough either way, and I was glad she'd stopped by.

I spent the next hour and a half fighting with my Christmas tree. It was no wonder why I never put the darned thing up. It was one of those fake trees that you screwed in each branch, piece by piece, before fluffing them out. I'd tried to make piles based on the sizes of each branch—they were color coded, which was supposed to make it easier—but Misfit kept diving into them, scattering them all over the living room. I ended up having to go in search of each individual piece every time I snapped one into place.

Once the tree was up—with only one missing branch I assumed had found its way under the couch—I returned to the laundry room for the decorations. I had rope tinsel because it was the least likely to be swallowed by a mischievous cat, though I preferred the loose stuff. The same went for the other decorations. Everything I used was cat safe and approved.

Eventually, everything was up, the movie was over, and Misfit was curled up beneath the tree, asleep. My back was barking at me, but I felt a sense of satisfaction that I managed to get the tree up without a disaster. It gave the room a cozy feeling, one that would have been accentuated by a fire, but since I didn't have a fireplace, and candles were too much of a risk with a long-haired, curious cat, it would have to do.

But yet, something was still missing. It only took me a few minutes to figure it out.

I hurried to the spare bedroom where I'd put Dad's and Misfit's gifts. I pulled them out and carried them to the tree. Careful not to disturb the slumbering feline, I placed the packages underneath. I stepped back and nodded in satisfaction.

"Perfect," I said. Misfit's ears twitched, but he appeared to be out for the long haul.

With nothing else to do—shopping for gifts would have to come later—I decided to sit down and watch *The Santa Clause.* I'd been hoping for something a bit more classic, like the original *Rudolph, the Red-Nosed Reindeer,* but the Tim Allen flick was the only Christmas movie I could find.

By the time it was over, I was starting to get a little antsy sitting around, doing nothing. I considered calling Dad to see how his trip was going, but wasn't sure he'd even gotten there yet. Instead, I picked up the phone and called Will. I got voice mail, of course. He was likely at work, though it would have been nice to hear his voice.

Glancing at the clock, I decided I could always head to the theatre a little early. Maybe if I got to know more of the cast better, more of them would help me get through the play without making a complete fool out of myself.

Thinking of the cast, it did make me wonder if I

should take the time to buy gifts for some of them. Prudence seemed nice enough, but who else did I really know? Robert was out. He'd take the gift the wrong way. And everyone else was practically a stranger.

No, it would probably be better not to. If I got something for one person, I'd have to get something for everyone.

"You be good," I said as I put my coat on. Misfit was still zonked out under the tree, but I had a feeling the moment I was out the door, he'd be halfway up the tree, batting at the ornaments. His kitty snores didn't fool me.

Bundled, I left the house, glancing quickly at the Winthrow place. The binoculars were gone, which felt a little strange. Eleanor was always there, watching. I almost didn't know what to do with myself without her watchful gaze keeping tabs on me.

I got into my car, started it up, and then reconsidered my plan. I couldn't take sitting around the house any longer, but it was still too early to go to the theatre. I doubted anyone would be there yet, so I'd end up hanging out alone for at least an hour or two. No, thank you.

It didn't take me long to figure out where to go, however. After my long day of decorating and indulging in cheesy Christmas movies, I thought I deserved a reward for all my hard work, and I knew exactly what it was I wanted.

4

"Krissy! What are you doing here? I thought you were leaving town for Christmas?"

"Hi, Jules." We shared a quick hug. Jules Phan was my next door neighbor, and owner of Phantastic Candies, where we now stood. "Canceled. I'm sticking around Pine Hills this year."

"There's nothing wrong, is there?" he asked, brow creasing in concern.

"Not a thing. Dad has a date, so instead of intruding, I get to stay here."

Jules beamed as if I was the one with the big date. He was wearing an elf costume, which made his smile that much more infectious. "That's fantastic. Lance," he called, raising his voice. "We have company."

Lance Darby exited the backroom, a half broken down box in his hands. "Hi, Krissy." He was wearing the same elf outfit as Jules, though his fit a bit snugger, thanks to his muscular build. He tossed the box aside and came over to wrap me in a strong hug. "It's good to see you."

"You both look great." Their costumes were far

nicer than what I had to wear for the play. It made me a little jealous, to be honest. They looked like movie extras, while the play outfits looked as if they'd come from a cheap Halloween store.

Jules actually blushed at my compliment. "It was Lance's idea. I was going to come in to work today as Santa."

"But that's done to death," Lance said. "And while elves are also a bit cliché this time of year, I think Jules looks especially nice in tights."

I didn't want to say what I was thinking since Lance's boyfriend, Jules, was right there, so I simply nodded. Let's just say Lance kept himself extremely fit and he filled out his own pair of tights nicely.

I turned away and looked around the candy shop. "Phantastic Candies is looking great," I said, impressed by how good the store looked. A waterline had busted a few months back and the store had flooded. Instead of simply fixing things, Jules had decided to do a complete remodel. The colors were more vibrant, the candy displayed in fun ways that would surely make the kids smile. Everything looked just the way it should, much to my sweet-tooth's relief.

"I know, doesn't it?" Jules said, looking around himself, hand on his hip. "I was worried at first, but the community really bonded together for the reopening. And it did allow me to make some changes I'd been wanting to do for years."

I took a quick walk around the room, mouth watering in approval. I picked up a bag of chocolate covered cherries and carried them to the counter. "I think I could use these for tonight."

"Oh?" Jules asked, ringing up the sale—applying a huge discount as he did.

"I agreed to fill in for a sick girl in the local Christmas play," I said. "I think I'm in way over my head."

"Nonsense," Jules said. "You'll be fantastic."

"If you can deal with Lawrence Jackson," Lance put in.

"I didn't know you knew him," I said, surprised. "I've only been at one practice, but he does seem a little tough on everyone."

"He's a slave driver," Jules said with a shake of his head. "I used to take part in the plays a good, I don't know, five or six years ago. I couldn't handle Lawrence yelling at us all the time. He made more than one person go home crying in my time, and from what I hear, he's the same way now, if not worse."

"Really?" I said. I'd felt like crying myself, but that had little to do with Lawrence and a lot to do with my poor, battered body.

"There was this one girl, Mandy Ortega. He used to berate her all the time, just because she had trouble keeping her weight down."

"As if that even matters," Lance grumped.

"That's who I'm replacing," I said.

"She's probably had enough by now," Jules said. "I'm surprised she's lasted this long without popping him in the nose. If he would have talked to me like that, I know I would have."

Speaking of popping, I opened my bag of chocolate-covered cherries and popped one into my mouth. It was absolute bliss.

"I'm not sure I'm going to make it through this," I told them once I swallowed. "It's a musical, which no one bothered to tell me before I signed up, by the way.

I feel like someone has run me over with a very large truck, multiple times." I rubbed at my back, which was smarting just thinking about it.

"You'll be fine," Jules said. "Be sure to hydrate often. And if you aren't taking any vitamins, I'd suggest starting to do so now."

"And get lots of sleep," Lance added.

"Thanks," I said, chewing on another cherry. "I'd better get going. Practice starts soon and from what everyone keeps telling me, the director doesn't like it when you're late."

"Keep with it," Jules said as I headed for the door. "You'll be thankful you did."

"I hope so," I said, before waving and leaving Phantastic Candies. I felt much better with candy in hand, yet I had a feeling it wasn't going to do me much good onstage.

I drove to practice and pulled into a lot that was a lot fuller than I'd expected at this hour. I checked the time to make sure I wasn't late, and found I was still almost an hour early. I got out of my car and started for the entrance when I noticed Lawrence talking with Randy, who appeared to have sobered up. They were standing near the front of the building and didn't see me. I hoped Randy was apologizing for how he acted yesterday, because maybe then Lawrence would treat the rest of us better.

I left them to it and headed inside the cast entrance. Prudence was leaning against the wall just inside, looking weary.

"Am I late?" I asked, glancing around. There were quite a few people here, all of them already in costume.

"Not if you didn't get a call from Lawrence," she

said. "He wanted a few of us here early to get some painting done. I should have known it was a smoke-screen. He had us up onstage running lines within minutes."

"Good." I breathed a sigh of relief before realizing how that must have sounded. "I mean, good about me not being late. Not so good he tricked you." I paused and frowned. "Why didn't he call me?" If he thought anyone needed more practice, I should have been at the top of the list.

"Probably didn't have your number," she said before nodding toward the back. "You should get dressed before he sees you out of costume. Maybe he'll think you've been here the entire time and will go easy on you."

"I can hope," I said, starting for the back, but stopped when I noticed Robert red-faced, standing with Santa and Trisha. I edged closer, not wanting to be seen, but curious as to what was going on.

"Leave her alone," Robert was saying, voice tight as if he'd been saying it over and over again for quite a while. "She's not interested in you."

"Give her time," Santa said. "It's not like she has any better options around here." He covered his smile by taking a drink out of huge mug.

Robert took a threatening step forward. It was surprising to see him defend someone else so vehemently. I'm not sure he would have ever done the same for me back when we'd dated. "I'm warning you . . ."

Trisha put a restraining hand on his arm and whispered something into his ear. Robert smiled and pointed a finger at Santa, yet another warning, but at least he didn't rush him, fists flying. Not that I thought Robert could hold his own, or had ever been in a fight in his life. Chances were good that if he were to pick a fight with Santa, he'd lose.

It should have ended there, but Santa couldn't seem to help himself. "You know," he said, turning to face Trisha. "We should spend more time together outside of practice to work on our chemistry. We're supposed to be married, and I don't think it comes off onstage."

"I don't think so," she said with a disgusted look. She was in full Mrs. Claus attire, but was anything but the loving wife at the moment. Then again, Santa wasn't being a very good Mr. Claus. He wasn't Billy Bob Thornton in *Bad Santa* bad, but he was getting there.

Robert ground his teeth together. "Don't make me hit you, Chuck, because I'll do it."

"Oh really?" Santa—Chuck, apparently—stepped forward and puffed out his chest. "Let's see where that gets you."

I was about to step in when the good-looking elf I'd noticed yesterday appeared and put his arm around Trisha. "You know, you don't have to deal with these losers if you don't want to."

She shrank away from his touch and moved closer to Robert. "I'm fine right here, thank you very much."

"Suit yourself." He turned to Chuck, seemingly unperturbed by her rejection. "I need to talk to you for a few minutes." He started back to the dressing rooms without waiting for a response.

Knowing I'd be caught eavesdropping if I remained standing there, I hurried down the hall and slipped into the women's dressing room. I closed the door, and then put my ear to it so I could listen in if they stopped outside to talk. I was the only one in the room, thankfully.

The sound of footfalls approached. I waited, but the door to the men's dressing room across the hall opened and closed. I held my breath and waited, hoping to catch a word or two, but if Chuck and sexy elf were talking, they were keeping their voices down.

With a shrug, I turned and started to get dressed myself. I didn't even know why I was interested in their conversation. I didn't care about Robert anymore, so it wasn't like I was worried about how his love life was progressing. And when it came to the conversation happening across the hall, it was unlikely it had anything to do with him or Trisha anyway.

Maybe Rita was rubbing off on me; she *was* the gossip queen and would love to know about all the drama going on backstage. If I slipped her a few juicy bits here or there, she'd go easier on me the next time I did something stupid.

My costume was sitting on the counter with my name written on a sticky note sitting on top of it. Someone had taken it in overnight, like Lawrence had wanted. I half-feared it would be too small now, but when I slid it on, the outfit fit perfectly. Whoever had done the job had done good work. Lawrence himself had been the one to pin it before I left the night before, so I wondered if he was the one who'd fixed it. The man *had* to have some redeeming qualities, didn't he?

I left the dressing room—pausing only a second outside the men's door, but it was quiet inside—and headed out front just as Lawrence called everyone to the stage. I took my place beside Prudence after sneaking another chocolate cherry. She looked me up and down and gave me a thumbs up and smile.

"Looks good," she whispered before turning to the front to await Lawrence's command.

He paced up front, scowling and rubbing at his forehead like he had a killer migraine. He kept glancing at the stage and muttering to himself. I guess his talk with Randy hadn't gone all that well. Maybe it hadn't been so much an apology as a last-ditch effort to regain his role.

Finally, Lawrence stopped and bellowed, "Where is everyone?"

I glanced around the stage. Neither Mr. nor Mrs. Claus was present. Nor was Robert. The good-looking elf was frowning down at his feet, so he was done talking with Santa in the back, though the not-so-jolly man wasn't on stage with us.

"Uh-oh," Prudence said. "Lawrence hates it when there's a no show."

Sure enough, the director busted a gasket. "What is wrong with you people? Don't you understand how pressed for time we are? Do you want to make me look like a fool while you bumble around the stage like a bunch of middle-schoolers who never bothered to learn your lines?" He sucked in an angry breath and turned to Dean, the poor crewman he'd berated yesterday. "Find them." And then he spun and stomped off.

Uncertain what to do, the cast wandered away, talking in low voices. I saw Asia and Prairie huddled together, talking to one another. I stuck with Prudence, since she was really the only friend I seemed to have here.

"Where do you think they went?" she asked, thoughtfully. "Chuck was here earlier. I can't imagine him skipping out now."

"I don't know," I said. "I saw him arguing with Robert earlier. He's missing too."

"As is Trisha."

"Maybe they've decided to duke it out," I said with a shrug. It sounded like something Robert might suggest, but I doubted he'd ever go through with it. "That elf over there was talking to Santa in the dressing room just before we started, so maybe he knows what happened to them."

"Let's find out," Prudence said. "I'd like to get practice started soon. Lawrence will hold us all night otherwise, and I have things to do this evening." She started for the good-looking elf, who was currently standing alone, still frowning.

I was about to follow her when I caught a glimpse of Robert heading for the side entrance. He had a backpack thrown over one shoulder, and while he was still wearing his elf outfit, his green shoes were gone. He didn't so much as look behind him as he hurried out the side door.

An odd sense of loss pooled in my gut at the sight of him leaving. While we might not get along, he *was* one of the few people I knew here. It was strange to think I could be upset about seeing Robert's back, but there it was.

I headed for the door, hoping to call him back, or at least ask him why he was leaving. I get that he was upset about Santa hitting on his newest girlfriend, but was it worth throwing away his role in the play? I had no doubts Lawrence would fire him on the spot the moment he realized what was happening.

I pushed open the door and flinched against the blast of cold air that rushed inside. A car—Robert's I imagined—fishtailed as it sped out of the lot and down the street. I was already too late.

A scream tore through the building behind me then, causing me to jump. I spun and saw the flood of people heading to the back, toward where the scream had originated. Not to be left behind, I hurried to catch up with Prudence.

"What happened?" I asked her.

"I don't know."

Just as we reached the dressing rooms, one of the female crew members staggered out of the men's side, hand over her mouth. She was only able to point back into the room, before she rushed away, tears streaming down her face.

Prudence and I looked at each other, and then started forward as one, most of the rest of the cast following at our heels. I pushed open the door and saw the nightmare-inducing tableau that lay on the other side.

5

"Why would anyone want to kill Santa Claus?"

I stood next to the cast entrance, arms crossed over my chest, listening to the shocked murmurs of the cast and crew in a state of disbelief. Asia wasn't the only one who couldn't believe Santa was dead. A part of me had known what to expect when I'd opened the door, but to see it was nearly enough to kill my childhood memories.

Sirens were nearing and they couldn't get there fast enough. I was shivering, standing in my elf outfit, by an open door in mid-winter, without a coat. The backstage area had felt oppressive with it closed up, hence the open door, but I was beginning to wonder about the wisdom of the decision. Still, while it might be cold and windy outside, there was something to say for natural light. It kept the shocked gathering from getting *too* down.

Lawrence was pacing back and forth in front of the dressing rooms, not letting anyone inside. He appeared beside himself, but I don't think it was because of the dead man as much as it was the fact his play was ruined. He'd cursed poor dead Santa at least twice in his nervous ramblings, which said a lot about his character, if you asked me. I mean, who does that?

"Who do you think did it?" Prudence asked, coming to stand next to me. She'd pulled on a shawl and was huddled in it, looking more like a fragile old woman now than she'd had since I'd met her.

"I don't know," I said, though I was pretty sure I did. Robert was gone, as was his girlfriend, Trisha. The good-looking elf who'd gone into the dressing room with Santa was standing near the stage, frowning at the floor hard enough, I was surprised it didn't crack. Did that mean he knew something? Had he been inside when Robert had burst in on their conversation? Maybe he was beating himself up because he let the two men fight it out, and now, one of them was dead, the other on the run.

Of course, that was all speculation. Maybe Robert had a perfectly good excuse for sneaking away quickly like he had. But whatever it was, it had better be a *really* good one or else he would be in some serious trouble.

"Can't say he'll be missed much," Prudence said with a shake of her head. "It's still a shame, of course, but he wasn't well-liked."

I nodded absently. I kept trying to imagine Robert attacking Santa, or as he should be known, Chuck. I couldn't seem to do it, however. It wasn't the sort of thing Robert did.

A pair of police cruisers pulled into the lot, an ambulance right behind them. I pushed the door open the rest of the way and steeled myself for what was to come. I was hoping Paul Dalton would be one of the responding officers; he always made these sorts of things easier for me. Much to my dismay, however, it wasn't Paul who stepped out of the nearest cruiser.

"Here we go again," Officer John Buchannan said as he approached the door. "Can't you stay out of trouble, just once?"

"I didn't do anything," I said, eyeing him. He'd never liked me all that much, and while he'd stopped accusing me of every crime in town, there was still a distrust behind his eyes I didn't like. I doubted it would ever go away, no matter what I did.

"The victim inside?" Officer Garrison asked, joining us. Her voice was as husky as ever and she smelled vaguely of smoke. She, much like Buchannan, wasn't my biggest fan, and I wondered if he had something to do with that. She wouldn't even look my way when she spoke, choosing instead to address Prudence.

"He is," I answered, loudly as to get her to look at me. "No one's touched anything since we found the body."

Buchannan motioned for the paramedics, who'd stopped outside, and as a group, they headed for the men's dressing room where Lawrence was waving them over. Buchannan paused, lowered—and surprisingly, softened—his voice and said, "Make sure no one leaves."

With a nod and a shiver, I closed the door and planted myself in front of it, Prudence at my side. It wasn't the only entrance to the building, but it was the most accessible. I wasn't even sure the front doors were unlocked since Lawrence made such a big deal about them yesterday. Everyone was hovering around backstage—everyone but Chuck, Robert, and Trisha that was.

"I bet Randy did it," Prudence said, rubbing her hands together to warm them.

"Why do you say that?" I asked. I'd seen him outside earlier that evening, talking with Lawrence, but hadn't seen him since. I supposed he could have snuck inside and waited for Chuck to be alone, and then struck, but it seemed a little far-fetched at the moment, especially considering Robert's flight.

"He wasn't happy about losing his part in the play," Prudence said. "He blamed Chuck for it, as if the other man was responsible for his drinking. Did you know he used a vodka bottle to dent Chuck's car door? Then, when it broke, he tried to stab it through the tire, but was too drunk to finish the job."

"When was this?"

"Second night of practice. Man has shown up ever since that night, drunk as a skunk. If anyone had it in for Chuck, it would be him."

Admittedly, he did sound like a likely suspect. If it wasn't for the fact I'd seen Robert fleeing the scene, I'd think he'd be the most likely. It would have been hard for Randy to get inside, kill Chuck, and get out without anyone seeing him, but it was possible. If he'd waited in the dressing room, he could have hidden away until the good-looking elf left the room.

I glanced at the man in question and wondered if he *had* seen Chuck's death, but disliked the man so much, he was willing to hide it. He'd sounded a little tense when he'd told Chuck they needed to talk.

"Maybe he wasn't murdered," I said, unconvincingly. It would be kind of hard to stab yourself in the back.

Prudence didn't even bother to respond to that, though she did perk up as Buchannan stepped out of the dressing room. I prayed he'd go straight to Lawrence, who was busy berating poor Dean again, as if Chuck's death was somehow his fault. Instead of heading for the director, however, Buchannan strode straight over to me.

"What happened?" he asked, as if I'd personally witnessed the murder.

"I was on the stage with everyone else," I said. "I didn't see anything. In fact, I didn't even realize Santa was missing until Lawrence said something."

Buchannan's eyes narrowed. Apparently, something I'd said didn't sit right with him. "What did you see?" he asked, putting on his angry cop voice.

I sighed. As much as I disliked Robert, I didn't want to get him into trouble. Maybe he had a perfectly good explanation as to why he and Trisha had left so abruptly.

Or maybe, he actually did kill Chuck. Protecting him would be doing no one any favors, myself included.

"Can you at least tell me what you found first?" I asked. "It might help me remember something."

Buchannan gave Prudence a meaningful look. She nodded once, and then with a squeeze of my arm, walked away. He turned back to me, still frowning.

"Santa was stabbed to death."

"Chuck."

"What?"

"His name was Chuck."

Buchannan removed a pad of paper and a pen and scrawled Santa's real name. "I don't know if there is any evidence on the knife, and I won't know for a little while yet. There was some sort of liquid contaminating the scene." His nose wrinkled as if remembering the smell.

"It was eggnog," I said.

Buchannan's eyes narrowed. "How would you know this?"

"I could smell it." I shuddered, hoping the memory of finding Santa lying in a pool of not just his blood, but a puddle of spilled eggnog, wouldn't put me off it for good. "Chuck was carrying a large mug with him. I'm guessing he was drinking eggnog and when he was stabbed, he dropped it."

"I see." Buchannan wrote something down. Once finished, he looked me up and down, and then asked. "Can I see the bottom of your feet?"

"Excuse me?"

"Your shoes," he said, gesturing toward my elven pull-ons. "Let me see them."

I pulled off my elf shoes and handed them over. I realized then I might not need them now that our Santa was dead. Would be kind of hard to have a Christmas play without him.

Buchannan checked the bottoms of my shoes, as well as the insides, and then handed them back. "They're clean."

I knew for a fact they were filthy from the back-stage floor, but knew that wasn't what he'd meant. "Why did you want to see my shoes?" I asked, pretty sure I knew why, but wanted to hear him say it.

"There's a footprint by the body," he said. "Was shaped funny, with no tread. I'd guess it was around a size ten or so."

Robert was a size ten. My entire body clenched, including my teeth. Could Robert have actually killed Santa over a girl? I mean, I'd dated the guy for *way* too long and not once did I ever think him capable of murder. Cheating and lying, sure, but not killing anyone.

"What do you know?" Buchannan asked, adopting a stubborn stance that told me I wasn't going to get away until I told him.

I glanced around to make sure no one was listening before speaking. There were quite a few eyes on us, but no one was close enough to hear what I had to say. If I was wrong about Robert, I didn't want to spread rumors about him, knowing it would somehow bite me on the butt if I did.

"I saw someone fighting with Chuck earlier. Before he died." I winced, realizing how unnecessary that last bit was.

"Who?" Buchannan had his pen poised above the pad of paper and was giving me an intense stare. If I was wrong, Robert was going to kill me.

"A guy named Robert Dunhill," I said, reluctantly. "He's my ex."

Buchannan gave me a surprised look, as if he couldn't imagine me ever having a boyfriend, before he scribbled down Robert's name. "What was the fight about?"

"A girl. Her name's Trisha. I don't know her last name. She's playing Mrs. Claus this year and Santa was acting quite un-Santa-like toward her."

Buchannan raised his eyebrows at me.

"He hit on her," I said, hating every second of this. "Robert and Trisha are dating, I think. Chuck and Robert argued before they went their separate ways. The guy over there talked to Santa in the dressing rooms afterward." I nodded toward the good-looking elf. "And then we all met up onstage."

"Was everyone but the victim there?"

"No." I swallowed. It was really starting to sink in that my ex might have killed someone. "Robert and Trisha are gone. Neither was Chuck because by then he was . . . well . . ." I couldn't bring myself to say it.

Buchannan glanced back at the elf I'd indicated before turning back to me. "Do you know where Robert and Trisha are now?"

"No," I said. "I haven't seen Trisha since the fight, but I did see Robert leave right before we found the body." I blinked my eyes to keep back the tears. "He wasn't wearing his shoes. His elf shoes, I mean."

Buchannan's eyes grew even more intense. "Are you sure about that?"

I nodded and couldn't seem to stop. "He's dressed as an elf and was wearing his shoes earlier. I . . . I can't believe he would do such a thing! Robert's a jerk, but kill someone? It can't be him. I mean, maybe someone else snuck in and did it. Robert could have forgotten he had a doctor's appointment and took off and . . ." I trailed off at Buchannan's frown. I was babbling, defending a man who'd made my life miserable for years, yet I couldn't seem to believe he was capable of murder.

"Garrison!" Buchannan called once I fell silent. She'd just come out of the dressing room and had started to speak to Lawrence when he'd called to her. He glanced at me, muttered, "Thank you," and then hurried over to where she stood.

I sank down to the floor, head spinning. Never in my life had I thought Robert capable of murder, yet here we were. Who else could it have been? Randy? That good-looking elf? If he killed him, then why was he still here?

I watched as Buchannan talked to Garrison, Lawrence looking on nervously. She nodded, glanced at me, and then nodded again. Somehow, I didn't think what he was saying was very flattering.

They parted a moment later, Garrison coming my way, Buchannan toward the good-looking elf whose name I had yet to learn. I started to rise, but Officer Garrison wasn't interested in me. She pushed open the door, letting in a blast of cold air, as well as Rita, before stepping outside.

"Oh my Lordy Lou," she said, shaking off her puffy coat. Apparently, it had started to snow since the police had arrived. "What's happening here? There's an ambulance and police cars outside!"

"Someone killed Santa," I said. Buchannan had the good-looking elf lift his feet to show him there was no blood on his elf shoes, before asking him some questions.

Rita gasped, hand going to her mouth. "Here? In the theatre?" She said it like she couldn't imagine anyone defiling a place like this with murder, even though it often was depicted onstage.

"It happened in the men's dressing room," I said, automatically. I was in shock, but this time, Paul Dalton wasn't there to comfort me. "You can't go in."

"Why would I want to do that?" Rita asked, appalled. "Oh dear, what are we going to do? Lawrence!" She waved at the director and hurried over to him, much to his apparent annoyance.

I remained seated, mechanically watching as

Buchannan moved from person to person, asking questions. I had a feeling most of the questions involved Robert. And by the occasional glances I received, a few were about me.

I'm not sure how long I sat there, stunned. More people showed up: cops and paramedics, but none of them were Paul. He would have known what to say, would have made me feel better, despite the situation. I'd call Will, but he'd still be at work. If I remembered right, this one was one of his long days, though lately, they all seemed to be long.

Eventually, Chuck was brought out on a stretcher, a sheet covering his body. That was my cue to get up and move away from the door. Buchannan had finished with his questions and was making sure everyone kept back. Garrison hadn't come back, so I was assuming she was off looking for suspect number one: Robert. I moved to stand with Prudence as the paramedics and cops all left together, leaving the shell-shocked cast and crew alone in the theatre.

"Everyone!" Lawrence called as soon as they were gone. "Gather 'round, please."

We were all pretty much standing in a loose huddle already, so hardly anyone moved.

"A terrible tragedy has befallen our production tonight," Lawrence said as we fell silent. "A murder most foul. Death." He pressed his hand to his mouth, dramatically.

"A little much, isn't it?" Prudence muttered.

Someone snorted behind her, which drew a sharp look from Lawrence, but he went on speaking, unperturbed by the interruption.

"Chuck's death is a blow to us all, a stain on our

sterling reputation." He sucked in a breath and looked like he might cry before continuing. "Many of you must be asking yourselves, 'How can we go on after this?' I admit, I myself have thought the same."

"He can't possibly . . ." Prudence whispered, sounding shocked.

"I have decided that the show must go on!" Lawrence proclaimed. "I've already contacted someone to replace our poor, departed Santa. There is no reason for us not to continue on, in his name, and make this the greatest Christmas play ever to grace our beloved theatre!" He finished his proclamation with a flourish, closing his eyes and throwing back his head like he expected applause.

We all just sort of stared at him, uncomfortably, until he sighed and lowered his head.

"That will be all for tonight," he said, sounding annoyed we hadn't thrown roses at him. "Practice tomorrow is canceled while I arrange things with the police. The men's dressing room is off-limits until the murderer who invaded our beloved theatre to commit this heinous crime is found. See you in two days." And with his grand declaration complete, Lawrence spun on his heel and walked out the door.

6

"I mean, really, Misfit," I said, picking up another ornament—this one from the kitchen. "I can't leave you alone for five minutes without you causing a mess!"

The cat in question sat on the couch, watching me with a contented gleam in his eye. The tree was thankfully still standing, but half the ornaments were strewn around the house. It's hard to believe one cat could cause so much mischief in such a short span of time. You'd think one ornament would be enough, but no, he had to try to bat them all around, as if looking for the one that would make the most satisfying crunch when it collided with the wall.

Yet, for all my complaining, I wasn't truly mad at him. When I'd put up the tree, I fully expected him to lose his mind right then and there, so it was good he at least waited until I wasn't in the room. Shiny round objects tend to draw felines like bouncy ones make dogs race across the park.

But I was tired, and it was making me grouchy.

I picked up the last ornament and deposited it back

onto the tree, knowing I'd find it on the floor again in the morning. I wondered if it would look too trashy if I used duct tape on the ornaments to keep them attached to the tree. Knowing Misfit, he'd just chew it off, leaving a bigger mess than he already had.

I plopped down onto the couch beside him with a heavy sigh. He eyed me a moment to make sure I wasn't angry with him before climbing into my lap and curling into a fluffy orange ball. I stroked him absently, mind already elsewhere.

Robert. A murderer.

Did I really believe that?

All the evidence pointed at him as the doer, at least, the evidence I was aware of. The size ten shoe print. His own missing elf shoes. His flight. His argument with Chuck right before Santa ended up dead.

And, of course, Robert was a cheating, lying jerk.

But did that make him a killer?

When we'd dated, I never once saw him do or say anything that would make me think he was capable of it. He'd never even been in a real fight as far as I was aware. When confronted, he usually wilted.

But hadn't there always been something off about him? It went deeper than his inability to remain faithful or take a hint. He was a terrible boyfriend, a not so good person, yet he always seemed to land on his feet. Maybe I'd never seen the true Robert because he never truly cared about me as much as he cared about Trisha now. I had been the victim of his pushy nature when it came to women, and while it wasn't murder, it felt darn near to it at the time. He'd tried to kiss me when I didn't want him to, and had no problem pushing me around in an ill-guided effort to win me back, so he did do some selfish stuff sometimes.

Maybe Robert the killer wasn't so far-fetched after all.

Misfit's warmth and the rumble of his purr had a calming effect on me. I settled back and instead of turning on the TV in search of yet another Christmas movie, I chose to stare at the tree. The lights didn't flash, yet something about the way they reflected off the ornaments, and the soft glow in general, was hypnotic. Within minutes of sitting down, I found myself drifting off to sleep.

A loud pounding startled Misfit, who went flying off my lap, back claws digging painfully into the soft flesh of my thigh. I yelped and leapt to my own feet, eyes wide, head swimming from my all too short nap. My heart was pounding and my leg was barking, though I don't think Misfit drew blood.

Panting, I looked around, not quite sure what had woken me. Had something fallen somewhere in the house? Did a truck go down the road, loose load banging around like thunder? It had happened before, and since I was off in dreamland, it was hard to say for sure exactly what it had been.

The pounding came again, startling another yelp from me, before I realized the sound was coming from the front door.

Still drowsy despite how I'd been woken, I eased over to peer out the window. It was dark outside and my front stoop light was off. Thanks to the heavy cloud cover, there wasn't even any moonlight to make out much more than a faint dark outline where someone stood outside my house, hand raised to knock again.

I hurried to the door and opened it before my visitor could knock the darned thing down. I opened my mouth to speak, but was nearly barreled over as my guest rushed inside, shoulders hunched.

"You've got to help me."

"Robert?" My heart sped up again, and I considered making a run for it before he could turn on me. If he *had* killed Santa, then he very well might have decided to go all in and kill everyone who'd ever done him wrong.

Don't panic, I told myself as I looked him up and down.

Robert was a mess. He was still wearing his elf outfit—minus his shoes, of course. His backpack was flung over one shoulder, stuffed completely full, as if he'd grabbed as much as he could before coming here. I wasn't sure if he'd walked all the way to my house, or if he'd driven. Glancing outside, I didn't see a car, but that didn't mean there wasn't one out there somewhere.

"What are you doing here?" I demanded, taking a chance he wouldn't kill me, and closing the door.

"I didn't do it," he said, eyes meeting mine. They were wide with shock and fear. "I swear, I didn't kill him."

"Then why did you run?" I asked.

Robert frowned and ran his hand through his hair. He had flakes of snow in it and his fingers and ears were bright red, which hinted at a long walk in the cold—not a warm drive. He shivered and licked dry, cracked lips, further confirming my guess.

"I freaked. And I knew what people would say. It . . . I . . ." He shook his head and squeezed his eyes closed. He sniffed as his nose started to run. Now that he was in a warm room, every part of him was starting to drip.

Murderer or not, I couldn't stand to see someone I knew suffering. I kept out of his reach as I worked my way around him, into the kitchen. I put on a pot of coffee, making sure not to turn my back on him as I did. Robert watched me work, but made no move toward me.

"The police are looking for you, you know?" I said. "You really should turn yourself in and tell them what you know before they make up their own minds about you."

"I didn't do anything," he said. He moved slowly toward the island counter, dropped his backpack onto the floor, and then plopped down on a stool. He buried his head in his hands as he continued speaking. "When I found him, he was already dead. I panicked. I know I shouldn't have, but what else was I supposed to do?"

"You could have told someone. If you didn't kill him, the police would have had no reason to blame you for his death."

"You're the only person I could turn to," he whined, giving me his best pleading look. "No one else understands me like you do."

I wasn't buying it. I crossed my arms over my chest and stared him down. "What about Trisha? Why not go to her?"

"I don't want to get her into trouble."

"But it's okay to get me into trouble, is that it?"

"It's not like that," he muttered, sullen. "She's my girlfriend."

I know I wasn't being fair, but I was still mad at him for how he'd treated me over the last few years. "How about you tell me what it's like, then? Otherwise, you should go bother someone else."

He frowned down at his hands. "You've helped people before." He said it like it pained him to admit it. "You've solved other murders, found the real killer when no one else could. I want you to do that for me."

"Robert, I'm not a detective. And there's mounds of evidence against you, evidence you made more compelling by running off like you did."

"Please, Krissy," he said. If he wasn't sitting, I had a feeling he would have dropped to his knees to beg. "I can't go to jail. I'd never survive."

I didn't know what to say to that, so I turned and filled two mugs full of coffee. I handed one to him before grabbing a cookie for my own. I knew he preferred cream and sugar, but I wasn't about to offer him any. I was giving him the coffee for the warmth, not the pleasure.

He took the coffee with a muttered, "Thanks," sipped, and then grimaced.

"Turn yourself in," I said.

"I can't." He shook his head. "I won't."

"You can't stay here." I glanced at his backpack and wondered if that's what he'd been hoping for. "It's bad enough you're sitting here now." Knowing Buchannan, he'd probably slap me with a harboring a fugitive charge for even letting Robert through the door.

"I know." He stood, looking as defeated as I'd ever seen him. "I should go. I'm sorry I bothered you." He started for the door.

Watching him walk away looking as if I'd kicked him caused indecision to flare through me. If Robert was guilty, I couldn't let him go. He needed to pay for his crimes. But what if he was telling the truth? If someone else killed Chuck, then Robert might be able to help solve the case. Maybe he knew something that would point to the real killer. If he left now, I might never get the chance to ask him.

"Wait," I called, just as he reached the door. "Don't go."

Robert stopped and turned, a sly grin on his face. "I knew I could count on you."

I bit my lower lip to keep from calling him a name and kicking him out. The whole depressed, defeated man had been an act to get me to feel sorry for him. I should have known it from the start.

Still, letting him go would only get in the way of justice, whether he was guilty or not.

"Go wash your face," I said. "You're filthy. The bathroom is right down that hall. We can talk once you get back."

He nodded, dropped his backpack by the counter. "Thank you, Krissy."

Don't thank me yet, I thought, but wisely kept my mouth shut.

Robert strode down the hall, whistling. I waited until I heard the sound of running water before grabbing my phone. I hurriedly clicked on Paul's name and typed him a quick text before shoving my phone back into my purse. Robert returned just as I was back where I'd started, sipping my coffee with a slightly shaky hand.

"You don't know how relieved I am," he said, walking into the kitchen to stand next to me. "For a minute there, I thought you were going to leave me hanging."

"The murderer needs to be caught," I said.

He nodded and grinned, the old Robert showing

through. "Think I can get a hug?" He spread his arms wide, as if he expected me to leap at the chance.

"Not on your life."

His smile faltered before he shrugged and sat down. "It's okay. Trisha wouldn't approve of you coming onto me anyway."

I took another long sip of coffee to hide my grimace. I'd felt bad sending the text to Paul, but the more Robert spoke, the less bad I felt.

"How are you going to do it?" he asked. "Clear my name, catch the bad guy?"

"You need to come clean with me, Robert," I said, setting my mug aside. "If you killed Santa, you need to tell me right now. And if you didn't, I need to know who might have."

"Of course," he said. "It was Brad."

I stared at him, waiting for him to go on. "Brad who?" I asked when he didn't.

"Brad Clusterman." He stared at me, then sighed as if annoyed I didn't know who he was talking about. "The guy who thinks he's hot stuff. He was hitting on Trisha earlier."

Ah, the good-looking elf. "Why do you think Brad did it?"

He shrugged. "He seems the type, doesn't he?"

I closed my eyes and counted slowly to ten. Then to twenty, when that didn't work. "You can't accuse someone of murder, just because you think they 'seem the type.'"

"Well, he does."

"And you can't accuse someone just because you don't like them either. This is serious business." I took a deep breath and let it out slowly. "Did you see or hear anything that would indicate someone wanted Chuck dead?"

Robert shrugged, pouting. I think he wanted me to rush off and accuse Brad of murder, just because he didn't like how the man had hit on his latest girlfriend. Considering the fact that Chuck had done the same thing before he ended up dead didn't look good for Robert. It made it sound like he had a vendetta against anyone who so much as looked at Trisha. It wouldn't be too much of a stretch to think he'd killed Chuck and hoped to blame Brad, just to get them out of the way.

"Robert," I said, growing not just annoyed, but exasperated by his lack of cooperation. "I can't do anything if you don't help me."

"You're supposed to be good at this stuff," he said.

I wanted to scream, but before I could, a siren rose in the distance and was rapidly getting closer. Robert didn't seem to notice at first. And then, slowly, he raised his head to look at me, brow furrowed.

"You called the cops?" The hurt in his voice almost made me feel bad.

Almost. "No," I said, wishing Paul would have come without sirens blaring. I'd texted them, so it wasn't exactly a lie.

Robert rose to his feet, grabbed his backpack. "I need to get out of here."

"Robert, you need to stay and explain yourself. Everything will be fine if you're honest."

"I can't." He looked wildly around, as if unsure which way to run, before breaking for the door.

Well, crap. I'd hoped this would go smoothly, that Paul would arrive and take control of the situation, and Robert would tell us everything, but now, the man who very well might be a murderer was looking to bolt.

I couldn't let that happen.

Knowing it was going to end badly for me, I rushed forward and grabbed Robert by the arm, just as he opened my front door. I yanked as hard as I could in a vain attempt to drag him back into the kitchen where I'd sit on him until Paul arrived if I had to.

It would have been a good plan if I'd spent more time doing push-ups over the last few months instead of sitting around watching Christmas specials.

Robert jerked his arm free and threw the door the rest of the way open. He looked panicked now, which would only make him do something else stupid if given the chance. I had a feeling that if he ran now, he would not only drag himself down, but Trisha and me as well.

The sirens were close, but not so close I thought Paul would get here before Robert was gone. Steeling myself for pain, I forced myself to act. I dove through the doorway, tackling Robert from behind. Surprised, he went down easily, and we went flying off my front stoop, which was thankfully not very high off the ground. We hit with a pair of grunts, pain shooting up my arm where my elbow hit the frozen ground. We rolled so that I was on my back, Robert on top of me, back facing me. I immediately wrapped my legs and arms around him, clinging to him as if for dear life.

"Krissy, stop it!" he whined, fighting against my hold.

But I refused to relent. "You've got to face this," I said, wincing as his elbow glanced off my cheekbone.

It wasn't on purpose, but it made me angrier at him. "Stop fighting me!"

Thankfully, the police cruiser pulled into my driveway just then, but it wasn't Paul. Officer Garrison got out of her cruiser and approached, hand on her gun, but she didn't draw. She frowned down at us, not quite sure what to make of us now that Robert had gone limp atop me.

"He's the man you're looking for," I said, air being pressed from my lungs. Robert was heavier than he looked.

Garrison hesitated a moment longer before removing her zip strips. She pulled Robert to his feet, read him his rights, and zipped him up, before leading him to her cruiser. She returned a moment later to ask me a few quick questions, all of which I answered honestly.

Then, with a backward glance that said she still didn't quite trust me, Garrison got into her cruiser and drove off, Robert sitting sullenly in the backseat.

Body aching, I watched them go. Robert glanced up once before they were gone, eyes so full of hurt and betrayal, I actually felt bad.

Turning away in shame, I headed back inside, idly noting both Jane and Eleanor Winthrow standing outside, watching me. So much for giving her a better impression of me.

With a tired sigh, I entered my house, closed the door behind me, and being thoroughly fed up with the day, I prepared myself for bed.

7

I didn't sleep well that night. Between my aches and pains from practice, and the memory of Robert's accusatory gaze as the police drove him away, I couldn't get my mind to relax. I was surprised to find I believed him when he said he didn't kill Chuck, which was funny since I'd wanted nothing more than for Robert to go away ever since he'd moved to Pine Hills. Now that it was looking like he wasn't just going to go away, but quite possibly, be put away, I found I sort of missed the idea of him being around.

Weird how the mind works.

I got out of bed nice and early, still sore, still tired, but with my brain working overtime, laying around wasn't happening. I needed a distraction, something that would keep my mind off Robert and his predicament. It was out of my hands now. The police would do everything they could to make sure the real killer was put behind bars. There was nothing left for me to do.

Yet, why wasn't I convinced?

After a quick shower, I got dressed, grabbed my purse and keys, and headed out to brave the biting cold.

Death by Coffee had a decent amount of business this morning, despite the chill in the air. Even though I'd only had to walk a short distance from my car to the front doors, my nose and ears were stinging and my eyes were watering like fountains. The wind ripped right through my coat and settled into my bones, causing me to shiver nearly nonstop. Once inside, I hurried to the counter where Jeff was taking orders.

"What can I get you, Ms. Hancock?" he asked, forcing a smile. His voice only quavered a little this time, which was an improvement. Ever since he'd started manning the register on his own, his nerves seemed calmer, though I doubted he would ever truly be comfortable talking to strangers. I mean, he could barely look *me* in the eye half the time.

"Black coffee and one chocolate chip cookie," I said, choosing my usual, rather than the eggnog. After the murder, I wasn't quite ready for it yet. I eyed the display case and considered getting something else to eat as well, but my stomach was doing odd little flips. I wasn't sure I could keep anything down; not until I got my mind off everything that had happened. "That should be it."

Jeff hurried back to fill my order. Vicki was upstairs, hanging more Christmas decorations around a shelf dedicated to holiday books. A small Christmas tree stood in the corner with a pair of gifts beneath it. The idea was that customers could donate gifts that would remain beneath the tree until Christmas Eve. Then, we'd have a small party where we'd hand them out to kids whose parents couldn't afford to spend much money during the holidays.

I should have been here to help. Guilt made my face warm as Jeff returned. I paid him, and then turned to head upstairs.

"Krissy," Vicki said, giving me a quick hug and smile. "What brings you in this morning?"

"I should be here," I said. "I want to help out with all of this." I nodded toward the tree.

Vicki beamed. "I just put it up this morning. It wasn't hard, so don't worry yourself. A couple of older ladies asked about it the moment we opened the doors. They bought a few books on the spot. Thankfully, they had wrapping paper in their cars because I forgot to bring some in."

While I was glad people were already buying for the kids, it didn't make me feel any better. "It might get busy," I said. "I could help decorate so you don't get overwhelmed."

Vicki shook her head the entire time I talked. "We're fine," she said when I was done. "Jeff and Lena can handle most everything now, and I don't mind being here. I love this time of year." She sucked in a happy breath, eyes practically glowing. "You are going to enjoy your vacation. I don't want to see you in here for anything but a quick visit."

"But . . ."

Her hands went to her hips and she gave me a stern look that was ruined by the twitch of her mouth as she fought back a grin. "We can handle it. If you want to help pass out the gifts on Christmas Eve, that would be great. Otherwise, no!"

I sighed, but relented. I wasn't even sure why I was so intent on coming back to work. Vicki was right; they were handling things just fine. A break would probably do me a lot of good, especially since I was committed to the play.

Shoulders slumped, I said my good-byes, and carried my coffee out into the cold. It was time to do what I'd originally set out to do.

Shopping has always been a problem for me. Money had never really been an issue when I lived at home, and even now, I could afford to buy gifts for everyone without stressing about my bank account.

But for some reason, the moment I stepped into a store to buy a gift for someone, my mind went blank. Nothing seemed right. I always felt I was letting my friends and family down and struggled to come up with the perfect gift, despite the fact they told me I was overthinking it. I couldn't help myself. I didn't want to disappoint.

Pine Hills didn't have a mall in which I could wander aimlessly for hours. Instead, various locally owned shops lined the downtown area. I had yet to go on a full blown shopping trip since I'd moved here, and found it oddly refreshing to visit smaller shops where I often knew the owner and employees, at least by sight. Sure, there might not be as much in the way of brand name stuff in the mom and pop stores, but there was definitely something to be said for hand-made items, a certain love for the craft you didn't find in mass manufactured goods.

I was browsing a knick-knack shop that had once been a clothing store named Tessa's Dresses. The previous owner was long gone, and had been replaced by a friendly older woman, who sat behind the counter on a daily basis. Everything inside had been made locally and I was careful not to knock anything over as I looked for something that would be a perfect gift for one of my friends. Who? I had no idea. As I was examining a ceramic cat, someone tapped me gently on the arm.

"You're the new girl, aren't you?" the woman asked.

I only paid her a quick glance before saying, "I'm just browsing," and going back to the cat. I wondered if Vicki would like it. It was short-haired, and didn't have the white spot under his nose, but it did kind of look like Trouble.

"I don't work here," the woman said with a fluttery laugh that I recognized from somewhere. "You're Krissy, right? Remember me? Asia?"

"Oh!" I said, looking at her fully now. I hadn't recognized her without her elf costume and two tag-along friends. "Asia! What are you doing here?" I glanced at the price tag on the cat and then quickly put it back on the shelf before I accidentally broke it and was responsible for the outrageous price.

"Looking around, I suppose," she sighed. "Trying to get my mind off things. I'm still a little shaken up, to be honest. I can't believe something so terrible happened right there." She shuddered.

"It was pretty horrible," I said.

"I heard you used to date the killer." Her voice turned interested as she followed me down an aisle full of Christmas ornaments. "Did you ever suspect him of being capable of such a thing? I spent these last few weeks with him and never once did I think Rob could kill anyone."

Rob? He never used to like it when someone called him that, but I guess that was just something else he was trying to change about himself. "I'm as shocked as you are," I said, feeling mildly uncomfortable talking about it. It's one thing to know a killer. It's an entirely different animal to have actually dated one. People always looked at you like you should have known.

Of course, I still wasn't entirely convinced he was the one who'd offed Chuck.

"I was talking with Greg and Prairie earlier. They are both positive Rob killed him. They've heard the awfulest things about him recently."

I was curious as to what they'd heard, but didn't want to get involved. "I'm sure a lot of it has been blown out of proportion," I said, wishing Asia would drop it and let me go about my shopping in peace. Was this how people felt when I started asking them about people involved in a crime? If so, I was really going to have to reconsider my methods.

"Well, a few of us are thinking of having a memorial for Chucky. He might not have been anyone's best friend, but he *was* one of us. You should come!"

"I don't know," I said, feeling guilty for some reason. I mean, I didn't know anything about most of the cast, let alone Chuck. I was an outsider, having just joined the group. Robert was the only one I'd known before the play, but he was now in jail. And while Prudence had been showing me the ropes, it didn't equate to being fully integrated within the cast.

Going to the memorial would make me feel more like a fraud than I already did. Yet to turn it down would make it seem like I didn't care about the man's death.

"We'll see," I said, going for the middle ground.

Asia clasped me on the arm and gave me a warm smile. "I'll get you the details as soon as they're finalized." And then she spun away, tiny purse hanging from the crook of her elbow, finally leaving me alone.

I tried to continue shopping, but my mind was now firmly stuck on Robert, and by extension, Chuck's murder. It's kind of hard to get into the Christmas spirit when you kept seeing Santa lying there with a knife in his back.

Giving up for the day, I left the store and made the cold walk back to my car. It felt colder, but that could simply be because of where my head was rather than an actual drop in temperature.

I drove home, preoccupied, barely seeing anything around me. It was a wonder I didn't drive off the road and into a ditch. This was supposed to be a time of joy and giving, yet I was thinking about murder and death. I wasn't normally a morbid person, but this time, it hit a little too close to home.

I parked in my driveway and was halfway out of my car before I noticed someone getting out of a smart car beside me. She wore a furry, hooded coat, which left her face mostly concealed. I caught a flash of blond hair and a pair of wide, pretty eyes, I recognized.

"Trisha?" I asked in a surprised gasp. "What are you doing here?"

She looked frantically around before hurrying over to me. "Do you mind if we talk inside? It's cold, and well . . ."

I nodded and led the way to my front door. "I'm surprised to see you here," I said. "You vanished during practice yesterday and I thought . . ." My hands shook as I tried to get the key into the lock. I quit talking so I could not only focus, but try to decide what it was I *did* think about her flight from the theatre after Chuck's murder.

Trisha stood so close behind me, I could feel her body heat. It was mildly uncomfortable and made it that much harder for my frozen fingers to maneuver the key into the lock. Eventually, I got it and pushed my way inside, gently using my foot to scoot Misfit away from the door. Trisha followed me in without a word, and deep down, the paranoid part of me started screaming that she could very well be the killer, come to finish me off, just like she did Santa.

I squashed the little voice as I closed the door, shutting out the cold. I turned to find her with her hood pushed back, staring at me, panicked.

"He didn't do it," she said, practically pleading. "He couldn't have. I know him. Robert would never do such a thing." Her words came out rapid-fire, very near hysterical.

"Coffee?" I asked, moving to the kitchen to put a pot on for myself. "I always find it calming." I smiled at her in the hopes it would cause her to relax. She looked just about ready to blow.

Trisha nodded vigorously before moving to sit on the stool where Robert had sat last night. She didn't say anything more right away, choosing instead to pull off her gloves and worry at her fingers, which were red from the cold.

I kept myself busy getting the coffee ready, mugs down, sugar out. I wanted Trisha to have time to calm down. I wasn't sure why she'd come to me, but was willing to let her talk through it. Maybe it would help me set my own mind at ease about Robert, though it's never a comfortable feeling to be alone with your ex's current girlfriend.

The coffee finished percolating. I filled two mugs, carried them to the island counter, before grabbing the sugar and cream. Sadly, I was out of cookies—a travesty during Christmastime—and was relegated to doctoring my coffee like everyone else.

Trisha thanked me and sipped her coffee black. She visibly relaxed and gave me a shy smile. "Sorry about that," she said. "I worked myself up while I waited for you to get home and lost my head a bit there."

"That's okay," I said, taking a sip of my own coffee with a grimace. It just wasn't the same.

"Robert told me to come to you if something were to happen to him. He knew they'd blame him for Chuck's death." Her jaw clenched for an instant before releasing. "He said you would be able to help."

"I'm not sure how," I said. "Robert stopped by last night before he was . . ." I reddened since I was the reason he was currently sitting in jail. "The police will work things out," I finished, lamely.

"That's the thing," Trisha said. "He's positive they won't. They'll claim they have evidence against him, and he's pretty sure it'll be hard to shake on his own."

"He was seen fleeing the scene," I said, blushing again since I'd been the one to see him running away and had tattled on him. "And there was a bloody print next to the body that matched his shoe size."

"I know." Trisha leaned toward me, eyes pleading. "That's why we need your help. You're the only one he trusts to get to the truth."

Flattered as I was—not to mention, surprised—I didn't see how I could help him. Robert not only fled the scene and left a bloody footprint, he'd also fought with the victim mere minutes before the murder. It was all circumstantial, sure, but without any other evidence, it might be enough to convict him.

But I couldn't turn Trisha away without hearing her

out. As much as Robert annoyed me, we did have a history. I didn't want him to be guilty.

"Tell me everything," I said.

Trisha breathed a sigh of relief and sat back. "He was with me when it happened," she said. "I know no one will believe me since I'm his girlfriend." She glanced at me then, as if checking to see how I'd react to the declaration. I merely nodded at her to go on. "But it's the truth. We were together, so there was no way he could have killed Chuck."

"Was it his footprint?" I asked. "I saw him leave without his elf shoes. Everyone else still had theirs on."

"It was." Trisha frowned, and then shuddered. "After the fight with Chuck, we found a quiet corner to calm down together. Robert was still angry and no matter what I said, I couldn't get through to him. He said he needed to say one more thing before he could practice that night, so we went to find Chuck." She paused, swallowed. "He was dead when we got there. Robert ran over to check his pulse and . . ."

"And he stepped in the blood," I finished for her.

She nodded. "He kind of freaked out then. He took off the shoes and told me to go, that we needed to get out of there. I wasn't thinking straight, and I know he wasn't either. I went to the car and started it. He came out a few minutes later and we left. I don't know what he did with his shoes."

"Why didn't you tell someone?" I asked. As much as I wanted to believe her story, it seemed strange she wouldn't have at least called the cops or yelled for help when they'd found Chuck.

"I was scared. Robert was saying they'd blame him right from the start. He watches *CSI* all the time. He said we needed to lay low for a little while because you'd figure things out and would clear his name. I wanted to call someone, I really did, but since Chuck was already dead . . ." She shrugged. "It wasn't like there was anything anyone could do to save him."

"If you were laying low, then why did Robert come here last night?"

"I don't know," she said. "He didn't think we should hide together." She made a face like she thought the idea of hiding at all disgusted her. "I was at home, waiting for someone to come knocking on my door, when I heard he'd been arrested. I knew I'd have to come see you."

She stood suddenly, like she just realized she'd left the stove on at home. "Please help him," she said. "He didn't kill Chuck." A pair of tears rolled down her cheeks. "I don't know what I'll do if they don't catch the real killer and end up putting Robert away forever."

I took a long drink of my coffee to give myself a moment to think. While I wanted to believe Trisha, she *was* Robert's new fling. She could be lying to protect him. Chuck had been pretty rude to her, and their argument *had* centered around her.

But even I had my doubts about Robert's guilt. Didn't he deserve a fair shake? Just because he was often a jerk, didn't mean he was guilty.

I set down my coffee mug, resigned.

"Okay," I said. "I'll look into it."

Trisha squealed, her misery forgotten. She hurried around the edge of the counter and wrapped me in a hug. "Thank you so much." She pulled away, wiped at her eyes. "I promise we won't forget this." She snatched up her gloves and hurried to the door, presumably to tell Robert the good news.

I slumped onto a stool and thumped my head down onto the counter. I was pretty sure she was right when she said neither of them would forget it. I was just hoping that by the time it was all said and done, *I* wouldn't be regretting it.

8

It's one thing to say you are going to do a thing, and another to actually do it. After Trisha left, I didn't immediately jump to looking into Chuck's murder. I had no idea where to start, and honestly, I wasn't even sure I *should* be sticking my nose into it. I was too close to this one, and had once had a personal relationship with the accused killer. Even if I did find evidence that Robert was innocent, there would be quite a lot of people who would wonder if I was supporting him because of our past.

Then again, if I found him guilty, there'd be just as many people wondering if I'd planted evidence to convict him. I'm not sure there was any way I could do this without looking bad.

Besides, it wasn't like I knew everyone involved at the theatre. I still thought of the murdered man as Santa half the time. I couldn't simply waltz up to the cast on the streets and start asking questions. I imagine most of them had no idea who I was and wouldn't appreciate the intrusion.

And then there was the police. If anyone would hate my involvement, it would be officers Paul Dalton and John Buchannan.

I was so screwed.

I spent the rest of the day puttering around the house, watching Christmas specials and baking cookies. It felt good not to have to worry about anything for a few hours. Even Misfit behaved himself, choosing to nap under the tree, rather than *in* it.

I was just settling in to watch *Home Alone* with a hot mug of cookie doctored coffee when there was yet another knock at my door.

"Getting popular," I muttered, rising from where I'd just sat down. I couldn't remember the last time I'd had so many visitors in such a short span. Usually, my house was populated by me and my cat with a guest stopping by once a week or so. I was normally the one who went out to visit others.

I opened the door and was surprised to see Jane Winthrow shivering on my stoop.

"Hi, Krissy," she said, rubbing her hands together. She wasn't wearing gloves. "I noticed you were home this evening and thought you might like to have that sit down we'd talked about."

"Tonight?"

"If you're free." She glanced past me, toward the TV. "If you're busy, we can always do it another night."

"No, tonight would be great." I wasn't sure how much I'd enjoy having a chat with Eleanor Winthrow and her daughter, but it had to be more interesting than watching a movie I'd seen at least a dozen times before. "Give me a minute to grab my coat and lock up."

Jane smiled. "Take your time. I'll head back over and tell Mom the good news. Come right in when you're done here. There's no need to knock."

"Will do."

Jane gave me a thumbs up and then turned to head back to her mother's house.

I closed the door to the cold and took a big drink of my coffee. It was still on the hot side, but I refused to let it go to waste.

"No movie tonight," I told Misfit as I rinsed out the mug. He had yet to move from beneath the tree and had barely lifted his head when I'd opened the door. I guess the cold was getting to him, too.

I shut off the TV, threw on something that didn't have smears of chocolate and batter on it, followed by my coat, and then headed out for dinner with the Winthrows.

It had grown steadily colder as the day progressed, and when the sun went down, it only got worse. The sky was darker than it should have been, thanks to heavy cloud cover, but at least there was no snow yet. It sure felt like it would be starting up soon, however.

I felt strange just walking into Eleanor's house, despite the invitation to do just that, so I knocked on the door before pushing it open and calling out, "It's just me!" to let them know I wasn't a burglar or anything.

"We're in the kitchen," Jane called as I closed the door and took a quick look around.

Eleanor's house was small, and felt even more so from the inside. A blue armchair that looked to have been made in the '70s sat by the window, turned so she could easily see outside. A folding TV tray stood beside that, stacked with at least twenty newspapers.

Eleanor's binoculars sat on the arm of the chair. The TV was one of those old box sets that needed rabbit ears to work. More newspapers sat stacked atop it. The orange shag carpet was dirty and faded in a path leading from the kitchen, to the chair, the door, and then down the hall, toward the bedrooms. It was brighter along the edges, as if something had been stacked there, but had recently been removed.

As I moved to the kitchen, I glanced down the hall. There were only three doors that way. The first on the right looked to be the bathroom. I caught a glimpse of stacks upon stacks of newspapers in the room on the left. There had to be hundreds of them.

"Thank you so much for coming," Jane said, meeting me just outside the kitchen. "Mom's a little uptight this evening, so don't take anything she says personally."

"I won't." Eleanor had never liked me much, not that she ever truly got to know me. Most of what she knew came from watching my house constantly. I'm sure she meant well when she called the cops on me all those times. I suppose I could see how she could misinterpret a lot of what goes on at my house. Maybe sitting down with her and hashing things out would put an end to all those misunderstandings.

Jane gave me a reassuring smile as she led the way into the eat-in kitchen. The appliances all looked to have come from sometime before Nixon was president, as did the old flower print wallpaper on the walls. Eleanor was seated at a table covered in a ragged tablecloth, scowling at me like I'd forced my way in.

"Hi, Eleanor," I said, hoping to break the ice by calling her by her first name. "It's good to see you."

She harrumphed and glared at her daughter.

"Please, sit," Jane said, playing the part of the hostess. "Meatloaf okay? It's all I could convince Mom to eat."

"Meatloaf's fine." I sat. The chair was rickety and an ugly yellow color.

Jane went about getting the food ready, so I focused on Eleanor. She looked older than when I'd last seen her, as if having her daughter around had aged her a decade. I guess having someone fuss over you could have that effect if you were used to living on your own. I knew Eleanor's husband had died of an aneurysm some years ago, though I'd never learned his name, or even how long ago he'd passed. She could have been living on her own for the last twenty years.

Jane served the meatloaf with a side of lumpy mashed potatoes. She sat to my left, watching both her mother and I, as if waiting to see which of us would snap first. Eleanor sat across from me, doing her best to look as if we'd conspired against her.

I guess, in a way, we had.

After a long, silent few moments, Jane asked, "Mom, do you have anything to say to Krissy?"

Eleanor snorted. "The neighborhood was nicer when she wasn't around."

"Mom!" Jane looked to me. "I'm sorry about that. She's angry with me and is taking it out on you."

"It's fine." And it was. Eleanor felt trapped, and was lashing out. I'd have done the same thing if it was me.

"No, it's not." Jane turned back to her mother. "Tell her what we discussed."

Eleanor huffed, before looking down at her liver-spotted hands. "I shouldn't be so nosy all the time."

"And?"

Eleanor responded by shoving a heaping helping of mashed potatoes into her mouth.

"This isn't necessary," I said, feeling awkward. It was obvious there were issues between mother and daughter, and I'd somehow been dragged into it.

Jane sighed. "I know, but I thought it might help if you two got along better. Mom has been . . ." She frowned. "She's been having a tough time as of late. She's always collected newspapers, but used to keep them in order. She was proud of them, treated them like relics. I'm sure you saw some of them when you came in."

I nodded. "She has quite the collection."

"They were stacked halfway up the wall when I showed up," Jane went on, disapprovingly. "I've spent nearly every last waking moment here trying to tidy up. It's as if she stopped caring." She bit her lip, went on. "I'm starting to get worried."

"I'm fine," Eleanor grouched. "And I'm sitting right here, you know?"

"She doesn't get out anymore," Jane said, patting her mom's hand. "Her hip has been bothering her more and more as she gets older. I keep telling her it's because she sits in that chair all day, watching the neighborhood. She needs to exercise, needs to spend more time with friends."

Come to think of it, I couldn't remember the last time I saw Eleanor away from her property. It had to be lonely sitting around the house, without anyone to talk to, day in and day out. No wonder she was always peeping through my window with her binoculars. Seeing her TV, it was likely I was the only source of entertainment she had left.

"What about Judith Banyon?" I asked, focusing on Eleanor.

She shrugged. "She's too busy for the likes of me these days." She looked down at her plate, jaw working before going on. "Only calls once every two weeks or so anymore. Usually to complain about something. Doesn't care about me."

"It's why I keep saying you need to get out more," Jane said, before turning to me. "I was going to take her to a Christmas play, but I heard on the news one of the actors was killed and she refuses to go."

"Yeah, I was there."

Jane's eyes widened. "That's terrible. I heard they caught the man who did it, but that doesn't make it any better, does it?"

"No," I said, glad it didn't appear she'd put two and two together and realized that was why the police were at my house last night. "We're still going to try to have the play. I think they're casting a new Santa, so if you want to come, you're welcome to."

Eleanor's eyes narrowed. "I hope you're not considering Randy Winter again."

Her comment caught me by surprise. Apparently, Eleanor wasn't as sheltered as it appeared. "Why's that?" I asked, though I had a pretty good idea why. No one wanted Santa to be a slurring drunk.

A fire lit in Eleanor's eye as she leaned forward. It was the same sort of look Rita got when she was about to reveal a juicy piece of gossip.

"I wouldn't be surprised to learn he had a role in that man's death," she said. "He's a no good scoundrel who will ruin the sanctity of Christmas if allowed to portray one of its icons."

"Mother," Jane said. "It's not nice to talk about

people that way." She gave me a sideways look that made me wonder if she'd heard the same thing about me.

"Well, it's true," Eleanor went on, stubbornly. "Randy the Rancid we called him. Always in his drink, always trying to scheme so he didn't have to do a lick of work. He didn't get paid for his role as Santa in those plays, but he used to get other paying jobs where he could sit on his fat fanny. Jolly my tush. I worked with the man!"

"Mom, that doesn't make him necessarily a bad man," Jane said.

"I heard he was talking down at the Whistling Wet Weasel about getting his old role back." Eleanor leaned forward, eyes gleaming like I had never seen them before. "And then that night, who ends up dead?" She spread her hands and nodded like she'd said it all.

"They already caught the killer, Mom," Jane said. She sounded frustrated with Eleanor. I was starting to get a better picture of their relationship, and I can't say I felt Jane was handling her mom right. Sure, Eleanor needed some help, but I think she was lonely, not losing it.

"Actually," I said, knowing I probably shouldn't add fuel to the fire, but wanting to know more. "I'm not so sure about that."

Both of them stared at me, causing me to redden now that I had everyone's full attention.

"I kind of know the accused," I said, leaving out the fact we'd dated. Knowing how the gossip train worked around here, it was a moot point anyway. Everyone would know by tomorrow. "He's got an alibi and I'm inclined to believe him."

"He was at your house," Eleanor said, narrowing

her eyes at me like I was suddenly under suspicion. "That's what all the ruckus was about last night."

"He was," I admitted. "He came to me for help." Then to redirect, "I'm also the one who called the police on him. Since then, I've learned more about what happened that night, and I'm starting to believe Robert might be innocent."

"So, it could be this Randy guy Mom's talking about?" Jane asked.

"I knew it!" Eleanor cackled and rubbed her hands together. Her eyes darted to an old wall phone as if she was anxious to call someone and spread the word.

"I don't know for sure yet," I said, hoping to stem the tide before it got started. "He's shown up at practice a few times, looking tipsy, so I suppose it's possible he lost control." I turned to Eleanor. "Do you really think he's capable of killing someone?"

She shrugged, took a bite of meatloaf, and grinned. "Being Santa was his life. Losing his role in the play damaged his reputation around town. I heard he wasn't even hired on at some of his other gigs out of town because of it. You know, mall stuff."

"But that's not enough reason to kill someone," Jane said, sounding shocked by the whole mess.

There was a time when I would have agreed, but lately, I wasn't so sure. People tended to lose their minds when their livelihood was threatened. By the sound of it, Randy Winter didn't just *play* Santa; he lived it. He had to resent the man who'd stepped in to fill his big black boots. And while it was more the fault of the director who'd cast someone else, and Randy for his inability to stay sober, it's easy enough to blame the replacement.

And I *had* seen Randy there the night of Chuck's murder, so it put him on the scene.

"I don't like all this murder talk," Jane said, even though she'd been the one to bring it up. "We should focus on the good in the world, not the bad."

Eleanor rolled her eyes and went about eating, seemingly happy she'd gotten a chance to gossip. I wondered if she ever talked to Rita. I imagine the two of them had enough in common they'd hit it off splendidly if given the chance.

Of course, I'm not sure how ready the town would be for *that* pairing.

I had further questions, but I let the matter drop for now. Tonight was supposed to be about instilling good feelings between neighbors, and while the topic of conversation might not have been the most dinner worthy, it had given both Eleanor and I something to talk about. Baby steps and all that.

And besides, I now had a suspect at the top of my list who wasn't named Robert Dunhill. Tomorrow, Randy Winter and I were going to have a little chat. I intended to find out how jolly this Santa really was.

9

I went home that night, head full of ideas. Not only did I feel like my relationship with my neighbor was on the mend, but she'd given me quite a lot to think about when it came to possible suspects in Chuck's murder. At this point, I wasn't sold on anyone just yet, not knowing enough about anyone to make any real judgments, but I was starting to see who could have done it, and why.

When I went to bed a few hours later, I couldn't focus on sleep. My dreams were full of Santas and elves, each looking guiltier than the last. Even Rudolph made an appearance in one disturbing dream where Santa had been stabbed with antlers, not a knife.

When I woke, it was to a white world. Misfit was sitting in the window, staring wide-eyed at the fluff falling from the sky. We didn't get this kind of weather where I'd lived in California, and while he'd seen snow just last winter, we'd never really had a good white snowfall. Last winter was mostly a mix of wet snow and rain that made things muddy, not pretty.

Tired, I got up and made my morning coffee, still

in my PJs. I didn't have anywhere to be just yet, and wanted to enjoy my morning without thinking about murder or plays or Robert. Once my coffee was done and properly doctored, I stood at the window and watched the snow fall. It really was beautiful, though I dreaded having to drive in it. To someone who was used to it, the snow wouldn't be a problem. For me, it might as well have been a solid sheet of ice. I'd be lucky not to slide my way directly into a ditch.

Eventually, I made myself a real breakfast and got myself cleaned up for the day. The hot shower beat away most of my weariness and by the time I was dressed, I was ready to face the world.

I started by seeing what I could dig up about Randy Winter. There was quite a lot of references to him online, almost all about his work as Santa over the years. He was very nearly a local celebrity in that regard. I found his home address easily enough and decided I'd pay him a visit before I headed into practice. Maybe he'd be able to give me some insights into the cast. Or, if he was the killer, would give himself up once confronted.

As if I'd ever be so lucky.

Not sure what else I could do until it was time to go, I pulled out a holiday crossword puzzle book, sat by the window, and waited for the plow to go through as I worked through the puzzles. There was no way I was going to leave until it did.

It took a little over two hours before I heard the scraping, rumbling sound of the plow. It zoomed right past my street, going faster than expected. Dirty snow and ice flew to the side of the road. I watched the plow go, hoping the driver would turn around, but instead, he turned left and continued on until he was out of sight.

I guess I shouldn't have been surprised he'd skipped my street. I lived on a dead end residential road. It's not like there was ever any through traffic, and really, it wasn't all that long of a street. I'd be driving in fluff for only about twenty seconds.

Bundled up as if I was going on a trip to the North Pole, I headed out. My car started up with only a mild protest and I sat in it, waiting for the windshield to defrost. When it did, I put the car in gear, and backed out, slowly so my bumper wouldn't get an up close and personal introduction to my mailbox.

I drove slowly, which earned me quite a few honks along the way. At one point, I got passed by an elderly man whose face was nearly touching his windshield. He wore glasses that looked as thick as bottle caps, but that didn't stop him from glaring at me on his way past. I decided to speed up a touch.

It still took me twice as long as it should have to reach Randy Winter's home. I was surprised to find he lived in a cute little cottage. It was small and looked well-tended from the outside. His drinking apparently didn't stop him from keeping up maintenance on his home. His lawn ornaments consisted of reindeer and a wooden Santa on a sleigh filled with gifts. The windows were decorated with stick-on snowflakes. I fully expected to see lights strewn from one end of the cottage to the other, but they were currently absent. It made the place seem a little sad, as if the former Santa couldn't get up the energy to finish the job.

I pulled into the short driveway and frowned. Tire tracks led from the car port at the side of the house, telling me someone had left sometime after the snow had stopped falling. There were no other cars in the drive, meaning I'd likely missed Randy. The car port was only big enough for one vehicle, so he either lived alone, or whoever he lived with didn't drive.

Undeterred, I got out of my car and headed for the front door, leaving three-inch deep footprints in my wake. I knocked, wincing as my frozen knuckles impacted the hard wooden door. I waited a good minute, knowing I was wasting my time, but holding out hope that he lived with someone who was still inside.

"You looking for Randy?" a middle-aged woman called from the house next door. She was wearing a bathrobe, slippers, and her hair was in curlers, yet she didn't look as if she was cold. Steam curled from the coffee mug in her hand, making me want some myself. "He's not home."

"Do you know when he'll be back?" I asked.

"When the beer runs out, I'd wager." She chuckled at her own joke. "I'd try back again late tonight, though I doubt he'll be in any condition to talk by then."

"Thanks," I said, thinking it was a bit early to start drinking, but who was I to judge? The man had lost the one role he apparently lived for. That couldn't be easy, though I wasn't a big fan of drinking to forget. There were other, less destructive ways, to get over disappointment.

The woman raised her mug to me in salute before vanishing back inside.

Trudging back to my car, I considered giving up for the day. I could always try to catch Randy really early the next morning, before he had a chance to hit the bars. Or I could stop by on my way home after practice. Then again, he'd shown up every single practice since the start, begging for his role back, so I might just have to wait for him to make an appearance and talk to him then.

But I wasn't thrilled about the idea. Not only would he be in a foul mood—and likely drunk—but everyone else would be there as well. It would be much better to have our little chat where someone couldn't eavesdrop.

It was then I remembered what Eleanor had said last night. She'd said he'd talked about trying to get his part in the play back, and he'd done it in a very specific place: the Whistling Wet Weasel.

The name didn't make the bar sound very appealing, and there was no guarantee Randy frequented the same place every day, but it was worth a shot.

Back in my car, I did a quick Google, and then was on my way. I drove slowly down the streets, which were already getting snow covered again, until I found the bar. It wasn't exactly a dive, but it was a near thing. During the summer, I could imagine a lot of motorcycles lining up outside, but in the snow, there were only a handful of cars. Muffled country music came from inside. The windows were decorated with beer signs and posters. There were no smashed bottles or tough looking characters outside, so I took it as a sign I wouldn't get myself killed asking questions of one of the patrons.

Or so I hoped.

Grimacing, I got out of my car and headed inside. I was met with a warm blast of stale beer and sweat. The place was so hot, I was surprised it wasn't on fire. Other than the heat, the bar wasn't so bad inside. There were tables where a handful of patrons were enjoying a meal, without a beer between them. I had to admit, the burgers and fries smelled pretty good. It was already well past lunchtime—closer to dinner, in fact—and my stomach was starting to protest.

I stopped just inside the door, in a puddle formed by the rapidly melting snow, and glanced around. It took all of two seconds to spot Randy at the bar, shoulders slumped, beer in hand. I made my way over to him, hoping he was sober enough to talk without slurring. Then again, drunk, he might let something slip, like, I don't know, whether or not he killed Chuck.

"Hi, Randy," I said, sliding up onto the barstool next to him.

He glanced at me, frowned. "Do I know you?"

"I'm Krissy." I stuck out a hand he pointedly ignored. "I'm one of the elves in the Christmas play this year." When he didn't look impressed, I added, "I'm filling in for someone who's sick."

Randy eyed me a moment, then shrugged. "Good for you." He turned back to his beer, though he didn't raise the bottle to his lips, just spun it slowly in his hands.

The bartender sauntered over. "Can I get you anything?" she asked.

"It's a little hot in here," I said, a bead of sweat rolling down my face. "A water would be nice." I considered adding something to eat, but decided I didn't quite trust bar food, no matter how good it smelled.

"Thermostat's broke. It's either hot as hell or cold as the Antarctic. No in between." She wandered off to get my water.

I waited until she pushed a sweating glass in front of me before turning back to Randy. "Did you hear what happened to Chuck?" I asked it as nonchalantly as I could.

Randy didn't respond right away. He took a slow sip from his bottle before nodding. "Can't say it's a shame. Got what he deserved for stealing my life out from under me." He turned on his seat, spread his arms. "Look at me. What else can I do but play Santa."

He was right. Randy Winter had the belly, the beard, the ruddy cheeks. Add a red suit and spectacles, and he'd be the spitting image of Santa. He even sounded a bit like Saint Nick. I had to fight down the urge to ask him to give me a hearty "Ho, ho, ho."

"Have you heard anything from Lawrence?" I asked. "He says he's going to go through with the play, despite what happened."

Randy snorted and turned back to his beer. "Why wouldn't he? He's probably found some other hack to fill in. Despite everything . . ." He glanced sideways at me, then shook his head.

"You two were talking the other day, and it seemed pretty civil," I said. "I thought you might have mended your relationship and he might give you a call. In fact, he said he'd talked to someone about filling in, and I figured he'd called you."

Randy frowned hard at his beer. "You didn't see anything. And I haven't heard a thing from Lawrence." Something about the last didn't ring quite true.

"So you're saying your conversation with Lawrence had nothing to do with your role as Santa? I know Chuck was still alive then, but maybe Lawrence was already looking to replace him. He seemed pretty confident he'd have a new Santa by today."

His frown deepened. "Why would it? I was long

gone by the time the imposter was killed. If I'd known someone was going to off him, I would have stuck around." He looked at me. "What is it to you, anyway? You're just a lowly elf."

"Just a lowly elf?" I wasn't sure if I should be offended or amused. "I—"

A blast of "Jingle Bells" cut me off.

"Excuse me." Randy reached into his pocket, removed his cell, and then glanced at the screen. His eyes widened as he answered. He rose and hurried back toward the bathrooms, voice low so I couldn't hear much more than his greeting.

The bartender wandered over and I stopped her with a, "What can you tell me about Randy?" I gestured toward the man in question, who was standing by the bathroom doors, but hadn't gone inside.

"He's a good guy," she said with a shrug. "Drinks a bit much when he's down, but otherwise, he seems decent enough."

"He's been upset a lot lately."

She smiled. "Honey, he's been miserable ever since they stopped letting him play Santa. It was his life." She nodded toward my water. "Can I get you anything else?"

"No thank you."

The bartender shrugged and started wiping down the counter, leaving me to wonder if Randy was miserable enough or angry enough to kill the man who'd taken his role. He might not have meant to do it. If he drank too much and went to confront Chuck, he very well might have killed him without knowing what he was doing. And depending on how drunk he'd gotten, he could have forgotten it had ever happened.

But when I'd seen him that night, he hadn't appeared drunk. In fact, I thought he'd looked pretty lucid and calm.

Randy ended his call and hurried back over to the bar, slapping down a five as he grabbed his coat. "I've got to run," he said, grinning. Before I could ask him why he was so excited, he was heading out the door at a near run.

I frowned after him before glancing at his beer bottle. "Do you think he should be driving?" I asked the bartender who'd scooped up the five.

"He's been here for two hours, nursing that very same one," she said, picking up the half-full bottle. "Must have come into some good luck lately." She walked away.

I rose from my stool and headed for the door. I had a feeling Randy's good fortune didn't come in the form of a lottery ticket. With Chuck dead, how easy would it be for him to work his way back into Lawrence's good graces in an effort to get his job back? Was that why he'd been there that night, cozying up to Lawrence? Did he already know Chuck was going to meet his end and wanted to show the director he could handle it? He knew the role, the words to the play. He was very likely the only choice left this close to opening night.

Randy was long gone by the time I stepped outside. The cold air instantly froze the sweat coating my body, sucking the breath right out of me. I hurried to my car, started it, and jacked the heat up to full blast to thaw out.

It was starting to look more and more like Randy Winter might indeed be involved in Chuck's murder. Glancing at the clock, I saw I still had a few hours left before I'd know for sure whether or not the call that had sent him scrambling was from Lawrence, offering him the part of Santa again. I had no doubts that when I arrived, I'd be proven correct.

And if that was the case, did that mean he'd killed Chuck?

My stomach grumbled and I decided it was time to step away from the murder a bit and get myself more into the holiday spirit. I glanced once more at the Whistling Wet Weasel, and wondered if Santa would be spending much more time there, or if he'd found a way to make his own Christmas wish come true.

10

I was happy to see business was brisk at Death
by Coffee, even if it meant waiting in line for my
eggnog coffee and cookie. It wasn't much of a meal,
but it was better than going hungry. Both Lena and
Jeff were working up a sweat as they took order after
order—mostly eggnog-related items. Upstairs, Vicki
was less busy. Her boyfriend, Mason Lawyer, stood at
the counter, talking to her while she rang up a book
sale.

As I waited for my turn in line, I glanced at the
tree upstairs to find even more gifts sitting beneath it.
It felt good to know there were so many generous
people in Pine Hills.

Lena gave me a tired smile as I stepped up to the
counter. "What can I get ya?" she asked.

I ordered my coffee and cookies and paid before
stepping aside to wait for Jeff. I'd have stood and
talked a bit, asking her how the day was going and so
forth, but the line continued on behind me and showed
no signs of easing up. Jeff finished putting my order
together and handed it over without seeming to recognize me.

I found an open table in the corner and grabbed it before anyone else could. I brushed away cookie crumbs left by the last guest who'd sat there, and then took my seat, feeling guilty. I should be working, not running all over town, shopping and investigating murders.

But Lena and Jeff did seem to have things under control. No one was forced to wait too long for their order, and when I tried my cookie, I found it to be still warm, so they were keeping up just fine with the baking.

"Can you believe what they've done to me?"

I jumped, sloshing a good portion of my coffee onto the table. Rita pulled up a chair and sat down.

"You should be more careful, dear," she said, with a disapproving look at the spill.

"Thanks," I muttered, rising to grab some napkins to mop up the mess. "What's wrong?" I asked Rita as I sat back down.

"I'm banned from the theatre!" Her hand fluttered at her chest like the mere thought gave her heart palpitations.

"Really? By whom?"

"Lawrence Jackson, if you can believe it!" She huffed. "He told me I was a distraction. Me! I mean, how dare he? After everything I've done for his production. And that's not to mention what I've done for the theatre. I was the one who'd discovered the wet spot on the ceiling in the women's room. If I hadn't, it could have caved in on everyone's head! And then I recruited you when they wouldn't have been able to find anyone to take Mandy's spot. I'm a blessing to that place and he simply can't see it."

I sat stoically through her rant before asking, "Why

would he ban you?" I was genuinely curious. Rita could be annoying, but her heart was in the right place. She truly did want the play to succeed, even if she often went about it the wrong way.

"I didn't do a thing to deserve it," she said. "All I did was ask Lawrence about why he was meeting with Randy Winter in the alley bordering the theatre yesterday. Something passed between them, and I'm pretty sure it was money."

I gaped at her. "A payoff of some kind?" Had Randy paid Lawrence to off Santa for him so he could take over the role? Why not just fire the man, if that was the case?

"I'm thinking drugs," Rita said with an assured nod of her head. "I mean, that man has to be on drugs to tell me not to come back. I'm the life of that theatre, whether he wants to admit it or not."

My eyes wanted to roll, but I kept them in place. "When did this happen exactly?" I asked. She'd said yesterday, but I found that hard to believe. Randy hadn't seemed thrilled when I'd brought up Lawrence, but then again, if there was blackmail of some kind going on, then I guess it made sense he might not be in a good mood.

Of course, that brought up the question: who was blackmailing whom?

"Just last night," Rita said. "I went to the theatre, thinking there might still be practice since no one told me otherwise. The doors were closed and locked up tight, so I was going to turn around and leave when I heard voices. I decided to do my civic duty and make sure nothing untoward was happening, and that's when I saw Randy and Lawrence. Once the money passed hands, I went back to my car and waited for

Lawrence to come slipping out of the shadows. He was parked right next to me, so I knew he'd have to come out eventually." She gave me a self-satisfied smile. "I confronted him right then and there."

"What did he say?" I asked.

"Nothing! Can you believe he denied it ever happened? I saw him as plain as day and he had the gall to call me a liar." She harrumphed. "Then he told me I'm not to return to the theatre or he'd call the police on me!"

My mind was racing. Why were Lawrence and Randy at the theatre on a night when there was to be no practice? They weren't supposed to like one another. You don't make shady alleyway dealings, especially right after a murder, if you didn't have something to hide. Could they be in on Chuck's death together? Or did one of them commit the crime and the other found out somehow?

None of it made sense. I simply didn't have enough information to go on without jumping to conclusions that would be better left for the police.

"Who gave whom the money?" I asked.

Rita started to speak, paused, and then frowned. "Well, now that I think about it, I'm not sure."

"What do you mean you're not sure?"

"It was dark. And they were all hunched together. Since it was in an envelope, I guess I can't be sure it was actually money. I was too busy trying to hear what they were saying to pay full attention to what they were doing. You know how it is."

I sighed. As far as we knew, Randy was giving Lawrence his favorite cocktail recipe. Since Rita had only seen an envelope, and she hadn't thought to check to see who was the one to pass it on to the other, that left me with practically nothing.

"Could you make out what they were talking about?" I asked, hopefully.

"As I said, it was dark." She said it like the quality of light would impact her hearing. "And they weren't talking loudly." She blushed and fanned herself off. "I only heard a word or two and none of it made much sense."

"So you don't know why they were back there?"

"Of course not, dear. Why do you think I had to confront Lawrence about it?" Rita heaved herself up. "I should be going. I need to make a few calls and let some very important people know they shouldn't attend this year's production. If I can't be a part of it, well then, no one is going to enjoy it!"

She stormed off, out into the cold, a woman on a mission. I felt bad for her, sure, but also felt bad for anyone who got in her way, including Lawrence. I don't think he realized what he'd done by getting on her bad side.

But if he was Chuck's killer, and was paying off witnesses, then my pity would be short-lived.

Noting Vicki and Mason alone upstairs, I finished off my light lunch and then rose. I headed upstairs to join them. Vicki was a theatre pro, so if anyone could fill me in on the ins and outs of theatre life, she was the one. And while she'd only done one play since moving to Pine Hills, there was a chance she'd had interactions with Lawrence Jackson, as well as some of the current cast. Maybe she'd be able to tell me what kind of people I was dealing with.

"Hey, Krissy, how's the acting?" Mason asked with a wide smile as I approached.

"Exhausting," I said. "No one told me it was going to be a musical. Every muscle in my body aches, and that includes my tongue from all the singing!"

Vicki laughed. "All plays can be grueling, but musicals are definitely worse. It's up to the director not to work you too hard."

Perfect, I thought. "Speaking of directors, do you know Lawrence Jackson? He's directing the play."

"Sorry," Vicki said with a shake of her head. "I've heard the name, of course, but nothing else. Why?"

I shrugged. "I was curious about him, is all."

"Does it have to do with the murder?" Mason asked, a knowing gleam in his eye.

"It might," I admitted. "He was seen making what one could construe as a shady deal in an alleyway last night. I was wondering if you knew if he was into gambling or anything."

"Can't help you there," Vicki said. "Are you still going through with the production? I'd heard it was still on despite the tragedy."

I nodded. "So far, we are. Though I'm not sure I'm going to make it." I rubbed at my lower back for emphasis.

"Drink lots of water," Vicki said. "And maybe throw in something with electrolytes. Since you're singing and dancing, you'll want to keep your energy up, as well as keep hydrated."

"Thanks," I said. My diet of coffee and cookies was probably not the best pre-practice fuel. "I'm worried about how tonight's going to go. Our Santa was just murdered, quite possibly by someone still working there. How can you get into the holiday spirit with that hanging over your head?"

"Are you going to be asking around about it?"

Mason asked, voice growing concerned. He wasn't stupid. He knew what kind of person I was, and that I wouldn't be able to leave a murder investigation alone.

"I don't know," I said, not meeting his eye. "I guess I will be. It'll be hard not to talk about it, so it isn't like I'm going to have to corner anyone."

"Want some advice?" Vicki asked.

"Sure."

"Don't throw accusations around. Theatre people are a tight knit group. Sure, everyone has their eccentricities, so there's always a little bit of gossip and jealousy going around. But if you start acting like you suspect cast mates of being involved in the murder, you'll be ostracized from the group and they'll start protecting one another."

"Okay," I said, not liking the sound of that at all. "What do you recommend?"

"Get in close to them," Vicki said. "You're new, so it won't seem strange if you try to get to know people by asking a few questions. If you hang out and listen, I bet you'll learn a lot more than if you try to badger a confession out of someone. But remember, if there's one thing theatre people love, it's drama! Don't be afraid to let a few juicy tidbits slip if you think it will get people talking."

"And try not to get yourself hurt," Mason added.

"I'll do my best," I said to his grin. "I should probably get going. Practice comes all too soon and I need to figure out how I'm going to do this."

"Do you have another minute to talk?" Mason asked.

I checked the clock and nodded. "Sure."

Mason glanced at Vicki before speaking. "We were

wondering if you'd like to have Christmas dinner with us at my place. Will is invited, too, of course. We thought it would be nice to have you two over for a gift exchange and meal. If you already have plans, that's fine. I know it's short notice, but we didn't make the decision until a few hours ago."

"I . . ." I was touched and found an actual tear in my eye. "I'll have to ask Will, but I'd love to go." I looked at Vicki, worried. "That is, if it's okay with you."

"Of course it is, silly." She came around the counter and gave me a reassuring hug. "We haven't spent Christmas together for years. I thought it was time we started it up again. You're like family to me."

I sniffed. It must be from the dust because I surely couldn't be crying. I wiped my eyes and smiled. "I'll be there." Even if Will couldn't make it, I was determined to make time for them. "Thank you."

Mason put his arm around Vicki's waist and drew her in close. "We'll see you then."

I left the two lovebirds before I started blubbering. When we were younger, Vicki and I spent every Christmas together. Our families would meet, share stories, and exchange gifts, laughing the night away. I hadn't realized how much I missed it until now.

I started for the door, but stopped myself short. Vicki was right; I needed to ingratiate myself with the rest of the cast or else I would end up dealing with a whole lot of cold shoulders. If I was going to help Robert, I couldn't have that.

Changing directions, I headed for the register, which was now empty. Lena and Jeff were currently slumped against the back counter, having finally made it through the line of customers.

If there's one thing owning Death by Coffee has

shown me, it was that people valued their coffee. If I wanted to win the affections of the cast and crew, what better way than to bring them fuel—and warmth—for the grueling evening of practice? And maybe, when it's all said and done, my gesture will help melt any cold shoulders I might otherwise have encountered.

11

"Hold the door, please."

Dean jumped at the sound of my voice, but held the door for me as I carefully made my way through the slick snow, into the theatre. I was carrying two large thermoses full of coffee in my hands, and had a sleeve of cups under one arm, a package of sugar and creamer under the other. Sadly, I didn't have enough hands for cookies or I'd have brought a few of those as well.

"Thanks," I said, slipping inside and shaking off flakes of snow. It had started up again, and was coming down in a fluffy sheet that had me worried about road conditions when it came time to go home.

"My pleasure," Dean said, taking the sleeve of cups from me before they fell from my loosening grip. He took a deep breath and grinned. "Is that what I think it is?"

"Sure is. Help me set up somewhere and you can have the first cup."

Dean scurried off, leaving me to hold the thermoses. I could hear voices throughout the theatre, but couldn't see anyone. I imagined most of the cast was in the back, getting dressed, while Lawrence was likely up front, making demands of whatever poor crew member he'd managed to snag hold of. I was kind of glad Dean had escaped him this time.

A moment later, he returned, carrying a folding table. I followed him to the back wall where he flipped it open, obviously having done it a time or two. I set down the thermoses and condiments the moment he had the table set upright, and then went about removing the cups from their sleeves. Dean picked up one of the to-go cups and looked at the label.

"Death by Coffee," he said. "You know someone there?"

"I'm co-owner," I said with just a hint of pride.

Dean snapped his fingers and looked me up and down. "That's where I recognized you from. I knew I'd heard of you from somewhere before, but couldn't place where. Now I know. You've been on the news. You helped solve a few murder cases, right?"

"That's me," I said, blushing. No matter how many times someone recognized me, I couldn't get used to the celebrity, no matter how minor. "But I'm here as an elf, so no murder investigating for me." My voice hitched on the last, and I hoped Dean didn't notice and take it for a lie, which it was.

"That's cool." He nodded slowly, glanced around the room, and then moved to the thermoses. "We used to keep coffee set up back here, but Lawrence didn't like it. Said it was a distraction. Too many of us would hover around, drinking and gossiping. When he's not directing the plays, we usually go ahead and have drinks and snacks set up."

"Do you think he'll disapprove of this?" I asked, not wanting to draw any more of Lawrence's ire.

"After the week we've had, I think he'll let it slide." He peered at the sticker on one of the thermoses and made a face. "Eggnog coffee?"

"It's actually pretty good," I said. "The other is regular, so if you aren't interested, you can have that instead."

Dean moved to the other thermos and filled himself a cup. He took a sip without adding cream or sugar. "So you aren't looking into Chuck's murder then?"

"They got the guy," I said with a shrug. "I just want to put it behind me and get on with the show. I really do need all the practice I can get."

"It's a shame," Dean said with a shake of his head. "I, like most people here, didn't much care for Chuck, but you never want something bad to happen to anyone you know, regardless of how they treat you. And now, the entire play is at risk. I know Lawrence wants to go through with it, but the Santa role can't be played by just anyone. There's just not enough time for a new guy to learn the part before show night." Another sip of coffee. "I should get to work before Lawrence finds me."

"He seems to be hard on you." I spoke hurriedly before he could walk away. "I never see him yell at any of the other crew."

Dean shrugged. "He expects a lot more out of me, I guess. I've been with the theatre for only a short while, but I work hard. Most of the time, anything that goes wrong, isn't my fault, yet I'm usually the one who gets blamed for it." His jaw clenched a heartbeat before he smiled. "Thanks for the coffee." He raised his cup before turning and walking off.

By now, others were coming in, both from the back, and outside. Prudence saw me the moment she was through the door and hurried over. The snow made her hair sparkle.

"Now, that's a sight for frozen bones." She reached for a cup, paused. "May I?"

"Help yourself."

She grabbed a cup and filled it will eggnog coffee. Unlike Dean, Prudence took hers with near fatal levels of sugar. She took a large swallow and sighed. "It's getting bad out there. Violet fell on her way in. Just about burst into tears, but ended up coming in anyway. Figured she might go home, rather than face anyone. She never could handle being embarrassed."

"Is Violet one of the elves?" I asked.

"One of the crew." She jerked her thumb over toward where Dean was assisting a female crew member whose backside was wet. "Mousey looking one. She's usually up in the booth with Zander, which is why you haven't met her."

"I see." It made me realize how little I knew about everyone. There were at least a dozen people here whose names I didn't know. And even when it came to the ones I'd met, I didn't know last names, Chuck's included, as bad as it seemed.

"Is that coffee?" Asia appeared from the back with both Greg and Prairie right behind her. She didn't wait for an answer before she started pouring.

"I thought it might help keep everyone warm," I said, though no one was listening to me. All three filled a cup to the brim. I was starting to worry I hadn't brought enough. While the thermoses were large, it wouldn't take long before they were empty. They were the only two we had at Death by Coffee. We kept them in reserve, just in case something ever happened, like the power going out, and wanted to keep some coffee warm.

Asia took a sip, smiled, and motioned to me with her cup. "We're going to have the memorial in two days. It'll have to be during the afternoon because of practice, which is a bummer, but we'll manage. I thought about having it here, but it seemed wrong somehow, like Chucky's ghost would appear or something." She rolled her eyes. "We're going to have it at my house instead." She produced a card from somewhere in her costume and handed it to me.

I flipped it open to find what I assumed was Asia's home address, along with a handwritten note that said, *"Memorial to be held in the honor of our dear departed Santa. Drinks and games will be provided!"* I raised my eyebrows at the mention of games, but let it slide. Maybe it wasn't such a bad idea to keep everyone's spirits up.

Asia glanced at Prudence and sighed. "I suppose you should have one, too." She handed over a card before turning back to me. "I expect to see you there!" And then she walked away. Prairie gave me a little finger wave and hair flip before following. Greg only glared, though it didn't stop him from taking a sip from his coffee as he left.

"Never liked her," Prudence muttered. "Always so full of herself. Never considers other people's feelings."

I shrugged. "I don't know. She seems okay."

Prudence snorted. "The girl thinks she should headline every production, yet she always ends up with a background role. She can't act, can't sing, and if you were to put a hammer in her hand, she wouldn't know what to do with it." She shook her head, almost sadly. "She's always putting on airs, acting like she cares. It's about the only acting she ever does." Another snort. "She's having this memorial only so she can throw a party. Don't let her fool you."

A man's death hardly seemed to be an appropriate reason to throw a party, but who was I to judge. Chuck didn't seem much liked, so at least someone was doing *something* in his name, even if it was for the wrong reasons. I wondered if he'd had any friends or family at all that were actually upset about his demise. If so, I had yet to meet them.

Prudence left then to get dressed. Much of the cast were already in costume and were wandering over to investigate the coffees. I watched, waiting to see if anyone showed any signs of guilt, but everyone simply seemed thankful for the hot drink and chance to socialize.

Trisha appeared a moment later, fully dressed as Mrs. Claus. She hurried over the moment she saw me.

"Have you found anything out yet?" she asked in a hushed whisper.

"Not really," I admitted. "I haven't had much of a chance to ask around."

Trisha frowned and worried at her hands. "Jail is no place for Robert. I'm scared something will happen to him."

"It's not like prison," I assured her. "He's probably a lot more comfortable there than the rest of us are out here." Not to mention, safer. If he wasn't the killer, that meant the real murderer was still out there

somewhere, and could quite possibly be planning yet
another attack. The thought caused me to shudder.

"You'll let me know if you learn anything, right?"
Trisha asked. "I hate not knowing what is going to
happen. I don't know how much longer I can do this.
It's so . . .." She trailed off, eyes going toward the stage.

I followed her gaze and found myself looking at
Lawrence. Randy Winter was at his elbow, dressed as
Santa, right down to his shiny black boots. Lawrence
said something to Randy, who belted out a hearty "Ho,
ho, ho," that drew every eye in the place.

"Is that . . . ?" Trisha shook her head. "I can't believe it."

I could, though it was still a shock to see him there.
He looked sober, though his cheeks were rosy. I
couldn't tell if it was makeup, or if he was just naturally
red-cheeked.

"Well, I'll be," Prudence said, coming to a stop
next to me. "Didn't think I'd see him dressed like that
ever again."

"I thought those two didn't like each other," I said.
I was having a hard time deciding what to believe.
First, I see them yelling at one another, and then later,
talking civilly. And then there was what Rita saw in
the alleyway, yet Randy didn't seem too happy with
Lawrence when I'd talked to him earlier that day. I
was royally confused.

"They don't, as far as I know." Prudence shook her
head. "It's a shame it took a man dying for him to get
his role back. He was always a better Santa. Well, most
of the time, anyway."

"I'll talk to you later," Trisha said, paying Prudence
a pair of quick glances, before walking away.

"You'd better get changed," Prudence said. "You don't want Lawrence on the warpath, especially not tonight. He's always harder on everyone after a day off."

I nodded and then headed to the dressing room, pausing to let a crew member I didn't recognize know about the coffee. He thanked me and hurried over, as if it might be his only chance, which it very well could be considering how popular it was. And if he was the mysterious Zander, he'd be spending the entire night in the sound booth anyway.

The men's dressing room was closed off with police tape and a box had been placed in front of the door, just in case someone got any funny ideas about going in. Curiosity had me moving that way anyway. I didn't know what I might find, but figured a little look-see could go a long way in discovering who'd killed Chuck.

I pushed the door open, careful not to disturb the police tape or box. The room was dark, making it impossible to see much of anything, so I leaned in just a smidge more to feel for a light switch on the wall. My fingers found plastic almost immediately, and I flipped on the light.

There wasn't much to see. It looked much like the women's dressing room, only messier. An ugly stain on the floor was the only indication as to where Chuck had died. There was no chalk outline or anything like that. Nor did I see anything in the room that would tell me who the culprit might be.

"We're in the other room, if you were trying to sneak a peek."

I just about flew forward through the police tape at the sound of the voice behind me. I caught my balance just before flipping over the box, and spun to find

Brad Clusterman—the sexy elf—standing a foot away, dressed in his elf costume.

"I was just looking," I said, clicking off the light and closing the door. "It's horrible what happened."

"Was it now?" he asked, not showing a hint of emotion. "I didn't know you knew him."

"I didn't really." I licked my lips, feeling nervous. Everyone else was up front, near the stage. I was left alone with a man who very well might be the last person to see Chuck alive. "But he was murdered. That's never a good thing."

Brad's eyes moved past me, to the closed door. "No, I suppose it's not." He swallowed, heavily. "But that's what he gets for breaking his promise." And with that cryptic turn of phrase, Brad walked away.

I sagged against the wall, breathing heavily. There was definitely something going on with Brad, something that had to do with Chuck, and quite possibly his death. If Brad was the killer, then it might serve me well not to let him know I was looking into the case for Trisha, lest I end up like our former Santa.

Taking a deep, calming breath, I entered the dressing room to find it sectioned off by an old flat, creating two small cubbies. No curtain hung on either, so anyone coming through the door could see, but at least the men would be separate from the women while changing. And it wasn't like you had to strip down to change outfits, so there was little chance of me walking in on anyone naked.

I quickly slipped on my costume, and then hurried out to meet with the others, who were already on the stage, getting instructions from Lawrence. He paused as I took my place next to Prudence, searing me with a look that could kill before finally going on.

"I know everyone is upset about the tragedy, but as I said before, the show must go on. Mr. Winter has agreed to resume his duties as Santa for this year's production and I hope everyone will respect him as they would anyone else."

Randy preened at mention of his name. Next to him, Trisha looked mildly uncomfortable, but not nearly as much as she had when she was next to Chuck. I think it had more to do with the fact we were doing this after a murder, and less to do with the new Santa. Randy Winter had to be an improvement over grabby Chuck.

"I do not wish to hear anyone speak of what happened here," Lawrence went on, pacing back and forth in front of us. "No rumors. No gossip. And certainly no prying." His eyes landed on me and held. "We are here to perform, and that is exactly what we are going to do. No distractions."

I looked away from Lawrence's gaze, only to find myself looking at Brad, who was staring at me as well. He didn't smile, didn't scowl, just stood there, staring at me like he was trying to make up his mind what to do with me.

"Now that that's cleared up, I want everyone to take their places. We're going to run through the entire play tonight and I want a flawless execution. No excuses!" Lawrence spun on his heel and went out to sit in one of the empty seats before shouting, "Places everyone!"

The cast and crew scattered, moving to their starting spots on the stage while Dean closed the curtains. I looked to where Brad had been standing, but he was out of sight, lost somewhere in the shuffle. Someone put a wrapped package into my hands—my main prop—and the lights went dim, signaling everyone to fall silent.

I took one last look around for Brad, but couldn't see him. And then the music started. The curtain opened and I was in motion, belting out the first line of song.

12

The snow had stopped by the time practice ended, but enough had fallen, I was nervous heading home that night. I didn't like driving in the dark at the best of times, and it was about a thousand times worse with snow on the road. I crept along at a snail's pace, earning myself a few honks, and one pickup truck flew around me, despite the fact his tail end swerved dangerously as he did.

I was thankful when I got off the main roads and was well on my way home. Here, traffic was nearly nonexistent, so I could plod along as slow as I pleased without angering anyone. My speedometer capped out at about twenty and I was leaning forward in my seat, putting myself so close to the steering wheel, I was very nearly resting against it. I imagined I didn't look much better than the old man who'd passed me earlier that day.

But I didn't care. I wanted to be safe. And it wasn't like anyone was going to be able to recognize me in the gloom.

Practice had gone well, all things considered. My

coffee was a hit and was gone before the first act. I'd hoped to learn more about Chuck and his relationship with everyone, but Lawrence wasn't kidding when he'd said there was to be no talk of the murder. Asia had gotten a tongue lashing because she passed out a few more invitations to the memorial party. She took the yelling stoically, and even though she rolled her eyes when Lawrence wasn't looking, she refrained from handing out any more invitations until practice was over.

I might not have found any evidence of who committed Chuck's murder, but at least I was coming up with a solid list of suspects. Robert was still high on the list, despite my hope he wasn't involved. All the evidence pointed right at him, and I couldn't take Trisha's word that he was with her at the time.

Then there was Lawrence and Randy. I knew Randy's motive, though I wasn't quite sure why Lawrence might be involved. Their alleyway payoff, or whatever it was, was definitely suspicious, however, which put them firmly in my crosshairs.

And, of course, there was Brad. He had a thing for Trisha, and wasn't shy about saying so. What better way to win her affections than to eliminate the competition? Chuck had been hitting on her, and now he's dead. And Robert, her boyfriend, was now sitting in a jail cell. It left Brad as the only available suitor, at least to his eyes. And with the way he'd been eyeing me during practice, and his strange words outside the dressing room, I was starting to think *he* might be involved.

That gave me four pretty solid suspects. Now all I had to do was try to place each one at the scene of the crime during the actual murder, and scrounge up evidence, all while avoiding getting in the way of the police. Easy peasy.

I wondered how many suspects Buchannan had interrogated since the murder. He'd barely talked to me, and had yet to contact me since that first night at the theatre. I figured after Robert had shown up on my doorstep, Buchannan and Garrison would hover around a lot more than they had.

I was so lost in thought, I very nearly didn't see the taillights off the side of the road. If I'd been going a reasonable speed, I likely would have passed the ditched car without noticing.

I slowed and pulled carefully off the side of the road. I turned on my hazard lights before getting out of the car, though so far, this was the first car I'd seen in the last five minutes.

"Hello?" I called, not seeing anyone at first. "Are you okay? Do you need any help?"

A head popped up near the back of the car, close to the back right tire. "Krissy?"

"Paul?" I crunched through the snow over to where he knelt. "What are you doing out here?"

Paul Dalton, police officer and one-time crush, came around to the back of his car. He was dressed in his uniform, but was wearing it casually, top buttons undone beneath his open coat. He was clearly off duty. He'd been driving his personal car, not his cruiser, which was why I hadn't recognized it right away. He had snow on his knees and his hair was a mess atop his head.

"I came to check up on you," he said, rising. "Hit some ice and slid off the road." He frowned, blushing. Or at least I thought he did; his color could be due to the cold. "Just finished digging out the tires and was going to try to push it back up onto the road."

"I could call a tow truck if you'd like," I said. "My phone is in the car."

"No, I don't think that'll be necessary." This time, he definitely blushed. "I'm pretty sure I can get it."

I considered ribbing him about his predicament, but thought better of it. It was embarrassing enough for him that I caught him out here. Plus, I wasn't sure how he'd take it, since we *did* have a history. Sometimes, I wondered if I'd made a mistake moving on from him. Other times, I realized how awkward it would be if we *were* a couple. I was always running afoul of the law, mostly because of my nosiness. And while having him around to bail me out of trouble all the time would be nice, it would make for some tense situations neither of us would enjoy.

"Let me help you," I said, moving to the back of his car.

"You don't have to do that," he said. "I can handle it on my own."

"You might," I said. "But two is better than one, right?" I put my hands on the bumper. I could feel the cold metal even through my gloves. "If you wish, I can always push it on my own."

Paul laughed. "Let me put it in neutral first. Wouldn't want you to hurt yourself." He hurried around to the driver's side and shifted gears. There was a crunch of snow as he worked the wheel so the tires faced toward the road. Thankfully, the ditch wasn't deep, though he'd managed to get the back tire stuck in some mud, hence the need to push.

He returned a moment later, placing his own hands on the bumper. "Ready?"

"Shouldn't you control it from up there?" I asked. "That's how they always do it in the movies."

"Probably," he said, smiling at me. "Ready to push?"

I felt myself warm at his smile. It always affected me that way. "Just give the word." I dug my heels into the soft fluff, worried I wouldn't be able to find traction, or that my tired muscles would give out on me, but it was too late to back out now.

"On three. One. Two." An exaggerated pause, then, "Three!"

Both of us heaved at the exact same instant. The car lurched forward with a crunch of snow. The sudden motion startled me and I didn't take the requisite step forward to compensate for the longer gap. I went down hard, face-first in the snow, yelping as I went. Biting cold shot through my face as snow went up my nose. I rolled over onto my back instinctively, choosing the wrong direction in my panic, and barreled into Paul's legs. He staggered back, almost caught his balance, and then crashed down beside me. Snow sprayed across my already frozen face, getting into my eyes.

Unable to contain myself, I burst into laughter, and grabbed a handful of snow. I tossed it at Paul as he started to sit up, hitting him square between the eyes.

He rolled over, back to me, and for a moment, I thought I might have hurt him. The snowball hadn't been packed tight, but cold snow to the eyes couldn't have felt good, and there might have been small stones in it. I opened my mouth to apologize just as he rolled back over and flung two handfuls of white fluff at me. I screamed and gasped as a large portion of the snow went into my mouth, giving me an instant cold headache.

I sputtered, laughing, despite the pain. I grabbed my own handfuls, but Paul wasn't about to let me throw them at him. He rolled over to me, grabbing both my wrists and held them down, his body pressing against mine. His face was inches from my own, cold breath pluming into my face as he gasped for air.

We lay like that, frozen, looking at each other from inches apart, for a good long couple of seconds. I was keenly aware of his warmth, his strength, and the feel of his hands on my wrists. My lips ached with cold, and maybe an urge to lean forward, to reduce those inches to nothing, and kiss him until all the snow in Pine Hills melted.

Paul must have been thinking the same thing because he was suddenly on his feet, looking like he'd done something illegal. "I'm sorry," he mumbled, brushing snow from his jeans.

I lay there, panting, a moment longer, not quite able to catch my breath, before rising. My legs were shaky and I was cold through and through. Paul's car was now blocking off the entire road, it having bumped out of the ditch and coasted into the oncoming lane. We were lucky it hadn't rolled back and crushed us while we'd thrown snowballs at one another.

I brushed myself off, but it was a futile exercise. My hair was thick with snow, nearly frozen into one solid lump. The only way it was going to come out was if it melted. Paul's own hair was sticking straight up, snow making it look almost white in the light from my headlights.

He started for his car and a sudden fear he'd get in

and pull away without saying another word gripped me. I rushed forward and stopped him with a hand on his arm.

"Don't go. I'm sorry."

He glanced at me and flashed me those dimples of his. I swear the snow melted off me almost immediately as my entire body warmed. He really needed to stop doing that.

"I need to get the car out of the middle of the road," he said.

"Oh." This time I warmed with a flush. "We should get cleaned up," I said, desperately needing to change the subject. "Do you want to stop by and have some coffee? You shouldn't drive soaking wet."

Paul looked as if he might say no, but changed his mind. I think the way he was starting to shiver had more to do with it than anything else. "I'll see you there."

I got back into my car, both jittery and freezing my tail off. I waited for Paul to get his car back onto the right side of the road, and then followed him the rest of the way to my house, wondering what I was thinking inviting him over in the first place. Sure, I hadn't seen Will in what felt like forever, but that didn't mean I needed to sate my loneliness with another man.

Nothing is going to happen, I told myself, firmly. We were just two adults, needing to warm up and dry off. And while it might be Paul Dalton, there was nothing left between us. Whatever spark we'd once shared, had long ago faded. Or, at least, it was being dutifully ignored since we were both seeing other people. Well, *I* was. I wasn't sure if he was still seeing Shannon or not. Their relationship had been rocky of late, which Shannon blamed on me.

After what I'd just experienced, I was beginning to wonder if she might not be right.

We reached my house without either of us losing control again. I got out and unlocked the front door. Paul knocked snow off his boots before following me into the kitchen. He gave Misfit, who was sitting on the island counter, a quick scratch behind the ears. The orange cat eyed him distrustfully for a moment before giving in and demanding Paul focus on his back.

"I didn't mean to drop in on you like this," Paul said. "I was on my way home and thought I'd see how you were doing. I know you have a past with this Robert guy and . . ." He looked down at his feet and fell silent.

"I'm fine," I said, getting the coffee I'd promised him ready. I peeled off my coat and found I'd somehow gotten snow inside it. No wonder I hadn't been able to warm up on the ride home. My shirt was soaked through, as were my pants. "We barely talk to each other anymore."

"I see."

I looked at him to find Paul was still staring at his feet. His cheeks were bright red, hair dripping wet. He was making a puddle where he stood. Come to think of it, so was I.

"Be right back." I hurried out of the kitchen and got into the closet for a couple of spare towels. I carried them back to the kitchen and handed one over.

"Thanks." Paul ran the towel through his hair, wiped off his face, and then placed it on the floor to stand upon it.

It wasn't until he was done that I realized I'd been standing there, watching him. I looked quickly away and did my best to dry off before filling two mugs with steaming hot coffee. I handed one over and took a sip, black, needing the heat more than I needed sugar.

"Do you have any more suspects in Chuck's murder?" I asked.

Paul gave me a blank look before shaking his head. "I'm not really involved with this one," he said. "Buchannan is handling everything with Officer Garrison. I'm not sure he wants me to be involved, to be honest."

I guess I wasn't surprised. There always seemed to be a bit of competition between the two. "So, you have nothing to do with the case at all?"

He shrugged. "If I'm needed, I'll talk to some people, but I think Buchannan is pretty confident he has the right man locked up. I haven't been asked to do much of anything."

I lifted my mug to my lips and muttered, "He didn't do it."

"What was that?" Paul asked, setting his own mug aside.

"I said, I don't think he did it."

"Now, Krissy, just because you two have a past, doesn't mean he's innocent of the crime. People do bad things sometimes, even people we know."

"I know that," I said, growing a little angry at the insinuation. "But I know him. Robert wouldn't kill anyone. He's a jerk, don't get me wrong, but he's not a killer."

Paul frowned at me and crossed his arms. His foot tapped on the towel, a clear indication he was waiting for me to go on.

"Trust me," I said. "You should look into it some

more. Robert came upon the body *after* the man was murdered. He stepped in some blood, which was why his elf shoes were covered in it. Robert's not too bright, so instead of letting someone know, he ran."

"And you know this how?"

Hmm. If he was asking that, then it was unlikely anyone told him that Robert had been arrested at my house. "His girlfriend told me," I said, deciding to play it safe.

"Krissy, you can't trust her word. People often lie to protect those they care about."

"I know that too. It's just . . ." How to explain it to him without sounding like I was out investigating the murder behind his back? In the end, I simply shrugged. "I just know he didn't do it."

Paul walked around the island counter, his wet boots squeaking on the linoleum. He hesitated a moment, and then pulled me into a damp hug. "I know this has to be hard on you. When I found out you knew the guy . . ." He left the rest unsaid.

I let him hug me longer than I should, enjoying the warmth of him. And besides, if he thought I was acting the part of a distraught friend, then perhaps I could use it to my advantage.

"I want to talk to him," I said.

"What?" Paul pulled back to look me in the eye.

"I said I want to talk to Robert. I need to hear his explanation straight from his own two lips."

Paul stepped back, fully releasing me. It got suddenly colder in my kitchen. "I'm not so sure that's a good idea."

"It's not just for me," I said. "Maybe if he sees me, he'll confess. Or maybe he'll be more willing to talk. He might say something that will help Buchannan with the case." I lowered my voice, pleading. "Please, Paul. Just a couple of minutes. That's all I'm asking for."

He sighed. "I'll have to check with Chief to make sure it's okay, but no one said he isn't allowed visitors." He raised a finger the moment I opened my mouth to thank him. "But it will be a monitored visit. You won't be alone with him and I don't want you milking him for information. You aren't investigating this, right?"

"Of course not."

He stared at me and I gave him my best innocent smile before he heaved another sigh. "Be there first thing tomorrow morning." Paul picked up the towel, wiped away a few more small puddles of water, and then handed it over.

"I'll see you then," I said.

He nodded, looking mad at himself for caving.

I walked Paul to the door and bid him a good night. There was a moment when I thought he might kiss me on the cheek, but he thought better of it and left without so much as a handshake. I watched him go, a strange sense of longing churned in my gut.

Then again, maybe that was hunger.

He got into his car as I closed the door. With a sigh of my own, I turned and headed back inside. I peeled my way out of my wet clothes, dried off completely, and then changed into something warmer before heading into the kitchen to find something more substantial than a cookie to eat.

13

Police Chief Patricia Dalton met me outside the station house the following morning. She was in full uniform, hat tipped back so the winter sun shone directly into her face. She was a short woman, yet seeing her now, she looked larger than life, kind of like a sheriff in an old cowboy movie. It might have been how the sun hit her wrinkled face, or simply how she was standing. Either way, it gave me a bad feeling.

As I got out of my car, she squinted at me, a frown crossing her lips. "I'm not sure what you said to him, but I'll be the first to say, I don't like it."

I gave her my best innocent smile. "I don't know what you're talking about."

"Uh-huh." She sighed. "We put him in interrogation room one. Officer Dalton . . ." She trailed off, her frown growing. "Paul is going to be in the room with you the entire time." She raised a hand when I started to protest. "No argument. This man is a murder suspect and I'm not going to leave you alone with him. We're doing this not because we want you involved, but because he is allowed visitors and there is no reason not to let you talk to him."

Which I could tell wasn't exactly true. I think she wanted me to talk to Robert, see if I could weasel anything out of him. If they haven't charged him for murder yet, that meant they didn't have enough evidence for a certain conviction.

"Buchannan's holding off on charging him then?" I asked.

"*Officer* Buchannan wants to make sure he has all the facts before he commits. We can't hold Mr. Dunhill much longer without charging him, which if nothing new crops up very soon, will happen in the next day or so. Once that happens, you're not going to be allowed to talk to him, so you'd better get everything off your chest now."

"Okay," I said. "Thank you."

Chief Dalton eyed me a moment longer, then took a step toward me. "Don't make me regret this."

"Have I let you down before?"

She snorted. "Depends on how you look at things, I suppose."

And with that, she turned and led the way into the police station.

I followed her in, thankful she hadn't rejected my request to see Robert outright. My relationship with the Pine Hills Police Department wasn't exactly a loving one. Chief Dalton had once tried to set me up with her son, Paul, but that was before I started snooping into every murder that happened in town. Now, I don't think she liked me very much, which made me sad. She was gruff sometimes, and wasn't always trusting of me and my methods, but I liked her.

I was worried Buchannan or Garrison would be

waiting for me inside, but when I entered the station, I didn't see either. I hoped they were out questioning other suspects, not just trying to pin the crime on Robert. I could see Buchannan forcing evidence to fit with Robert, just because I'd once dated him.

But then again, he *was* a good cop. He might not like me all that much, but I doubted he'd intentionally ignore crucial evidence just to get at me.

Chief Dalton led me down the hall to the door to interrogation room one, which to my knowledge, was the only interrogation room in the place. Paul was standing outside, arms crossed. As soon as I stopped in front of him, he put his hand on the doorknob, though he didn't turn it right away.

"You sure you want to do this?" he asked.

"Positive."

His eyes flickered to his mom. She must have nodded from behind me because he sighed and pushed open the door. He led the way inside, waited for me to enter, and then closed the door behind us.

The room was exactly as I remembered it. A table with plastic chairs around it sat in the middle of the room. A couch was against the wall, dartboard above it. I think the darts were still in the same places as when I was last inside the room, telling me they didn't play it very much these days.

All in all, the room was kind of cozy, which fit with the Pine Hills Police Department. The town wasn't huge, and the police force reflected the laidback personality of Pine Hills. Sometimes, that was a good thing. Other times, it made things more challenging.

Robert was sitting at the table, hands atop the wood. His wrists were bound with handcuffs, not the zip-strips the local police usually used when arresting someone. His head was drooped and his shoulders slumped in a way I'd never seen them before. He looked defeated, as if he had absolutely no hope of beating this thing. Was it a sign of guilt? Or, like many people in Pine Hills, did he not believe the police capable of solving a crime?

"Robert," I said, moving to the opposite side of the table. Paul remained by the door, watching.

Robert lifted his head and glared at me. "This is all your fault, you know?"

"Mine? You shouldn't have run."

He snorted and lowered his gaze. "Why's that, exactly? They would have stuck me in here if I would have stayed. At least running gave me a chance."

I sat down slowly. The plastic chair creaked and listed to one side. One of the little metal feet was missing, making the whole thing wobbly. Every subtle shift of my weight made the chair jerk alarmingly, but it was unlikely to collapse.

"But it also made you look guilty," I said. "I mean, what did you think you'd accomplish by hiding?"

He shrugged, refused to meet my eye.

I glanced at Paul before leaning forward and lowering my voice. I expected it would carry across the room, yet I hoped some of what I had to say would go unheard by anyone but Robert.

"Trisha came to see me."

At his girlfriend's name, Robert perked up. "Is she doing okay?"

"She's fine. I don't think the police believe she had anything to do with the murder. I imagine they've talked to her by now and she's told them her side of the story. As long as you are telling me the truth, it can only help."

He nodded, managed a weak smile. "She'll collaborate my story."

"Do you mean corroborate?"

"Whatever."

I bit back a not so nice response and said, "Trisha seems like a very nice person."

"She is." Some of the old Robert came back in his smug grin. "Very nice."

I rolled my eyes, continued. "She asked me to help you. She said you didn't kill Chuck, and I'm of the mind to believe her."

This time, the smugness was aimed at me. "See, I was right. You made a mistake calling the police on me. I'm here because of you. Do you know, they are calling me a flight risk? It's why I haven't been able to walk out of here already. If it wasn't for your betrayal of my trust, I wouldn't be in this situation."

"Hardly," I said. "You ran, you pay the price." And then, before he could say anything else to annoy me, I said, "I'm helping you not because I like you, but because I believe that if you are innocent, then the real killer needs to be caught. I want to make sure no one else gets hurt."

Robert smiled at me, and then winked, as if we were sharing some deep dark secret.

"Robert, I'm serious."

"Okay, okay." He glanced back at Paul and then sat back in his chair. He tried to cross his arms, but the handcuffs made that impossible, so he settled on dropping his hands into his lap. "If you want to help me so badly, then why are you here? Shouldn't you be out there, catching the bad guy?"

"I need some information from you," I said, watching Paul to see how he'd react. Other than a brief tightening of his jaw, he showed no reaction to what was being said. "What can you tell me about Trisha?"

Robert looked startled by the question. "Why do you want to know about her?" Then the grin returned. "Jealous?"

I started to stand. "If you can't be serious . . ."

Robert's eyes widened and he sat forward. "No! Wait! I'm sorry."

I hesitated, and then sat. "I need to know more about her in case it becomes important somehow."

Robert let out a relieved breath. "I don't see how it could be," he said. "Trisha's a good girl. She doesn't have any enemies, if that's what you are asking. Everyone likes her. And she had no reason to want Chuck dead, so . . ." He shrugged.

"He had been hitting on her though, hadn't he?"

A tic under Robert's eye jumped. "Yeah, there was that." And then realizing how that must have sounded, he added, "It's still no reason to want him dead."

"From what I gather, Chuck wasn't the only one interested in Trisha."

"Brad Clusterman." Robert's nostrils flared. "I told you he did it."

"You also told me you'd never cheat on me, and well, we saw how that turned out."

Robert blushed. "Sorry about that." He cleared his throat and leaned in closer. "Brad has wanted to date Trisha for like, forever. She says he used to stalk her when they were kids. He'd show up outside her house, offer to drive her to school, and then later, practices."

"So they went to school together?"

"Yeah. He thinks that means they have a stronger connection than what she has with me." He snorted a laugh like he thought the mere idea preposterous. "She told me how he was, how he still is. The guy's a creep."

"Do you know why he would be so moody lately?"

"He's probably feeling remorse for what he did. Killing Chuck has only solidified Trisha's and my commitment to one another."

I ignored that, lest I say something more about Robert's ability to commit to anyone. "Do you know what Brad wanted with Chuck when he interrupted your fight the other day?"

"He wanted to kill him, duh. The guy was the last person to see Chuck alive, right? He had to have done it."

Knowing I wasn't going to get any real information on Brad, other than the mostly groundless accusations Robert was throwing around, I moved on. "What about the director, Lawrence?"

"What about him? Dude's cool enough, I suppose. Kinda mean when things don't go his way, but he's never yelled at me." He puffed out his chest. "I'm going to be a star, he says."

I ignored that, too. "Do you know why he would be seen exchanging an envelope with Randy Winter?"

Robert frowned. "That's the drunk Santa guy, right?"

I nodded in affirmation.

"No, that's not right. Those two hate each other."

"I have a reliable source that says otherwise."

"Can't be." Robert shook his head and sat back.

"Randy took a swing at Lawrence one practice. Knocked the d-man on his ass."

"Do you know why?"

He shrugged. "Probably because he was still whining about losing his job as Santa. Said it was Lawrence's fault, that if he hadn't walked in on him some night, then none of this would have happened."

"Wait. What night? Seen him doing what?"

"Beats me. They were yelling at each other in the parking lot on the second day of practice. Trisha and I showed up late and saw it all go down. No one else was out there, and since that Randy guy left immediately after, I didn't think nothing more of it." He paused. "You think it could mean something?"

Did I? How did Randy and Lawrence go from fistfighting to Randy getting his role back and everything seeming hunky dory between them? Did it have to do with that envelope? What was it Lawrence had seen that had caused the other man to lose his job? I'd always assumed it had to do with the drinking, but could there be another reason the two didn't get along?

I stood and stepped back from the table. Robert's eyes widened and he himself started to rise, but Paul cleared his throat, so he sat right back down.

"Don't leave me," he said, panicked. "I can't stay here much longer."

"I'll come back if I learn anything more," I told him, keeping my voice low. "Stay strong." I reached out, hesitated, and then patted Robert awkwardly on the arm. He looked surprised by the gesture, almost as much as I was.

I hurried away and went to the door. "I'm done here for now," I said.

Paul opened the door for me and followed me out into the hall. When I tried to keep walking, he stopped me with a hand on my arm.

"Krissy, wait." He waited until I turned before saying, "About last night . . ."

"What about it?" I asked, warmth making my toes tingle.

"I . . . I shouldn't have . . ." He shook his head.

"It's fine. We had a little snowball fight. Nothing more. I think we both needed the stress relief."

He looked me in the eyes for a long moment before nodding. "Now, about what he said in there . . ."

"What do you mean?" I asked, all innocence.

"You don't think he did it."

I shrugged, noncommittal. "It's not for me to decide. If I were to guess, I'd say no."

"And what was all that about two people getting into a fight?"

"It might not mean anything," I said. "I'm sure Buchannan is all over it." Actually, I wasn't sure anyone else knew about it, which made it unlikely Buchannan was asking the right questions. But who was I to tell him? If I were to try to tell Buchannan who to talk to, what to do, he'd likely do the exact opposite, just to spite me.

"You'll stay out of trouble, won't you?" Paul asked. "I can fill Buchannan in on what little I overheard in there. There's no reason for you to involve yourself."

"Don't worry about me," I said. "I'm focusing on the play. If I hear anything that might help, I'll be sure to let you or Buchannan know, but I won't go looking for it." I hoped he didn't see my fingers cross.

Paul looked doubtful, but nodded. His hand left my arm and I was surprised to realize it had been there the entire time. I was far too comfortable with him touching me, and I wasn't sure I liked it. I was with Will, a man who had everything a woman could want.

But where is he now?

I left the station, feeling guilty, and needing to talk to Will in the worst way. Calling him was out of the question—he was working and wouldn't answer his phone.

But if I made a quick little stop at his practice, he'd have to see me, wouldn't he?

I got into my car, started it up, and with my mind squarely on the man who *should* be number one in my life, I drove away, determined to lay my guilt to rest once and for all.

14

Butterflies swirled in my stomach as I made my way to the door of Will's practice. I was so nervous, I felt like I was on a first date rather than visiting a man I've been dating for months. The lack of communication between Will and I as of late had me worried there was more going on than simple scheduling. It was a miracle I'd even landed him in the first place, considering my usual track record with men. Exhibit A: Robert.

Nurse Bea sat at the front desk when I came in. The eighty-year-old woman looked at me over her bifocals and scowled. She knew I wasn't there for an appointment, and clearly disapproved of my arrival. I smiled at her as I walked up to the desk.

"I need to speak with Doctor Foster for just one minute, please."

"He's busy."

"I know." I glanced around the waiting room. Besides me, there were only two other people here. "It'll only take a couple of minutes. I promise."

Bea stared at me, expression locked in an annoyed

scowl. I stared right back, smiling away like I didn't notice. The desk nurse was always like this when I came in, even when I had an appointment. I hoped we'd eventually call a truce since I planned on spending quite a lot of time around Will in the future, and my own doctor worked here.

Finally, Bea heaved a sigh. "Fine," she huffed. "Take a seat and I'll let him know you're here. I can't promise he'll be able to see you right away, so you could end up waiting a while."

"That's fine, thank you."

Bea turned away and picked up a phone. I took it as a dismissal and found a seat.

I was hoping Will wouldn't be mad at me for showing up unannounced. The only time I ever came here was when I needed to see my doctor, Paige Lipmon. I knew Will's friends, Carl and Darrin, worked here with him, but I had yet to see either of them. They all put in time at the hospital the next town over as well as keeping hours here at their own practice, so maybe I just timed my visits wrong.

The door opened and I started to rise, but it was only a nurse. He called for "Jeremiah," and a middle-aged man who was sitting next to me rose and followed the nurse into the back. That left me with a heavyset girl who was busy swiping furiously at her phone. It was kind of hypnotic to watch, and was far more interesting to watch than the muted *Fox News* on the TV.

Of course, watching someone play *Pokémon Go!* could only hold my interest for so long. After only a few minutes, I removed my own phone, but instead of clicking on the only game I had installed—*Mahjong*, unsurprisingly—I chose the Facebook app.

I am admittedly bad at social media. I never

post, never check it for anything more than research anymore. As a stalking tool Facebook can be great, depending on permissions. I can't stand it for anything more these days. There were too many memes out there, and too many people who never really think about whether what they post is mean or offensive or downright wrong. I decided one night to not bother reading most posts anymore because I'd much rather keep my friends, estranged or not, than to start disliking them because of some poorly worded post.

I clicked on the search bar and typed in "Randy Winter." The very first hit was the one I wanted, since we had a couple of mutual friends from town. Unfortunately, like so many Facebook pages these days, I couldn't even click on his photographs without being his friend, let alone read any of his posts. So much for cyber stalking my suspects.

With a sigh, I closed the app and shoved the phone back into my purse. I could have tried to look up Lawrence, Chuck, and Brad, but didn't want to waste the time. Even if their pages were open to the public, I doubted I'd find much that would help with this particular case. Besides, I needed to be focusing on what I was going to say to Will, not worrying about the murder.

The door to the back opened again, but instead of the nurse, Will poked his head out this time. "Krissy?" he asked, sounding concerned. "Is there something wrong?"

I rose and hurried to the door. "I'm sorry for bothering you at work, but I had to see you."

In the movies, the man would soften at that comment and would sweep the woman off her feet with a kiss and a swell of dramatic music. Will, however, only frowned, forehead bunching. "I'm working."

"I know." I lowered my head, feeling dumb. This wasn't the movies. He had a business to run, patients to see, and here I was, getting in the way of that. It wasn't like Death by Coffee where I could take a break whenever I wanted and everything would be fine. If Will walked away at the wrong time, someone very sick might get worse and end up needing a visit to the hospital.

Still, I couldn't help but admire the sight of the man before me. His creamer-rich coffee skin tone, mixed with those dark eyes of his, melted away much of my worries. Coming here might have been a mistake, but at least it made me feel a little better about myself. If I could snag a man like this, I couldn't be all bad, right?

"I should probably go," I said.

"No, don't." He rested a hand on my arm. "I have a few minutes. I'm just surprised to see you."

I noted both Bea and the heavyset girl were watching us, but there wasn't anywhere for us to go unless he took me into one of the exam rooms. That sort of thing only happened on romantic dramas, however, so we stayed put.

"I won't keep you," I told him. "And really, I don't know why I came." I sighed, gave him an apologetic smile, and then asked, "What are your Christmas plans?"

He seemed surprised by the question. "The practice is closed on Christmas, so I won't be working unless there's an emergency. I figured we'd get together and have dinner, maybe watch a movie or two. You still want to do that, don't you?"

"I do," I said, happy he'd remembered. Our chat over the phone had been so brief, I could barely remember it happening at all. "But something else has come up."

"You have to cancel?" His face fell and he sounded disappointed, which actually made me feel even better about our relationship.

He truly does care! "No, it's nothing like that," I said. "Vicki and Mason invited us over for Christmas dinner and a gift exchange. Vicki and I used to do it every year when we were younger, but stopped once she moved away. We'd kind of like to start it up again and would love it if you would join in on the festivities."

Will smiled, looked like he wanted to give me a hug, but held off. We *were* still in his office. "Of course it's okay. Just text me the details and I'll make sure to be there. But for now, I need to get back to work."

"Okay," I said. "I'll get everything to you later."

He nodded and vanished into the back.

I practically skipped toward the door, I was so happy. All my worries that he was avoiding me or unhappy with me were just my paranoia sneaking in. My failed relationship with Robert had left me feeling unworthy and unwanted, and apparently, I had yet to get over it. I should have realized it was my own personal issues—not disinterest from Will—from the start.

I was about to step outside when the nurse stuck his head back into the room and called out, "Mandy."

I stopped, the name instantly pinging my interest. The heavyset girl made one last swipe on her phone screen and then rose.

"Mandy Ortega?" I asked, stepping back inside.

"Yeah?" she asked, looking me up and down. Just because she was large, didn't mean she wasn't pretty. Her hair was dark, and I could see her Mexican heritage in her face, which looked to be used to smiling and laughing. "Who are you?"

"My name is Kristina Hancock," I said, extending a hand. "I'm replacing you in the Christmas play."

She took my hand in a firm grip and shook. "I feel sorry for you."

"Why's that?" I asked.

"The director can be a real jerk sometimes."

"Mandy," the nurse said, a little more forcefully. "Doctor Lipmon is ready for you."

I felt bad for interfering since I knew from experience Paige hated it when her patients were late for their appointments, but I didn't want to lose this opportunity to learn something from someone no longer connected with the play. Mandy might be more willing to speak freely, especially about Lawrence, now that she wouldn't have to fear getting cut for opening her mouth.

"This will take just a sec," I said to the nurse, who gave Bea a bewildered look before vanishing back behind the door.

"I really should head back there," Mandy said, touching her stomach gently.

"Are you really sick?" I asked. "Some are saying you quit because of tension between you and Lawrence, not that you're actually ill."

"Gallstones," she said, holding her finger and thumb in a circle. "About as big as a quarter. Going in now to discuss my options."

"Ouch." I'd never had gallstones myself, but heard they could be painful. "Are you in much pain?"

"Sometimes." She paused, seemed to realize it was none of my business, and changed the subject. "Is there something I can do for you?"

"I was just curious to know what you thought about the people involved in the play. I don't know if you've heard, but the man playing Santa, Chuck, was murdered a few nights ago."

"I heard." Mandy frowned down at her hands. "He wasn't really all that bad of a guy if you could get past his crudeness."

"Do you know of anyone who might have wanted to hurt him?"

She shrugged. "There was a lot of tension going around this year. I know a lot of people didn't like Chuck because of the way he hit on some of the women, but it wasn't as bad as some of them would make you believe. He really only went too far with one person."

"And that would be?"

"Trisha McConnell." Another shrug. "She's the prettiest woman there, so it's no surprise."

"What about Brad Clusterman?"

"I don't think Chuck was interested in guys."

"No, I mean, did he make any untoward advances to Trisha? Maybe he resented Chuck for hitting on her, too?"

Mandy rubbed her foot onto the carpet, clearly uncomfortable with the gossip. "I don't know. I tried not to butt in on anyone else's business. I was there to act, not take part in any real life drama." She paused. "Although there was this one time when Brad and Chuck went off alone together. When Brad left the room, he slammed the door, though Chuck acted like nothing was wrong. I just assumed it was more tension between cast members. As I said, it's been happening a lot lately."

Interesting. Not only had Chuck and Brad gone off alone the night of Chuck's death, but had done the same before. Could something have been building between them that eventually led to Chuck's death? And if you consider Randy and Lawrence had their own private meetings together, it was starting to appear as if there indeed was quite a lot of secret dealings going on around the theatre.

"Mandy," the nurse said, opening the door again. "You need to come back and see Doctor Lipmon. If you would rather wait, we can reschedule . . ."

"I'm coming." She turned to me. "Sorry, I've got to go."

"That's okay. You've been a big help."

Mandy headed for the back and I made a quick prayer that her gallstones wouldn't require surgery. Any sort of invasive procedures came with risks, and she seemed like a really nice girl.

Another couple of people came into the office then. I caught the door before it closed and headed outside to my car. There was still a lot of time before I needed to be at practice, and I wanted to eat a good solid meal before tonight. I'd barely made it through last night.

Besides, I needed to think about how I was going to approach Randy, Brad, and Lawrence. While I hadn't learned anything that amounted to a smoking gun, I was finding the relationships between the various cast members to be more and more intriguing.

Why were Brad and Chuck going off alone to talk, not just once, but at least twice? What passed between

Lawrence and Randy and how did it affect their working relationship? How did Trisha and Robert fit in to all of this? Or were they simply at the wrong place at the wrong time? Or was there more to it, a sort of *Natural Born Killers* thing going on between them?

I shook off the thought, not only because I couldn't see it, but imagining Robert in Woody Harrelson's role simply wasn't happening. It would take time, but I was determined to figure out how all these secret meetings could possibly lead to Chuck's death, even if, no matter how ludicrous it sounded, Robert turned out to be the bad guy.

15

Bundled tight, I made my slow way across the theatre parking lot, watching every step I made as if it might be my last. Someone had shoveled away the snow, but didn't bother to scrape away the thin layer of ice that lay beneath. Footing was beyond treacherous, and I was worried I'd end up on my rear before I made it anywhere close to the door. As nice as it was to see snow, I was already ready for spring.

Just ahead of me, Prudence walked with the assuredness of someone who'd spent most of her life in this kind of weather. I was an admitted newbie, so I didn't feel too bad about my plodding, though I did envy her quick, shuffling pace. It wasn't just cold out tonight; it was bitter. I wanted to get inside where it was warm and I could dance away the chill that was making my bones ache.

Prudence opened the door and waited for me to work my way to her.

"Thank you," I said as I slipped past her, footing still iffy. The floor just inside the door was dirty and wet. While most of the snow and ice had melted off everyone's shoes, there were still slick spots where it had fallen off and the constant opening and closing of the cast entrance door was causing it to come close to freezing again.

"It's my pleasure," Prudence said, letting the door fall closed. The icy wind was immediately sealed off and a warm flush found my cheeks as I basked in the heat from the rickety unit that kept the place at least moderately warm. "If it keeps up like this, we might have to cancel a practice or two."

"Do you think Lawrence would do that?" I asked, skeptical. I mean, a murder had happened and he was till plowing full steam ahead. What was a little bad weather compared to that?

Prudence gave me a crooked smile and a wink. "Nope." And then she headed for the back to get changed.

I followed her to the dressing room, though my focus was on the cast and crew who were already out front. I could hear Lawrence yelling at someone on the other side of the stage. My guess was, it was poor Dean getting chewed out again. Either he was a really bad crewman, or Lawrence had it out for him. I didn't see Brad or Randy as of yet, so most of my suspects were currently missing.

The men's dressing room was still closed off, and the women's was uncomfortably busy, though it didn't take many people to make it feel full. Brad was sitting on the men's side, slipping on his elf shoes. He glanced up as Prudence and I entered, and then pointedly ignored us. I was guessing I wasn't going to be getting a Christmas card from him anytime soon.

Music drifted through the dressing room as I moved to the women's side. Asia was there with Prairie. They were smiling and talking animatedly with one another, both already fully dressed. The upbeat music was coming from a small speaker sitting on a stand set up on our side of the divide.

"Is that necessary?" Prudence asked, indicating the speaker with a grimace.

Asia glanced over at us and smiled. "I thought we could use some more cheer in here after everything that's happened. I figure I'll play something uplifting before and after each and every practice, so that everyone will leave with a smile."

The speaker seemed to pulse as the bass beat throbbed. It wasn't so loud as to hurt my ears, but it was definitely not my kind of music. All that was missing were flashing lights and an army of young people jumping up and down and we'd have a rave.

Prudence apparently felt the same way. "Couldn't you find something a little more appropriate?"

"No one else has complained," Asia said. "Right, Prair?"

"I think it's great," Prairie said.

Asia turned her gaze my way and I cringed, knowing what was coming. "You don't have a problem with it, do you?"

"It's not what I usually listen to," I said, hoping she'd drop it and leave me out of it. I didn't want to get on either woman's bad side over music.

Prudence grunted in annoyance and then started getting dressed, her movements quick and a little abrupt. I hoped I didn't upset her by not taking her side, but even though the music was kind of annoying, it did add a little life, something our production had been lacking over the last few practices.

Asia pulled out her phone and pressed a button,

causing the music to fall silent. "We've got to get out front anyway," she said. "Enjoy your silence."

Behind her, Prairie muttered, "Spoilsport," eyes flickering to Prudence, who pretended not to notice.

"So, are you coming tomorrow?" Asia asked me, shoving her phone into her coat, which was hanging from a hanger in a small closetlike cubby.

"To practice? I should be."

She rolled her eyes. "Not to practice, silly. To the memorial. I'd like to get as many confirmations as I can now so I know how many hors d'oeuvres to have on hand."

I glanced at Prudence, who was shaking her head, a disgusted look on her face. By her reaction alone, I wanted to say no to earn back some of her goodwill, but thought better of it. I very well might not get a chance to talk to anyone at practice tonight, or any other night for that matter. Lawrence ran us pretty hard. By the time we were done, most of the cast were dead on their feet and just wanted to get home—me included. And since Lawrence had banned anyone from talking about Chuck's death, even a few innocent questions could get me screamed at, if not barred from the place entirely.

But if everyone went to the memorial, I'd have more than enough opportunities to talk to them. It wouldn't seem strange for me to ask questions about Chuck there either, since the event was for him. I hadn't gotten a chance to get to know him, so if I seemed curious, no one would think anything of it. Plus, the real killer might show up and give something away. I doubted they'd gloat over Chuck's demise, but might say or do something suspicious.

No, this was far too good of an opportunity to pass up, even if it made Prudence mad at me.

"Sure," I said. "I'll be there."

"Fantastic!" Asia beamed. "I'll see you tomorrow then. It's going to be a blast." She motioned for Prairie, and the two women left the room together.

"Why are you going to that thing?" Prudence asked. "It's downright disrespectful if you ask me. It's all just one big excuse to have a party. It's sick. I thought you were better than that."

I bristled at her tone, but let it slide. She was right, in all honesty. If the shoe was on the other foot, I probably would have felt the same way.

"Can I tell you something?" I asked, keeping my voice down, though it still sounded far too loud in the newfound silence of the dressing room. Without Asia's music, every word seemed to echo.

Prudence raised a single eyebrow at me and frowned. She was fully dressed and ready to go and I hadn't even gotten my coat off.

"I don't think Robert killed Chuck," I told her. "I think the killer is still out there."

"What does that have to do with you going to a party?" she asked, clearly not impressed with my reasoning.

"I'm trying to figure out who killed him," I whispered. "I plan on keeping an eye on everyone and see if someone acts guilty or strange somehow."

She eyed me a long moment, her demeanor not softening in the slightest. "So you're saying you think someone here killed Chuck?"

"Could be," I said.

"And you believe someone in the cast could be responsible."

"It's a possibility."

"Is that why you're hanging around me?" Prudence's eyes went hard. "Do you think *I* could have killed Chuck?"

"Of course not!" I said, shocked she could even think it. "You were right beside me when it happened." Though, if I was honest with myself, there'd been more than enough time for her to sneak in and kill Chuck before I'd joined her on the stage.

But to imagine this kind, older woman being a killer . . . It just didn't make sense to me.

Prudence shook her head, almost as if she was disappointed in me. "You do what you have to do," she said. "It's none of my business." She gave me a stiff smile before getting up and leaving the dressing room.

I felt bad. I really did like Prudence, and my investigation was turning her against me. Vicki was right when she said the cast would pull together if someone started accusing them of murder. I only hoped Prudence would realize I was trying to help find a killer, not make enemies.

Feeling as if I'd made a mistake, I hurriedly got out of my coat and gloves, and pulled on my costume. I needed to come up with a way to apologize to Prudence without backing out of my promise to go to the memorial party. As much as I wanted to remain friends with Prudence, I wanted to find the killer more.

I was so lost in thought as I pushed open the dressing room door, I walked right into Dean, who was hurrying down the hall. We crashed into one another, causing him to drop an armload of cords he was carrying as he attempted to steady me.

"I'm sorry!" I said, quickly dropping to my knees to help him pick up the tangle. "I wasn't watching where I was going."

"Keep it down," he said. "Lawrence will rip me a new one if he finds out I dropped these." He gathered his load of cords and held them close to his chest.

"I'm sorry," I said again, this time at a lower volume. I looked at the mass of cords, many with strange connectors that looked nothing like the usual USB I was familiar with. "Did something break?"

"Someone took one of the soundboard connections. Happens sometimes."

"Just one? Why all of these then?"

Dean sighed. "Lawrence doesn't let us throw anything away. Well, the guy who runs this place doesn't, but Lawrence is the enforcer." He smiled, bitterly. "When something goes bad, he has us put it with the rest of the supplies in storage." He jerked a thumb toward a large set of doors. "Which, coincidentally, is where we keep all the stuff that actually works when we're not using it. Makes finding anything difficult, especially since not everyone is careful where they put things."

"Why not pitch the bad stuff when Lawrence isn't around?" I glanced back to make sure the man in question wasn't sneaking up on me before I said it.

"He'd know." Dean scowled. "I think he keeps a ledger somewhere. I thought things would get better after . . ." His gaze moved toward the men's dressing room and the police tape strung across the door.

"Why do you say that?" I asked, interested. I wasn't

sure how Chuck's death would make anything better, though I suppose someone like Trisha might be relieved.

"Well . . ." Dean looked like he wanted to say something, but shook his head. "Look, I'd better get these to the booth before Lawrence comes looking for me."

"Good luck," I said.

"I'll probably need it." He flashed me a smile and then hurried toward the front.

I gave the men's dressing room door a thoughtful look before moving toward the front myself. What had Dean meant when he'd said he thought things would get better? I mean, it was an obvious reference to Chuck's death, but if anything, everything had gotten *harder*. Was it because Dean didn't like how Chuck treated the women of the cast? Or was there more to it, something I had yet to discover about their relationship?

I cut my thoughts short when I noticed Randy, dressed as Santa, standing by the cast entrance. He had the door cracked open a sliver and was peering outside, as if waiting for someone. He was currently alone, which was practically an invitation for me to approach him.

"Hi, Randy," I said, joining him at the door. Without my coat, the cold air coming inside was nearly unbearable. I crossed my arms over my chest and hopped from foot to foot in a vain effort to stay warm.

Randy glanced at me, and then let the door fall closed. "Hey, I remember you. You're the one who came looking for me at the Weasel."

I smiled at him. "One and the same. How have you been? Must be nice to be back here."

He nodded and ran his hand down the front of his

suit. "It is. I didn't feel like the same person. Actually, I don't think I was." He chuckled.

"Five minutes!" Lawrence called from the front. Dean must have found the right cord because I saw him hustling to the back, carrying the remainder toward the storage room.

"We should be heading up front." Randy tried to step past me, but I got in his way.

"Can I have just a moment?" I asked. "I was curious about something I heard."

He heaved a sigh and crossed his arms, no longer looking like the jolly old man he was to portray. "Okay, what?"

"I was told by a few people that you and Lawrence don't get along," I said. "And one night, you two got into a fight that ended when you punched him."

"Yeah, so? We had a fight. I was drunk and angry and made a mistake. That sort of thing happens when you lose control of your life."

"It appears you two have made up."

"We have." He smiled, though it didn't reach his eyes. There was distrust there, which I guess I shouldn't be too surprised about. What excuse did I have for asking these sorts of questions of him? "We sat down, talked it out, and everything is just fine now."

"What about the money?" I asked, going for broke. I wasn't entirely sure it was money in the envelope that had passed between them, but really, what else could it have been? You didn't sneak into a dark alley to give someone a recipe.

Randy's face went carefully blank. "What money?"

Got ya! "There's been talk," I said, implying it was more than just Rita talking. "People are wondering how you and Lawrence mended fences so quickly." I stepped closer, lowered my voice. "Now, I'm not saying *I* believe it, but there are a few people wondering if it might have something to do with Chuck's murder."

"What?" His eyes widened and he took a step back from me. "That's crazy. Why would I want to kill the guy?"

"He did steal your role as Santa."

"He didn't steal it," Randy said, eyes darting around the room like a trapped animal's. "I messed up and lost it on my own. Was I mad at him? Sure. But I didn't kill him."

"Then tell me what's going on," I said. "I like you, but I'm afraid there are people getting the wrong impression. If I know what's happening between you and Lawrence, maybe I can set them straight."

Randy shook his head and I could all but see him closing down. "There's nothing to tell."

"Are you blackmailing him?" I asked.

"You have no idea what you're talking about." Randy calmed considerably. "Sure, Lawrence and I have talked privately. I wanted my part back, and at first, I went about it the wrong way. Once I stopped acting like a fool, he was willing to discuss it with me. He even admitted he'd made a mistake in letting me go. Then Chuck died, and while it's terrible, it did ease my transition back into his good graces."

There was something in his eyes that told me he wasn't telling me the full truth, but I had no idea how to get him to open up.

"Everyone to the stage!" Lawrence called from the front.

Randy glanced past me, smiled. "If that's all, we'd

better get up there. I, for one, don't want to get on Lawrence's bad side again."

"You go ahead," I said, not quite ready to face the rest of the cast.

Santa shrugged and walked away. I watched him go, trying to decide if a stupid role in a play was enough reason to kill. I mean, even he said it was his life, yet there had to have been an easier way to get his job back.

Randy was hiding something from me; I knew it. Was it because he knew something about Chuck's murder, whether he committed it or not? I didn't know. The only way I'd find out would be to keep pressing, though I wasn't sure going after Randy was the right way to go about it. Maybe after a chat with Lawrence, I'd see some discrepancy that would tell me what it was Randy was trying to hide.

"Places!" Lawrence shrieked.

I pulled myself out of my own head and hurried to the front to take my place, lest I end up getting myself cut, which would put an end to my not so subtle murder investigation. Randy flashed me a friendly smile, though the distrust was still in his eyes. I smiled back, waited for the music start, and then looked away to focus on my own song and dance.

16

Practice was grueling, and I think Randy must have had a word with Lawrence about my snooping at some point during a scene change because the director seemed to have it in for me. Every time I missed a step or flubbed a line in the song, he would scream at me like I'd personally offended him.

Admittedly, my mind wasn't entirely on the play, so it wasn't like I was making things any better. I kept sneaking looks at Randy and Brad, wondering if one of them could have killed Chuck. And then there was Trisha, trying her best to put on a strong face, but I could tell her heart wasn't in it. Mrs. Claus looked as dejected as I felt. What would she think if I told her the Santa standing next to her with his ruby red cheeks and belly shaking laugh might have killed the previous Santa in a fit of jealous rage?

As if hearing my thoughts, Randy glanced my way and smiled. It wasn't a sinister gesture, but something in it put me off and I ended up spinning left when I should have spun to the right. I just about bumped into Prudence who corrected her own spin so we wouldn't collide.

"No, no, no!" Lawrence shouted. "What are you doing?" He made a frustrated sound and threw down his script. "I've had enough. That will be all for tonight." He glared at me. "You. Come with me."

Prudence hissed in a breath and patted me on the arm. "Good luck," she whispered before heading to the back with the rest of the grumbling cast. Even though I'd been the focus of Lawrence's wrath, no one liked having their work stopped because of someone else's mistake. I mumbled a few apologies as I left the stage.

Lawrence headed straight for the sound booth, hardly paying me a glance as he went. He was steaming and I imagined he was keeping silent to prevent a full-on explosion.

He led me through a doorway and then we climbed a set of scary metal stairs that were far too small and far too steep for any sane person to want to use. Lawrence took them by twos with practiced ease, while I walked carefully, clutching the thin metal railing like it was the only thing keeping me from falling. My legs were shaking so badly, it probably was, to be honest.

The two crew members responsible for working the sound—Zander and Violet, if I remembered right—were waiting at the top of the stairs, watching me make my slow ascent. As soon as I stepped safely into the booth, they both whispered a few words of encouragement before heading down the stairs, not bothering to watch where they were going or use the railing. I fully expected one of them to fall, but they both made it to the bottom without trouble. Violet paused and waved up at me before chasing after Zander, her arm linking with his as they made for the door.

"What in the world were you doing up there?" Lawrence asked, spinning to face me. His face was beaded with sweat and was an uncomfortable looking shade of red. I wasn't sure if it was from the climb or my repeated mistakes.

"I'm sorry," I said, looking around the small booth out of both curiosity and a desire to avoid Lawrence's gaze. A board with what appeared to be hundreds of dials and knobs took up a good portion of the booth. Against the back wall were more dials and knobs, along with a CD tray, a tape deck, and a few other slots I couldn't identify. The place looked both old and high tech at the same time. "My head wasn't in it today."

Lawrence began messing around with some of the knobs on the board. The lights on the stage dimmed, while a light over the seats came on. "Do you realize how you jeopardize our entire endeavor with your behavior? If you can't handle yourself properly, we may need to replace you. If we were in the earlier stages of our work, I very well might have already, but with us being so close to opening night . . ." he heaved a sigh.

"I'll do better," I promised, not wanting to get fired. While my body might prefer to sit at home, on my couch, watching TV all evening, the play was important. If I was cut, it would significantly impact my ability to look into Chuck's murder. "It was just a rough night."

Lawrence flipped a few more switches, which seemed to do nothing as far as I could tell, before he turned to face me, eyes hard. "It would be much easier to focus if you came here with your mind on your role, not on things which do not concern you."

Well, crap. It looked like Randy *had* blabbed. "I wasn't trying to start anything."

"Really?" Lawrence crossed his arms over his chest and leaned his hip against the sound board. The entire apparatus groaned and tilted slightly toward the large window that looked out over the theatre. I had a frightening mental image of the entire thing, Lawrence included, crashing through and falling to the floor and seats below.

"I wasn't," I said, taking a step toward the back wall, just in case.

Lawrence huffed. "You throw unfounded accusations at the one man I could find to play Santa on short notice. And then you have the gall to come up here and tell me you weren't trying to start anything?"

"They weren't unfounded," I said, defensive. "And if you want my opinion, it's *your* actions that are risking the play. No one likes to be lied to." I narrowed my eyes at him. "What *were* you two talking about so secretively?"

"That, Ms. Hancock, is none of your business." Lawrence squared his shoulders and leaned forward. I had to admit, he could strike an imposing figure when he wanted to. "I'd appreciate it if you'd stop asking questions you have no right in asking. Keep it up, and you might find yourself incapable of continuing your flailing up onstage."

I suddenly realized how precarious my situation was. We were high up—really high up. The door was hanging open behind me, the stairs a steep drop to the hard floor below. Lawrence could easily shove me out without much effort. All he'd have to do was tell everyone I fell on my own and it was likely they'd believe him. I mean, Violet and Zander had watched my slow, painful ascent. It wouldn't be too hard to imagine me slipping on the way down.

I did a quick scan of the room, but there was nothing I could use to defend myself with if Lawrence made a move toward me. The sound board was too heavy to lift, and the wires plugged in all over the place wouldn't make much of a weapon.

But Lawrence made no move toward me. If he was thinking of throwing me out of the booth, he thought better of it, and instead took a step back. "I need to finish shutting everything down for the night," he said. "Think on what I said. I'm sure you'll see reason and make the right choice." He turned to the board and started powering things down.

I left him to it, thankful to be out of there. I wasn't sure if Lawrence's threat was a physical one, or if he'd chosen his words poorly and had only wanted to imply he'd send me packing if I kept poking my nose in his business. I wondered if Chuck had been given a similar speech before his death. Maybe he'd seen something that had cost him his life, something like a secret meeting between the director and a former cast member and had made the mistake of confronting them about it.

Even though I was anxious to be gone, I took the stairs slowly, both hands on the railing in a death grip. Lawrence might not have thrown me out of the booth, but that didn't mean I was out of danger yet. I slid one foot carefully from one step to the next, working my way down like it was coated in ice.

Once I was back on solid ground, I took a moment to settle my jangled nerves, before walking on wobbly

legs to the back. The place was eerily silent without
the cast and crew running around. Lawrence must
have control of the lights back here as well, because
there was only a faint glow from a single light by the
door, leaving the rest of the backstage area in gloom.

Nervous, I hurried to the back, and was thankful to
see light seeping from beneath the closed dressing
room door. At least I wouldn't have to change out of
my costume in the dark.

Just before I reached the door, a woman shouted,
"No!" and there was a crash of something hitting the
floor. A few muffled sounds followed, including
grunts, as if someone was fighting off an attacker.

Visions of a second murder flashed through my
mind. Chuck was killed in the men's dressing room,
and now, it looked like someone else was about to
meet their end in the women's room.

There was no way I was going to let that happen.

Ignoring the complaints of my overtaxed legs, as
well as my own sense of self-preservation, I threw
open the dressing room door, hands balled into fists.

Brad leapt back and spun to face me, face flush.
Behind him, Trisha was on her knees in the corner,
picking up a tray of stage makeup. Both were fully
dressed and looked as if they'd been on their way out.

"I thought we were alone," Brad said, as if that
explained everything.

I looked from him, to Trisha, who was refusing to
meet my eye. "Trisha, are you okay?" I asked, keeping my fists at the ready. I doubted I could take Brad
in a fistfight, but darn it, I wasn't going to sit back
and let him hurt her.

She wiped at her eyes and nodded. She gave me a

weak smile that looked even more pitiful because her makeup was smeared as if she'd been crying.

I turned my gaze to Brad, who was looking guiltier by the moment. "And what do you think you were doing?" I demanded.

He wiped his mouth with the back of his hand and cleared his throat. "I don't think that's any of your concern," he said.

"Really? Because if I'm left to my own imagination, I might come to the conclusion you were trying to hurt her."

"It wasn't like that," he said. "She was upset and I tried to comfort her. She knocked over the makeup kit, and that's it. Nothing else happened."

I looked to Trisha. "Is that true?"

She shrugged, tossed the last of the makeup into the kit, and then stood. "It's no big deal," she said. "Brad got the wrong impression and it's over."

Brad grunted and mumbled, "Led me on, is more like." Then he raised his voice. "She was crying in the corner and all I wanted to do was make her feel better. Next thing I know, she's clutching at me like she wants me to hold her. What was I supposed to do?"

"I never invited you to kiss me."

"Sounds like you overstepped your bounds," I said.

"It's her fault." Brad took a deep breath and closed his eyes. "I wouldn't have if . . ." His jaw worked and I could see he was both embarrassed and angry. "Look at what she's done," he said. "Her boyfriend is in jail, and another man is dead. Look what she's done to me!" He threw his hands up into the air.

"Brad, you know I'm not responsible for any of that!" Trisha looked genuinely hurt.

"Right." Anger was starting to win out. "You turn

men against one another. You toy with our emotions. I mean, what was I supposed to do?" He turned to me, ran his fingers through his hair. He took a few deep breaths, seemed to calm. "She needs stability in her life. You know that, right?"

"And you think she should get that from you?" I asked, growing angry myself. "Robert might have his issues, but it looks like he was doing a good enough job of keeping her happy."

"Before he killed Chuck, you mean," Brad said.

"I'm not sure he did," I said, and instantly regretted it.

Brad laughed. "Oh, you're on his side now? And what? Do you think *I* killed Chuck? Is that why you're acting like this? I wouldn't kill anyone for some girl." He shot Trisha a look like she wasn't worth his time, which was funny, considering what had just happened. "Give me a break. I'm sorry I tried to make you feel better. And I'm sorry you can't seem to control your emotions. But I'm done with this." With that, he pushed past me and out the door.

I let him go with a sigh of relief. I would have defended myself, and defended Trisha if push came to shove, but I was glad it was over.

"Thank you," Trisha said, picking up the makeup kit and setting it on the counter. "I'm sure he means well, but doesn't know how to show it."

"I'm not sure why you're defending him," I said. "I heard you scream."

"I know." She blushed. "He tried to kiss me and I panicked. He's always been a little awkward with women, especially back when we were in school. Admittedly, he's blossomed since." Her flush deepened. "But I'm not interested in him that way. He doesn't seem to understand that just because he looks better now than how he did in school, it doesn't mean I'm going to suddenly fall in love with him."

Still, I didn't think prior awkwardness was any excuse to try to kiss someone who isn't interested. And then to grow angry and defensive about it only made him look worse.

"You should avoid being alone with him for the time being," I said. "Robert thinks Brad might have killed Chuck." And after all I've seen, I was starting to wonder if he might be right.

"Brad?" Trisha chewed on her lower lip, and for a moment, I was sure she was going to defend him again, but instead, she nodded. "I'll be careful." Hope suddenly sprang to her eyes. "You believe me, then? Robert didn't kill Chuck."

I nodded without hesitation. "I do. I don't think he's capable of murder." And with how Randy, Lawrence, and now Brad were acting, I wasn't hurting for viable suspects either.

Trisha stepped forward and gave me a hug before saying, "Thank you," again. She sniffed, wiped at her eyes, and then started for the door. "I'll see you tomorrow."

"Sure thing."

Trisha left me alone in the dressing room. I waited by the door, ears peeled, just in case Brad decided to wait for her out in the gloomy backstage area. A few seconds passed, and then I heard a faint thump, telling me she'd left through the side door.

The silence that remained was heavy. Feeling creeped out, I hurriedly removed my elf costume, grabbed my coat, bundled up, and left the dressing room, shutting off the light as I went.

Lawrence was still banging around in the sound booth as I made for the door. I wondered if he'd heard Trisha's shout, or if the distance had been too far. Then again, no one had heard Chuck's murder taking place, and we'd been a lot closer. Did that mean he'd died without crying out? Or had it been too loud at the time for anyone to notice?

I pushed my way outside, into the bitter cold, and shivered. Tonight had been a surprisingly enlightening evening. I was more certain than ever that Robert was innocent of Chuck's murder.

But how to prove it?

I was running out of time. If Robert was charged, then it would be completely out of my hands. I was already an iffy witness, thanks to my history with the accused, but for now, I thought Buchannan would listen to me if I found evidence. But if he charged Robert with murder, I doubted he'd be willing to admit he'd made a mistake, no matter what evidence I managed to uncover.

As much as I loathed the idea, I was going to have to have a talk with Officers Buchannan and Garrison, and quite possibly, with Chief Dalton, and I was going to have to do it soon.

But not tonight.

With a yawn that made my entire body ache, I made my slow, cold way to my car, and then headed for home.

17

"Jingle Bell Rock" was playing on the radio. I turned it up and practiced my dance moves, much to Misfit's amusement. He watched me from the couch, ears perked, head cocked to the side, as if he wasn't quite sure what to make of my awkward gyrations and spins.

"I'm getting better," I told him in what I hoped wasn't just wishful thinking. I'd found I didn't actually *hate* the play, despite how miserable I felt during practice and how much I ached afterward. It was fun in its own way. Take away the murder and Lawrence's berating of me, and I might fall in love with it.

I'd slept surprisingly well last night and had a burst of energy for the morning, which I decided to use on dance practice. If I didn't give Lawrence anything more to complain about when it came to my lack of dancing and singing abilities, then maybe he'd leave me alone to focus on my not-so-official investigation into Chuck's murder.

I took a step to the right, spun, and very nearly tripped over the coffee table. Misfit gave me a look that said, "This is better?" before jumping down and heading to his food dish.

The song ended and I plopped down onto the couch in his place. I picked up a glass of eggnog I'd left on the coffee table and downed it, hating the fact I was so out of breath. Okay, so maybe I wasn't going to be dancing on Broadway anytime soon, but I *was* doing better. I was determined not to make a fool out of myself on show night, and if it meant I had to suffer a couple of bruised shins, I'd suck it up, although I might look into buying some shin guards.

I glanced at the clock, and seeing it was past noon, I picked up the phone and dialed Dad's cell. It had been a few days since we'd last talked. I was curious about how his trip was going, or even if it had started yet.

Besides, all the murder and mayhem made me long to hear his raspy voice.

The phone rang four times before he picked up and answered with a muffled, "Hmmm?"

I gasped as realization hit. "Oh, no. What time is it there?" I'd completely forgotten he was no longer on California time.

There was a rustle, followed by Dad's laugh, "It's actually a little after six."

"I woke you up, didn't I?" I cringed. By the sound of his voice, I was pretty sure when he'd said six, he meant in the morning.

"It's all right, Buttercup. I didn't mean to fall asleep." He yawned. "We're going to go out for dinner in an hour or so and I must have dozed off."

Apparently, Switzerland was ahead of Pine Hills. "Long day?" I asked, worried. Dad wasn't the type to fall asleep early. In fact, James Hancock tended to be more of a night owl.

"The time change has really messed me up. We went hiking earlier and by the time we got back, I felt dead on my feet." He cleared his throat. "Was there something you needed?"

"I was wondering how your trip was going, but it can wait," I said. "I really didn't think about the time difference. I didn't mean to bother you."

"No, I'm glad you did. I want to get ready before we head out. I need a shower." He laughed. "Hopefully Laura won't hold it against me if I'm a few minutes late."

"How is Laura, anyway?" I asked, uncertain. I still wasn't sure how I felt about them going on a trip together. I think it had more to do with me not knowing anything about her, rather than any real dislike of Dad dating again. I mean, I didn't even know they were dating until he called a few days ago.

"Good, good." More rustling as Dad got up and started moving around. "She's done this before, so she knows all the tricks in the books on how to get your body on the right schedule. Can't say it's working on me all that well, but she's doing great. I might be able to use some of this when I get back home and sit down to write." He paused. "So, how are things on your end? I really am sorry about canceling on you on such short notice. She kind of sprung it on me, too, but I should have handled it better."

"No, it's fine," I said, and meant it. "Don't be shocked, but I've landed a role in a local play. One of the elves got sick and I'm taking her place."

"Really?" He sounded surprised, but not as shocked as I would have expected. "I didn't know you were interested in the theatre."

"I'm not really, I guess. But I thought I'd help Rita out when she asked. You remember Rita, right?"

"How can I forget?"

"Well, she asked if I'd step in and I said yes. I don't have any lines, so it isn't anything special. But I have fun." *When I'm not whining about my back hurting, that is.*

"I wish I could be there." He sighed wistfully. "Have someone take some pictures for me, would you?"

"I will."

"Do you have any other plans this Christmas?"

"Vicki and I are getting together with Mason and Will for a gift swap. It's going to be like the good old days, just without you." The last came out sounding sadder than I'd intended.

"That sounds nice."

"It should be. I miss getting everyone together."

There was a brief moment of silence before he said, "Is that all, Buttercup? You sound . . . distracted."

I bit my lower lip and considered what to say. Dad would love to hear about the murder investigation. If he'd been home, he probably would have read something online about Chuck's death. Ever since I started getting involved in murder investigations in Pine Hills, he'd taken to checking the local news online, just to check in on me. He had to worry about me, but had never called to tell me to back off or anything. He knew me better than that.

But he was on a trip now, with a woman he might very well be interested in for more than a brief fling. This could be a long-term relationship, one just blooming. Did he need me worrying him about something he couldn't do anything about? Not only might it ruin his trip, but it would make me feel bad, especially since there really wasn't anything he could do to help.

"No," I said, regretting it only slightly. While I valued his insight, I could do without it this one time. "I only wanted to check in on you and see how you're doing. It sounds like everything is going great!"

"It is." There was a faint knock on the other end of the line. "Hold on a moment."

I waited while he answered the door. I could barely hear a woman's voice, which I assumed to be Laura's. I tried to strain to hear her better, not to eavesdrop mind you, but to get some sort of impression of who she might be. You can sometimes tell a lot about a person by the way they speak, how they phrase things.

In the end, her voice was too faint, and the conversation too brief. Dad returned a moment later. "I'd better get going, Buttercup," he said. "Laura says the place we're heading often gets busy and she wants to get a good seat. Apparently, there's going to be music."

"Sounds like fun."

"It should be." I could hear the smile in his voice. It looked like Dad really did like Laura, and more than just as friends.

We said our good-byes and I hung up with a vague sense of melancholy. Would every Christmas be like this from now on? Or was this a one-time thing? I missed seeing him, but if spending time with Laura made him happy, well then, I was happy. I've had him all my life; he deserved to spend time with someone else.

My eyes strayed to my Christmas tree, which was in something of a state of shambles, thanks to my cat. He'd stopped removing all the ornaments, choosing instead to focus on one at a time. I was already tired of picking them up every few minutes, and had started tossing them back onto the tree haphazardly instead of trying to find the empty spot from which they had originally come.

The gifts sitting beneath the branches looked lonely. Checking the clock once more, I realized I still had a couple of hours until Chuck's memorial. I could spend that time practicing, or I could go down to the police station and have a chat with Officer Buchannan.

Neither option filled me with much joy, so instead, I decided to go shopping.

It took only ten minutes for me to be ready. I was fully bundled, credit card in hand, and prepared to face the cold. I left a few treats in the bedroom for Misfit in the hopes he'd eat them and pass out on the bed instead of mess with the tree, and then I was off.

If there's one thing Pine Hills needed, it was a mall of some sort. Even a small one would do. Sure, I wasn't a big fan of all the in-your-face advertising, but at least it made it easier to find something for everyone without having to wander all over town in the hopes of spotting that perfect gift. If it wasn't so cold, I might not have minded as much.

My first few stops were a bust. I did buy a *Speed Racer* shirt for Vicki's boyfriend, Mason. If you'd ever seen him drive, you'd know why. Otherwise, I couldn't seem to find anything for anyone. The gifts were either too expensive for my admittedly limited budget, or I couldn't find what I was looking for; not that I had any real idea what that might be. I was wandering, at a complete loss as to what to buy, and with each passing minute, I felt my shopper's despair grow.

And then, finally, on my fourth—and last—stop of the day, I saw it.

It was stupid, really; just a coffee travel mug with a picture of Pine Hills on it. It was the sort of thing you could easily make on your own with a cheap mug and a printer, but something about it drew me in. I picked up the mug, turned it over in my hands, and instantly knew what had drawn my eye.

The photo of the town had been taken from above, but not so high as to be taken from a helicopter or plane. Maybe from a tall building, or perhaps a hill with a really nice zoom lens. It was just another day in Pine Hills, immortalized on a mug.

Front and center, however, was the police station. In front of it, mere moments from walking inside, were two figures. One a man, the other a woman, both wearing police hats and uniforms. I couldn't see their faces to be sure, but I was almost positive the photographer had caught both Chief and Officer Dalton heading in to work.

As I said, it was dumb, yet I felt I needed to have it. If nothing else, Paul would get a kick out of it. And since he spent quite a lot of his time in a car, the mug would come in handy. He could bring it to Death by Coffee every morning and I could fill it for him. Maybe I'd include a gift card so he wouldn't have to pay for his first few stops.

A little voice in the back of my head asked, *What would Will think?* People didn't normally buy gifts for their exes, but Paul wasn't exactly an ex. One date does not constitute a relationship. But I *have* seen the look in Will's eye whenever we're around Paul. Would he think less of me because I bought another man a silly little gift?

"It's Christmas," I muttered. If Will was *that* jealous, then we needed to have a serious talk.

Determined not to let my own imaginary guilt deter me, I carried the mug to the counter and paid for it. I still needed to find something for Will, but figured I could do that soon enough. I was going to put some serious thought into what I got for him.

The cashier handed me my bag and I made for the door. Just as I reached it, a fully bundled Jules Phan walked in, three stuffed bags already in hand.

"Krissy!" he said, giving me a hug, despite his load. "It's such a wonderful day, isn't it?"

"It's a little chilly for me," I said with a shiver.

He chuckled. "But the sun is out, as is my credit card." He winked and shook his bags. "I take it you are last minute shopping as well?"

I nodded, embarrassed. "I'm picking up a couple of small things here and there. I was considering stopping by Phantastic Candies in a little bit to pick up a box of chocolates." He didn't need to know I was going to get them for myself, of course. "Are you open?"

"Lance is taking care of the store while I'm out. He'll hook you up with our holiday discount."

"Thanks!" Make that two boxes of chocolates.

"It's my pleasure." He glanced at my bag. "Did you pick something up for the steamy Doctor Foster?"

I clutched the bag close, more embarrassed than ever. "Actually, it's for Paul."

"Really? Officer Dalton." He must have seen the mortified look on my face because he lowered his voice and asked, "Are you thinking of moving on from Will?"

"No," I assured him. "It's just a friendly gift. Silly, really."

"There's no reason to be ashamed," Jules said.

"Christmas is a time of giving. You should never be embarrassed about that. Paul Dalton is your friend, so you have every right to get him something."

"Yeah, but what if Will disapproves?" If Jules thought I might be considering a change in men, then Will might think the same.

"If he disapproves, then he's not worth your time. Trust me," Jules said. "If he can't let you have your own friends and live your own life, then he's not the man for you. Jealousy can be a good thing sometimes, but if it makes you afraid to be yourself, then it's a disease, one better removed than left to fester, if you know what I mean."

I nodded, wondering what I'd do if it came to that. Will was great and all, but what if he asked me not to talk to Paul anymore? Could I do that? Would I even want to?

"Thanks, Jules," I said. "I'd better get to Phantastic Candies. I've got a memorial to attend afterward."

"For the actor who died?"

"Yeah."

Jules grew somber for a moment. "Such a horrible thing to happen at such a joyous time of the year." He clucked his tongue and shook his head, before smiling. "I'd better not keep you then. Say hi to everyone for me."

"Will do."

Jules continued his shopping as I headed out into the cold, uncertain if I felt better or not. I was dreading having to see everyone at the memorial, especially since I hadn't known Chuck all that well. What if they started telling stories and wanted everyone to say something nice about him? Jules was right; this wasn't the sort of thing you wanted to think about during Christmas.

Which was exactly why I was getting the chocolates.

I deposited my purchase in the backseat of my car, and headed for Phantastic Candies, which was only a few blocks away. The candy had become a top priority because I had a feeling that by the time the day was done, I was going to need all the comfort I could get.

18

I opened the door to Phantastic Candies to the sound of a giant piece of candy being unwrapped. No, no one was opening up a mega gumball or one of those suckers that were as big as a fist. The door always made that sound when opened, or at least the speaker above it did. With my hunger for something chocolatey and decidedly unhealthy, the sound made my mouth water.

I stepped inside and immediately came to a halt. There were a few teenagers in the store, filling bags with candy. Lance watched over them, not quite distrustfully, but at least with interest. Candy was one object you could easily pocket, and while an individual piece wouldn't put Jules and Lance out of business, it did add up.

But it wasn't Lance or the teenagers that stopped me in my tracks. It was the person standing by the display of chocolates, studying them as if deciding whether or not to take the plunge. While she was dressed in normal clothes—a green turtleneck sweater and jeans beneath a calf-length coat—I'd recognize her stern face anywhere.

"Krissy!" Lance said, noticing me. "To what do I owe the pleasure?"

Officer Garrison glanced up and frowned before picking up a box of assorted chocolates. She considered it a moment before nodding to herself.

"I thought I'd stop in for a snack," I said, walking toward the display, wishing she'd go somewhere else. The chocolates were in red heart-shaped boxes, likely meant to be given to a loved one. I, however, intended to keep one or two for myself and hated the fact that someone else was going to see me buy them, even if she didn't know who I was buying for.

Garrison watched me approach without comment before carrying her box to the counter. I snatched up two boxes of my own, considered a moment, and then grabbed one for Will as well. Garrison's eyebrows rose and I think her gaze moved to my hips before she turned back to the counter and Lance, who was ringing up her purchase.

I moved to stand in line behind her, feeling only mildly self-conscious about my three boxes. Sure, I could stand to lose a little weight, but I wasn't overweight. Out of shape? Yeah. But if I kept with this play thing, I'd take care of that in no time.

"Oh, darn!" Lance said. "I'm out of bags. Let me run to the back and grab one." He hurried away, leaving Garrison and I standing in line, the teenagers still filling their bags behind us.

"Chilly day," I said to Garrison, who glanced back at me.

"It is," she said.

"Day off?"

A tic jumped in her left eye, as if my questions were annoying her, but she answered anyway. "I go in later this evening. Thought I'd get some shopping done first."

"Me too," I said, showing her my three boxes. "Everyone loves chocolates."

She gave me a strained smile as Lance returned.

"Sorry," he said. "Jules usually takes care of this. Took me a minute to find what I needed."

"That's fine," Garrison said. "I'm in no rush."

Lance bagged her candy and thanked her before looking expectantly my way.

Garrison started to leave, but as I put my boxes onto the counter, I realized I was letting an opportunity pass that I shouldn't. Garrison and I had gotten off on the wrong foot from the time we met, and if I could make peace with her, it might make my life a whole lot easier. Heck, it might even help Robert, if and when I figured out who'd killed Chuck.

"Hey, officer," I said, realizing I didn't know her first name. That was something else I should remedy.

Garrison stopped at the door and looked back. She didn't respond in any other way.

"Do you have time for a quick coffee?" I asked. "I have somewhere to be soon, but would like to sit down and, well, talk." I gave her a hopeful smile.

Garrison considered it a moment, and then shrugged. "Sure, why not."

"Would you mind meeting me at Death by Coffee in ten minutes?" I asked. "I can get us a discount."

"Sure." And then she walked out the door. I couldn't tell if she was intrigued by my invitation, annoyed, or thrilled. She was about as emotional as a robot.

"Know her well?" Lance asked, ringing up my candy.

"Not really," I said. "I'm trying to make her like me a little more." And if doing so allowed me to ask a few questions about where the police stood on the murder investigation, then even better.

Jules would have started asking questions about our relationship and quite possibly told me a little about Officer Garrison and her life outside of work, but Lance only smiled and bagged my candy, asking instead, "These for anyone special?"

"Will," I said. "And me." Though I wasn't about to tell him they were mostly for me.

"Candy is always appreciated," Lance said. "I do sometimes get a little tired of it since Jules always brings some home with him, but I still think it's the perfect gift for anyone. Who doesn't love chocolate?" He winked.

"Tell me about it," I muttered, wishing I didn't love it quite so much, before raising my voice and saying, "Well, I hope he likes it." I found I was actually a little worried about that. There are some doctors who don't like eating unhealthy. I didn't think chocolate was too bad on anything but your teeth, and maybe your blood sugar levels, but I wasn't sure. Since Will wasn't a dentist, I was hoping he didn't mind.

"I'm sure he will." Lance's gaze moved past me. "All set?"

I moved aside to make room for the teenagers. I gave Lance a farewell wave, and then hurried down the street to my car. While I could have walked to Death by Coffee from here, I wanted to unload my bags and see if I could park closer. Even a short walk in the cold made my face hurt.

Turning the heat on to full blast, I drove down the street until I found a parking spot only a couple of spaces away from Death by Coffee. I parked in it, careful to avoid the big truck that had pulled up a little too far. I wiggled my way in, albeit crookedly, and then headed for the warmth of the coffee shop.

Garrison was already there, seated, a tall cup of coffee held in both hands. Apparently, she hadn't wanted to wait for me and my promised discount. I waved to her and then went to the counter where Vicki was waiting.

"My usual," I said, and then, as she got my coffee, I asked, "How's business?" I glanced up the stairs to find no one up there. "You working alone?"

"Jeff's on break," she said, carrying my coffee to the counter and grabbing a cookie out of the display to plop inside. "He should be back in a few minutes. We've been pretty busy up until now."

"Good. If you need me to come in . . ."

"I'm going to pretend you didn't say that." She smiled at me and started to make a fresh pot of coffee.

I carried my drink over to where Garrison sat and took a seat. "Thanks for meeting me, Officer."

"Call me Rebecca. Becca, I guess."

"Becca then."

"I hope you're not going to try to talk to me about the murder case," she said. "John warned me about you. He said you have a tendency to get involved where you don't belong."

"I do," I admitted. "But that's not why I wanted to talk to you."

She raised a single eyebrow and took a sip of coffee. I was happy to smell eggnog flavoring. Maybe we'd have to consider making it a permanent part of our menu, or at least, see if it continues to sell after the holidays.

I considered where to start, glancing over my shoulder at the sound of the door opening to cover my indecision. I turned to find Todd Melville entering, mask covering his nose and mouth. He narrowed his eyes, glanced around to make sure Trouble was nowhere near, and then went to the counter to order. The guy was allergic to cats, yet continued to come here for his coffee, which I didn't mind, but wondered how he could stand it.

I turned back to find Garrison watching me with a frown.

"I'm sorry about how we first met," I said, which seemed to surprise her.

She lowered her coffee as her brow furrowed. "What do you have to be sorry about?" she asked. "That's all in the past."

"Yeah, but I fear it gave you the wrong impression about me. I don't go beating on cops or harassing old ladies. It was just a strained time in my life." And was mostly Buchannan's fault. And Eleanor Winthrow's when you got right down to it. Still, I should have handled myself better when I'd caught her peeping in on me and Buchannan wouldn't take me seriously. I'd like to think I've grown as a person since then.

"Don't worry yourself about it," Garrison said.

Behind me, the door opened, letting in a blast of cold air. A moment later, Todd strode by the window, removing his mask to take a drink from his coffee cup.

"You don't hold it against me?"

Garrison hesitated, frowned, and then shrugged. "Can't say I'm a fan of anyone who ends up in a cell.

The petty stuff gets to me sometimes. It gets in the way of the real work."

"Well, I'm sorry," I said. "I've been good since then and haven't ended up in jail, so that has to count for something, right?"

Garrison actually flashed me a smile. I think it's the first one I'd ever seen her give, even if it only lasted a second or two.

She looked like she was going to say something when the large black-and-white store cat, Trouble, came sauntering down the stairs. Garrison's eyes, which had always had a harsh edge to them, went immediately soft as she made an "Aww" sound.

Trouble must have either heard her, or sensed that there was someone there who'd give him the love he wanted. He veered over to where we sat, fluffing up his already fluffy tail as he strode our way, making himself look as friendly and inviting as he could.

"He's adorable," Garrison said, all of her rough edges falling away.

"He's the store cat," I said, sensing a weakness. "His name is Trouble and he's the brother to my cat, Misfit."

Garrison glanced up at me. This time her smile was warm and interested. "I love cats," she said, rubbing Trouble behind the ears. His purr was loud enough that it carried throughout the shop. "I have two of my own, in fact. My boyfriend doesn't like cats, though." Her face clouded over a moment before she broke back into her smile. "Makes me wonder if he's worth my time. How can you not love this face?" She scratched under Trouble's chin.

Soaking up the attention, he wound his way around her legs and then plopped down next to her chair. I knew I should coax him upstairs, but we were alone in the dining area at the moment, and I was afraid if I didn't strike now, I'd lose my chance to get something out of her.

"My ex wasn't a big cat person either," I said, careful not to emphasize the ex part *too* much.

Garrison sat up, leaving Trouble to groom himself at her feet. "Must have been difficult," she said. "Pets are just as much a part of the family as children, in my book."

"It was." I took a deep breath and went for it. "Robert was always difficult, but he's not a bad guy."

She understood where I was going with this right away. "John told me he was your ex. You're far too close to him, which was why we don't want you anywhere near this one."

"I understand," I said, curious about her wording. Was there a situation in which Buchannan would actually want my help? I couldn't imagine it happening, but I supposed it was possible.

But unfortunately, I couldn't think about that now. Later, though . . .

"I'm not too thrilled to have Robert back in my life in any way," I continued. "But I do hope you and Buchannan consider other suspects. I know what the evidence looks like . . ." I trailed off to Garrison's raised hand.

"We're going to do our jobs properly," she said. "I know you and John have a past, but he's not going to let that cloud his judgment."

I wanted to believe her, but a part of me was afraid he'd go after Robert even harder if he found out I was trying to prove him innocent—if indeed he *was* innocent.

"I know," I said. "It's just . . ." I took a deep breath to consider what I should say. "I've heard some things around the theatre and it makes me wonder if someone else might have committed the crime. No one seems to think Robert had any reason to do it."

"Sometimes people snap." Garrison shrugged as if it happened all the time. "Perfectly good people have been known to let anger get the better of them. No one ever sees it coming, but it does happen."

"I didn't say Robert was a good person," I said, knowing it probably wouldn't help his cause any, but needing to say it nonetheless. I didn't want anyone thinking I still liked him. "But I am almost positive he's innocent here."

Garrison reached down to pet Trouble, eyes going distant, before sitting back to regard me. "You know, something has nagged me about this one from the start. The evidence does point toward Mr. Dunhill, but something seems off." She stopped short of saying she thought him innocent, however.

The door opened again and Jeff came inside. He paused when he saw me, said, "Hi, Ms. Hancock," and then hurried back behind the counter to deposit his coat in the back. When I looked back to Garrison, she was getting to her feet.

"I should get going," she said. "I do hope that if you do hear anything regarding the case at the theatre, you'll come to either John or I. You don't need to be involving yourself, but I know how people love to gossip around this town. They tend not to divulge anything to the cops, but to you . . ." She shrugged.

"I'll let you know if I hear anything." And I guess

I meant it. Mostly. Sure, I'd learned a few things about Lawrence, Brad, and Randy that might be of interest to the cops, but so far, I'd discovered nothing that screamed "Murderer!"

Garrison buttoned up her coat, gave Trouble one last rub, and then took her coffee with her as she left.

I remained seated a few minutes longer, contemplating what I should do. Turns out, I kind of liked Rebecca Garrison. She tended to show only a strong, hard exterior when in uniform, but there was a kind person behind her cop persona. Could we eventually become friends? Maybe. Anyone who liked cats earned extra brownie points in my book.

But I wasn't ready to go running to her or Buchannan to tell them everything I knew, or at least, what I thought I knew. I needed to learn more, make sure I wasn't going to send them on a wild goose chase that would let the real killer get away.

And the one way to do that, was to keep poking around, despite what both Garrison and Paul Dalton had asked me to do.

Gathering my things, I rose, ushered Trouble back upstairs toward the books, and then made my way back into the wintery cold, more determined than ever to get to the bottom of this thing, if for no other reason than to prove to Garrison—and Buchannan if I was being honest—that having me on the case was in everyone's best interest.

19

Asia lived in an apartment complex inhabited mostly by young people who were living on their own for the first time. If there was a nearby college, I'd have called it college housing, but there wasn't. The complex was well-kept, not the kind of place where you'd find keggers or ugly porch furniture. There were three buildings in total, each housing five units. The units themselves were about the size of a small house, including an upstairs.

I'd driven past the complex quite a few times, which was how I knew the average age of its residents. There were always a few guys standing outside, throwing a football back and forth, or the occasional cookout where everyone looked fit and still of an age where they were trying to figure out what to do with their lives. I'd say most residents were in their mid-twenties, a few younger, maybe a handful older.

It reminded me of my youth. I wasn't a sorority girl, or even an occasional partier, but I'd seen it all. A part of me wishes I could go back to those years, relive them, and see if perhaps I could change a few of my least impressive moments of my college years. Another part was happy right where I was, and honestly, if changing something back then would cause my current life to change, I'd have to give it a pass. But it was nice to fantasize sometimes.

All of the parking spots in front of Asia's apartment were full, so I was forced to park at the far end of the lot, near a dead end turnaround not unlike the one at the end of my street, only smaller. A sidewalk fronted the units. There were no cracks in it, and all the ice and snow had been carefully removed, as in, completely taken away, not just tossed to the side.

I marveled at how nice the area was all over again. When people thought of apartments, especially ones mostly occupied by people under the age of thirty, they usually thought of college campus apartments with parties day and night, as well as iffy accommodations. Looking around, I thought that if I was ever forced to sell my house, this wouldn't be too bad of a place to go—even if I brought up the average age of the residents. The brick was clean, looked almost new. White, lacy curtains hung in many of the windows. There were flowers, green grass, and a sense of peace you wouldn't expect in a downtown residence.

The only noise was coming from Asia's apartment— a faint thump of music that wasn't too loud, but louder than what you'd expect at a memorial. I stopped outside her door and wondered if I should just walk in or knock. We didn't know each other all that well, and honestly, I was starting to wonder if I'd made a mistake in coming.

Before I could make up my mind on what to do, the door opened, and both Violet and Zander, the two booth crew members, came out with identical frowns on their faces. They both shook their heads at me, a clear indication they didn't appreciate Asia's way of doing things—and didn't think I would either—before hurrying off, not quite hand in hand, but close.

I considered walking away then. The music inside was upbeat, danceable, and entirely inappropriate for the occasion. The door started to swing closed, and I grabbed it, choosing to head inside, despite my reservations. I wasn't here to remember Chuck, but to see if I could learn why anyone would want to kill him. Walking away now would help no one.

Prudence had been right when she said Asia would use Chuck's death as an excuse to have a party. A table was set up across the room, snacks and drinks on top of it. The lights were dim, the music loud, and less than half of the people there were associated with the theatre, if that. It was hard to tell for sure since I was used to seeing everyone in costume.

"Krissy!" Asia called, spotting me. "I'm so glad you could make it." She looked at my empty hands and gave a little frown. "If you brought anything, it goes over there." She waved a hand toward the snack table. "We're getting a little low on drinks."

"Sorry," I said, guessing she didn't mean coffee or water. "I was pressed for time and didn't grab anything."

"No biggie." It was clear in the way she looked at me, it was. "I wasn't sure you were going to make it. A few cast and crew have been in and out, but not as many as I'd have liked." She pouted, jutting out her lower lip, before smiling. "But I guess that means more for us, right?" She laughed and waved at a young man who appeared to have just hit his twenties in the last few months. He was trying to grow a beard, but it just wasn't happening. "Ian!" She rushed over to him without another word to me, but I was okay with that.

I looked around the gathering in the hopes of spotting someone I knew and liked, but neither Prudence nor Trisha were in sight. It wasn't much of a surprise, really. Prudence had made her feelings about the memorial party clear, and Trisha's boyfriend was currently in jail. I doubted she was much in the partying mood.

Prairie and Greg were there, of course. They stood close together, talking with Greg's lips almost pressed to Prairie's ear. She was nodding and smiling, while he didn't look all that happy as he watched Asia socialize. While I'd figured they'd both be as excited and would mingle as much as Asia, it didn't appear to be the case. Or at least, it wasn't at the moment.

I found an empty spot by the wall and decided to simply watch the crowd for a few minutes and see if anything struck my interest. None of my suspects were in attendance, unfortunately. Not even Dean was there to talk to. While Asia had given out invitations to everyone, it seemed most of the cast and crew realized what she was doing and didn't bother to waste their time and come. She might have called it a memorial, but I didn't see anyone memorializing anything. There wasn't even a picture of Chuck anywhere in sight.

"Hi." A pair of guys moved to stand in front of me. "Are you one of Asia's friends?"

"We're in the same play together," I said, noncommittally. After seeing this, I wasn't sure I could ever be friends with her in any meaningful way. Our worlds simply didn't align.

"Ah." The blond of the two nodded. "She's a pretty good actress, isn't she?"

"She's definitely better than me," I said, which wasn't untrue. Granted, everyone was better than I was, but these two didn't know that. "Do you know her well?"

"We live two units down," the redhead said. Freckles covered the top of his nose and darkened the skin around his eyes, making him seem almost haunted. "She invited the entire complex to this thing."

"Did you know Chuck?"

The two guys looked at each other and shrugged. "Chuck who?" Blondie asked. "Is that one of her exes?"

I didn't know how to respond to that, but didn't have to. Two young, pretty women came through the doorway then, drawing both guys' eyes. They were across the room in an instant, nearly tripping over one another to be the first to introduce themselves.

I might have been offended by the sudden dismissal if I wasn't so relieved. I was starting to feel like the old stick in the mud who didn't belong.

I'd only been there for a few minutes, but the memorial party was already starting to look like a bust. Asia and her friends, Prairie and Greg, were about the only cast or crew remaining, and I had a feeling I'd get nothing important out of any of them.

The music changed as a slow ballad began to play. Nearly everyone partnered off and started dancing, as if we were at a high school dance. Unwilling to participate, I hurried over to the snack table and loaded myself up with unhealthy food before anyone could ask me to dance; not that anyone had so much as looked at me, but still.

I watched the couples dance as I ate my snacks—a pair of chocolate cakes that were to die for—and considered my exit strategy. I didn't want to just up and leave since it might offend Asia. I might not approve of her style of memorializing the deceased, but that didn't mean I wanted to upset her. I'd wait until she wandered over and would make up some excuse as to why I had to go.

"I'm surprised you came."

I jumped. "Greg! I didn't see you. Shouldn't you be dancing?"

He frowned, eyes on the dance floor, or namely, on Asia, who was dancing with the guy she'd called Ian. "I'm not much of a dancer," he said, and I could tell that if someone had asked him, he likely would have given it a shot.

I watched him a moment and wondered why he'd even come over to talk to me. I don't think he'd said a single word to me since I'd taken over for Mandy, and if he had, it hadn't been anything I would want to remember.

Greg wasn't all that bad to look at, but had a haughty look to his eye, like he thought he was better than everyone else. I supposed when you hung around Asia, who had the same sort of look, you inherited some of the attitude. Either that, or it was a requirement to be one of her friends.

"Sucks about Chuck," I said, not quite sure what else to say. And since we were at his memorial, I figured it was at least somewhat appropriate.

Greg glanced at me, face unreadable. "I suppose."

"Didn't like him either?" I asked.

He shrugged, eyes returning to Asia. "He didn't fit in," was all he said.

The song ended and the music picked back up. The partygoers went back to milling about, returning to their conversations as if the brief dance break hadn't even happened. Greg hardly paid me a second glance as he drifted over to Prairie, who'd broken away from a guy she'd danced with during the slower song. She didn't look happy about it. Neither did Greg, who started talking in her ear the moment they were back together.

The door opened as I stuffed my cake into my mouth, drawing my eye. Brad stepped inside, scowled at the people who were clearly not there to honor Chuck, and then he turned and walked right back out.

Brushing crumbs off my shirt, I hurried across the room and out the door, not wanting to miss this opportunity to talk to him outside the theatre. Maybe without Trisha and the others around, he might be willing to open up more.

"Brad!" I called as I stepped outside. He kept walking without looking back, so I raised my voice and jogged toward him. "Brad, can we talk for a second?"

He stopped and turned with a huff. "What do you want?"

"Were you here for the memorial?" I asked.

"What memorial?" he snorted. "That thing is downright disrespectful."

I had to admit, I agreed. "Asia has her own way of dealing with grief, I guess."

"You mean she's a selfish, arrogant kid who will never grow up." He glanced past me, toward the apartment, and shook his head before returning his gaze to me. "If this is about last night, you can stop right there. I have no interest in discussing it with anyone, let alone you."

"It's not!" I assured him. "But I thought we could talk a little about Chuck. You know, have our own little memorial out here."

He gave me a look as if I was crazy and rubbed his hands together with a shiver. "Out here?"

"Why not?" I said, adding a shiver of my own. "There isn't much memorializing going on inside and you seemed to know him better than some. If anyone else shows up, we can have them join us."

He still looked skeptical, but at least he didn't walk away. "You didn't even know him," he said.

"No, not really," I admitted. "I only had a few practices with him, and he seemed nice enough." If not a bit grabby with the women.

Brad rubbed at his chin. "He was a jerk most of the time," he said. "But you're not supposed to talk ill of the dead." His jaw clenched, as if he was holding in barely suppressed anger.

"Did he do something to you?" I asked. "Did you two get into a fight when you went off together the day he died?"

"No," Brad said. "Not really." He frowned at me. "I really don't know what business it is of yours what we did or discussed."

"It's not," I said. "But I'm trying to figure out why someone would kill him. If Robert didn't do it, then someone else did, and I'd like to know who before they decide to do it again."

Brad stared at me long and hard, as if trying to make up his mind whether I was accusing him of anything. I wasn't sure if I was or not, to be honest. He'd been acting strange lately, had been ever since Chuck had died. Sure, it could have everything to do with Trisha, but what were the chances his bad mood coincided with Chuck's death without them being connected somehow?

"How can you be so sure Robert didn't do it?" he asked, voice dropping low. "His footprints were there and he'd been arguing with Chuck right before he died."

"Circumstantial," I said, feeling good about myself for using a professional word. "Trisha says she was with him when Chuck was killed. They discovered the body together a little later and panicked. You trust her, don't you?"

Brad's jaw clenched a few times before he nodded. "I want it to be him so bad . . ."

"You really do like her, don't you?"

He gave me a bitter smile. "She never cared about me in that way. Ever since school . . ." He shook his head. "As much as I try, I can't seem to get her to notice me. She always goes for guys who will end up hurting her."

I had an urge to tell him about Robert's unfaithfulness, but decided I didn't need to be adding more fuel to this fire. "What about Chuck?" I asked instead. "If we assume Robert didn't kill him, who would have wanted to hurt him?"

Brad got a faraway look in his eyes. "It doesn't seem possible."

"What doesn't?" I prodded. By the look on his face, I was starting to believe we were getting somewhere.

Brad thought it through a moment longer before taking me by the arm and walking me farther away from Asia's apartment. No one had come out since we'd left, and no one else had gone in, but it was clear he wanted to be careful so he wouldn't be overheard.

We stopped beside a heavy duty pickup. We could see the door from there, but would be most blocked off from view if anyone were to peek their head out and look.

"Chuck came to me a few weeks back, talking about some sort of investment opportunity he'd become aware of. I thought he was joking at first, but after I looked into it some more, I realized he was on to something. He said he needed money up front and was willing to include me in on it, full partner. He didn't give me enough in the way of details so I could do it myself, not that I know anything about investing."

He paused when there was a loud cheer from Asia's apartment. After a few seconds when nothing else happened, he went on.

"He was asking for a lot, but I figured it was worth it. I gave him the money and he took care of the rest. Or, I thought he did. The day he died, he called and told me he needed more money than he thought. I was upset. It was too much, but I knew that if I could come up with it, we'd both be rich. That night, I took him aside to talk to him. You saw us go."

"And then he died."

Brad nodded, anger in his eyes. "I didn't think I could get the money and wanted to ask him if there was some other way we could do this. He said there wasn't, that we'd need to get a third involved, or else the money would be lost. *My* money. I was angry, but when I left him, he was alive. I swear I didn't kill him."

"Did he already talk to this third he mentioned?"

Brad shook his head. "He said he had yet to talk to anyone else about it. We were going to be partners, and I assured him I'd find a way to come up with the money, though I was angry he wasn't upfront with me from the start." His fists clenched. "Someone must have overheard us talking at some point and decided to kill him."

"But why?" I asked. "If someone caught wind of what you were doing, why not offer to be the third partner?"

"I don't know," Brad said. "Maybe they wanted to keep the money for themselves. Or maybe they went to Chuck after I left and he refused to listen. He was never good at dealing with other people at the best of times, and he was stressed because of the whole thing. Either way, my chance is shot now. I have no clue how to proceed without him. I'm not sure I even want to."

Now, this was a motive I could do something with. People did some crazy things for money, even if it wasn't a sure thing.

My brain pinged then. Money. The envelope that passed between Lawrence and Randy!

"Do you think Lawrence could have overheard you?" I asked, growing excited. It would tie everything together neatly if that was the case. Lawrence overhears Brad and Chuck talking, decides he wants in on it. Chuck refuses, so Lawrence gets rid of him.

But why bring in Randy afterward? If, like Brad, Lawrence doesn't know anything about investing, and Randy did, it would be make sense. Or perhaps it came right back to money. In order to invest in something, you had to have money to start with. Did Randy have money saved up and was willing to contribute, despite how poorly he and Lawrence were getting along at the time? Or did I have it all backward and it was Randy who'd overheard Chuck talking?

"I don't know," Brad said. "And at this point, I

don't care. I just want it to be over with." He stepped back from me. "If you see Trisha before I do, tell her I'm sorry. With everything that's happened, I lost my head a little and . . ." He shook his head, sighed.

"I will," I said. "Thank you."

He nodded and then got into the large pickup we were using as a shield.

I watched him drive away and wondered if what he'd told me was the truth. If it was, then I very well might have stumbled on the reason for Chuck's murder.

All I had to do now was figure out what to do about it.

20

Practice came both all too soon, and not soon enough. I was anxious to confront Randy and Lawrence about what Brad had told me, but I wasn't too keen on dancing and singing tonight. The memorial had been surprisingly depressing despite the upbeat music and interactions. It was sad to see that no one seemed to care about Chuck. I felt as if someone should be mourning him, even if it ended up being me.

Prudence was waiting for me as I entered the theatre, curiosity painted all over her face. "What was it like?" she asked the moment I was through the doorway.

"You were right. It was all an excuse to have a party. Hardly anyone showed up, other than Asia's neighbors and friends. I didn't stay long."

Prudence nodded knowingly. "That girl has no class. Always thinking about herself without a care about anyone else in the world. She can't even see what's right in front of her." She sniffed. "I bet she won't even show tonight. Probably wore herself out with her little party."

I was guessing Prudence was right. It wouldn't surprise me if the party carried on into the night. "I should have listened to you and stayed home." Though in doing so, I wouldn't have gotten the chance to talk to Brad.

Prudence patted me on the shoulder. "You'll learn. We old folk know what we are talking about."

I smiled, then glanced around. "Have you seen Randy yet?" Not only was Asia and her friends missing, but so were quite a few others. We were decidedly light tonight and I hoped that meant we'd get to go home early.

"Haven't seen him. Lawrence isn't even here yet." She sounded shocked by the last.

"What about Brad?" I asked, wondering if tonight was going to be a complete bust. It seemed like every one of my suspects had decided to take the night off.

"Same. I wonder if Lawrence called off practice without letting the rest of us know. Probably expects us to go on without him." She harrumphed.

I shrugged as I finally spotted someone coming from the dressing rooms. "I'll talk to you in a few," I told Prudence before heading over to where Mrs. Claus now stood, looking nervously toward the stage. "Seems slow tonight," I said to her.

Trisha hugged herself. "I hope no one else shows. I'm not in the mood for this. I went to see Robert earlier and he's extremely distraught about all this. He thinks his time is running out." She looked to me, eyes hopeful. "Please tell me you've made some progress."

"Some," I said. "But I'm not sure if it will help him

or not. I need to talk to Randy and Lawrence to clarify some things. Have you seen either of them yet tonight?"

She shook her head. "I've been in the dressing room since I got here. It's quiet back there. I . . ." She gave me a sad smile. "It's hard. I wanted some time alone to think."

"I understand how you feel."

She took a deep, shuddering breath. "Robert's terrified he's going to end up in prison for the rest of his life. I don't know what I'll do if that happens."

"He won't," I promised her, though I was starting to worry. "If you see Randy or Lawrence, please let them know I want to talk to them."

"Do you think they had something to do with Chuck's death?" she asked, hand going to her mouth as she realized what I might be implying.

"I don't know," I said, not wanting to start rumors, but wanting to assure her at the same time. "There's some interesting tidbits going around and I'd like to confront them about them to see how they react. It might be nothing."

"Or it could be everything," she said. "I can't imagine Lawrence being involved."

Of course, she hadn't seen him when he'd all but threatened me the other night. I checked to make sure no one was paying us any mind and then asked, "Have you heard anything about some sort of investment opportunity? Apparently, Chuck was about to get involved in one before he died."

"No, I haven't heard anything of the sort." She leaned forward, lowered her voice. "Do you think that's why he was killed?"

"Could be." And if it was, going after Lawrence and

Randy could be hazardous to my health. It would be a wiser course of action to call Buchannan or Garrison and let one of them handle it.

But it was unlikely Lawrence and Randy would be willing to tell the cops anything. I had a way of getting people to talk, which was probably why I wasn't very popular, but *did* get results.

"Well, I hope you figure it out soon," Trisha said. "Robert shouldn't have to stay one more minute behind bars for something he didn't even do. It's not fair."

"I'll do the best I can," I said. I started to walk away, and then remembered the message I was supposed to deliver. "Brad wanted me to tell you he's sorry for last night," I said. "I guess he's been under a lot of stress lately, though that's no excuse for what he did. Still, he said he was sorry, and I believe him."

Trisha looked surprised. "Oh, thank you, Krissy. I'll have to talk to him when he gets here." She got a contemplative look on her face, as if trying to decide if she should accept his apology or not. I mean, it would have been better coming from him, but at least now she might be willing to hear him out when he finally did get up the nerve to tell her.

I left Trisha then to go back to get changed. Everyone else was already dressed, so I had the room alone. Asia's speaker was sitting silently in the corner. I had half a mind to hide it so I wouldn't have to listen to her music whenever she arrived, but left it alone. I might not like it, but it could be soothing to some.

I changed, and then made my way back out front, hoping to catch Randy and Lawrence before practice officially started.

That was not to be.

The door opened and Randy came in, but before I could rush over to him, Lawrence followed him in with a man I didn't recognize. The man was tall, with a slight paunch. He wore a wool suit and had a few rings on his fingers. His hair was black, going on gray, and deep lines marred his face around his eyes and mouth.

"Who's that?" I asked Prudence, who was watching with me.

"Kenneth Purdy," she said, with clear disdain in her voice. "He controls how the money is spent for the theatre. There's rumors that he's squandering most of what we earn. It's been years since we've gotten a new script, let alone new costumes, so I'd believe it."

Lawrence led Kenneth toward an electrical box, opened it, and gestured toward the mess of wires inside. I eased forward to listen in, but didn't have to. When Kenneth spoke, he practically shouted.

"It's fine for now," he said. "You've managed to make it work this long, and I'm sure you can make it last a little while longer. Once the play wraps, I'll see what I can do."

"It might short out before that happens." Lawrence seemed beside himself, but kept his temper mostly reined in.

"I'm sorry," Kenneth said, not sounding sorry in the slightest. "But you know nothing can be done until after the play is done. Funds are low." He brushed imaginary lint from his shoulder. "I fully expect the show to be a success this year." He glanced back, saw me listening and huffed. "I do hope you'll stop wasting my time."

And with that, he spun on his heel and walked off.

Lawrence stood there a moment, watching as Kenneth left through the side door, before he slammed the electrical box closed and headed for the front, grumbling to himself. I guess I should have been happy he hadn't turned on me to vent his frustrations, but I wasn't. That mess of wires had looked dangerous, and if Mr. Purdy was supposed to be keeping the place running, he was doing a pretty poor job of it.

"It's like that every year," Prudence said. "It's about the only time I ever feel sorry for Lawrence."

"I can see why." Kenneth Purdy did not seem like a nice man.

"Places!" Lawrence shouted from up front. "Now! Dean, get those props into place!"

I scurried to the stage with the rest of the cast, or at least, the cast that was present. While the important roles were here, we were missing quite a few elves. It didn't take long for Lawrence to notice.

"This will not fly!" he shrieked. "Don't you people understand how close we are to opening night? If we want to have a successful show, we need everyone here doing their part!" He seethed a moment before throwing his hands into the air. "I suppose this will have to do. Lights!"

The lights dimmed, the curtains closed, and we were off to our places. As predicted, Asia and her friends hadn't shown, nor had Brad. Trisha was out of sorts, probably because of both my questions and Brad's absence. She flubbed her first line, which sent Lawrence off on another tirade about responsibility. I could only stand and watch in silence, though I did notice Dean standing off to the side, watching

Lawrence with a frown. The poor guy had been the target of his own share of tirades to know how it felt.

He glanced my way as if feeling my eyes, flashed a smile, and then vanished behind the curtains again.

Practice went on like that for a little while. No one had much energy or life, which caused Lawrence's frustration to build. Finally, having enough of it, he called for a break. He stormed to the front of the building, likely to blow off steam. Knowing it was my best chance to get him alone, I hurried after.

"Lawrence," I said, catching up to him right before he walked out the front door, presumably for fresh air, albeit frigid air.

"Ms. Hancock." He sighed. "Is there something I can help you with?"

"Was that the owner I saw you with earlier?" I asked, deciding to start small.

"He owns the building. Nothing else. Why?"

"No reason," I said. "I was just curious."

"Well, take your curiosity somewhere else. If that's all, I'd like to clear my head before we begin again."

"Actually," I said, stopping him before he could go outside. "I've heard an interesting rumor." I glanced back to make sure no one had followed us, and then lowered my voice, hoping it would give credence to my ploy. "I'd like in."

Lawrence frowned. "I have no idea what you are talking about."

"Come on," I said, edging closer. "You know who I am, what I do. I ask a lot of questions, learn things." I winked. "I'd like a part of it." I was careful not to say of what, wanting Lawrence to say it himself.

He eyed me, fidgeting. "Ms. Hancock, I can assure you, I am at a complete loss as to what you might be referring to. Now, if you'll excuse me . . ." He started to walk away, but I stopped him with a hand on his arm.

"You and Randy are in on it together, right?" I asked.

"That's none of your concern."

Bingo. "Isn't it? From what I hear, you'll both come out of this with some extra cash, and I, for one, could use some more money." And that wasn't a lie. Death by Coffee might be doing great, but that didn't mean I was rolling in cash. In fact, we often spent most of what extra we earned improving the place.

"You don't know what you are saying," Lawrence said, eyes darting all around. "You'd be best served to walk away right now and pretend you never heard a thing."

"Or what? I'll end up like Chuck?"

His eyes narrowed and it was his turn to lean in close and lower his voice. "If you press long enough, who knows?"

I swallowed nervously, but pressed on. "What are you investing in?" I asked. I refused to be put off so easily. Lawrence appeared to be *this* close to cracking and letting something slip. He'd already threatened me, albeit vaguely. If I could get him to admit more, I might be able to take it to Buchannan and be done with this whole thing.

"Investing?" Lawrence stepped back, frowned, and then broke into a wide smile. "You really do have no idea what you're talking about. This is all a front." He laughed. "You aren't a very good actress, you know? You can't fool me with your flimsy story." He spun on his heel. "I'd suggest returning to the back and practicing a bit before we move on because, quite frankly, you need it."

He pushed open the front door and a rush of cold air blasted in. Lawrence glanced back once, still smiling, and shook his head, almost as if in humored disbelief, before the door swung closed, leaving me alone in the lobby.

I couldn't decide if Lawrence's change in demeanor was because I was truly off base, or if I'd come too close to the truth, and he'd needed an escape. If it wasn't an investment that brought him together with Randy, then what was it? And how did it lead to Chuck's murder, if at all? I was back to wondering if I'd been right when I'd first thought it was blackmail, but if that was the case, why were they acting so friendly to one another now?

I headed back to the stage, mind on anything but the play. Dean was busy changing the flats to the post intermission side. He smiled and waved me over.

"Could you help turn this one?" he asked.

I obliged and took one side. We turned the flat to the other side—a frozen, nature scene, snow covering everything. Just the sight of it made me shiver in remembered cold.

"I saw you chase after Lawrence," he said, wiping sweat from his brow. "Is everything okay?"

"I guess," I said. "I'm trying to figure this thing out and it's just not making sense."

Dean glanced at the flat. "What? The play?"

"No, Chuck's murder." Then, realizing I'd basically admitted I was looking into it, I flushed. "Robert and I used to date and I'm pretty sure he couldn't have killed anyone. I figured I'd at least see if I could learn anything about who might have had a reason to kill Chuck, but I'm getting nowhere."

Dean studied me a long time before saying, "I don't see you as his type."

"Gee, thanks."

"No, I mean that as a compliment. Robert seems . . . shallow."

"That, he is. But that doesn't make him a killer."

"Yeah, well, I wouldn't worry yourself over it too much. Everyone gets what they deserve one way or the other."

"What do you mean by that?"

Dean shrugged, removed a handkerchief from his back pocket to wipe his face. While it was cold outside, and the heating unit wasn't all that great, it did get pretty hot onstage with the lights beating down on you.

"Chuck treated people poorly. He caused trouble and then blamed it on others to amuse himself. Look where it got him." He spread his hands. "And then you have this Robert guy, who thinks he's better than every other guy on the planet. I'm sure he's hurt a few women in his time." He gave me a meaningful look. "And look where it's gotten *him*."

"But if he didn't commit the crime . . ."

"I'm sure he's guilty of something," Dean said. "The police will take care of it. You shouldn't worry yourself over something that's really not worth your time." The door opened as Lawrence returned. "I'd better finish up before he pops a gasket." He gave me a brief smile and then hurried to the back for more props.

Practice went on from there, and much to Lawrence's dismay, it didn't get much better than the first act. No one's mind was on acting, least of all mine. I kept sneaking glances at Randy and Lawrence, both of whom seemed distracted in their own right.

Mercifully, it all ended well before our usual quitting time. Lawrence threw a disgusted hand in the air and demanded we all leave. Nearly everyone made a beeline for the back to get changed, thankful we wouldn't have to embarrass ourselves any longer.

I changed quickly and then lingered in the back, hoping Randy would appear, but apparently, he decided to leave, still fully dressed as Santa. I hadn't seen him go, but if he'd left while I was changing, I wouldn't have.

With a frustrated sigh, I headed for the door. I stopped when I heard muffled voices coming from the front. Curious, I crept to the closed stage curtains and parted them just enough so I could peek out.

Randy and Lawrence stood huddled together in the aisle, talking briskly amongst themselves. The crew was gone, including Violet and Zander, leaving just the three of us inside the building. Lawrence was animated, hands gesturing wildly as he tried to make his point. Randy just stood there, shaking his head, white ball on the end of his Santa hat bouncing.

I needed to get closer. While I could hear their voices, I couldn't make out a word of what they were saying. I was pretty sure the conversation had to do with me and what I'd said to Lawrence earlier.

But there was nowhere for me to go that wouldn't get me caught. The stage was clear of all but the flats and a few props. The two men were too far up the aisle for me to hear. Even if I tried to sneak around the side of the stage, I would be too far away to make out anything.

Randy said something then and pointed toward the lobby. Lawrence nodded, and together, they headed that way. I waited until they were gone, checked to make sure I was indeed alone, and then, knowing I was taking a risk that could put me in a lot of hot water, I followed after them.

21

Snow crunched underfoot as I followed after the coconspirators. Neither Randy nor Lawrence acted as if they were concerned about being followed. They'd likely thought they'd had the theatre to themselves so their conversation and brisk walk in the cold had gone unobserved. They hadn't stopped their animated discussion since they'd left the theatre, and to my eyes, it appeared Lawrence wasn't happy. He kept gesturing wildly, nearly smacking Randy upside the head twice in his agitation.

Sometime during practice, it had started snowing again and had yet to stop. It came down in a fluffy haze that obscured the streetlights and made it harder to see, which was probably good for me. If one of them were to look back, they might mistake me for a common pedestrian, though there was hardly anyone out, thanks to the snow. Only an occasional car coasted down the road, often well below the speed limit. It was good to see I wasn't the only one who was overly cautious when driving in this stuff.

I could think of only one reason why the two of

them would be out together on a night like this. I'd rattled Lawrence. He'd tried to play innocent, and had done a convincing job at the end making me believe I was on the wrong track, but this solidified my belief that both Randy and Lawrence had something to do with the investment that had likely gotten Chuck killed.

I slowed my pace as a new thought hit me. If I'd rattled Lawrence enough that he and Randy were sneaking off to have a little pow-wow, there was a good chance the topic of their conversation might be me, as in, "How do we get rid of that pesky woman?" sort of thing.

My mind immediately conjured worst case scenarios, such as knowing I was following them and were leading me away so they could dispose of me elsewhere, for example.

Determined, I continued on, squinting against the falling snow. I wouldn't let fear control me. There were no abandoned warehouses in Pine Hills, no big lakes within walking distance they could drop me in—even if they weren't all frozen over. And while I hadn't told anyone where I was going, I was pretty sure it would be easy enough to figure out what had happened to me if I were to suddenly come up missing.

Or at least I hoped it would be.

We hadn't been walking long before Randy motioned for Lawrence to stop. I did the same, moving to stand behind a streetlight, which did little to conceal me, but might make them overlook me if they did a quick perusal. My toes were frozen, as were my fingers and nose, but I refused to dance in place or rub my hands together lest I draw unwanted attention my way.

Randy put a hand on Lawrence's shoulder, spoke to him for a good thirty seconds, before pointing toward the church where Rita held the writers' group meetings—you know, the ones I'd been missing as of late. Lawrence replied with a sharp shake of his head. Randy continued to talk before, finally, Lawrence sighed, nodded, and they turned to head to the church.

Surprised, I followed after. I'd expected them to lead me to a dark alley or some other sinister location where dark dealings and murders could be planned. But a church? I seriously doubted the two of them were heading inside to pray for forgiveness.

I caught the heavy door just as it was about to close. I peeked inside to find both Lawrence and Randy at the top of the stairs, moving toward the room where the meetings were usually held. Randy's stride was confident as he disappeared inside. Lawrence, on the other hand, looked like a rabbit ready to bolt. Was it the church itself? Or was something else going on that made him nervous?

I waited until they were both well out of sight before I slipped inside, closing the door silently behind me. I took the stairs carefully, knowing exactly where to step to avoid the groans and creaks that went along with any old building. I reached the top of the stairs, somehow not drawing attention despite the few missteps I'd made, and moved to stand by the doors, just out of sight.

"Well?" Lawrence asked, clearly impatient.

"Well what?"

"This is pointless. You know my feelings on this woman."

"I also know how important this is to you, to the both of us." There was a dull smack, which I imagined was Randy slapping Lawrence's back. "Everything is moving along smoothly now. We just need a little extra cash to make it happen."

I edged closer, wanting to see the two men. I peered around the corner, ready to jump back if they were looking this way, but they weren't. Randy was standing in the middle of the room, his back to me. Lawrence was pacing in front of him, rubbing at his temples, eyes to the floor.

"Why here?" he said. "She could have come to us."

"You know that wouldn't have worked," Randy said. He ran a hand through his beard and flicked the water he'd pulled from it to the floor. "People would have started asking questions. Where would we be then? All it would take is one person finding out and then *he* would know. You know what would happen then."

Lawrence glanced up to scowl at Randy. I slunk back into the shadows, mind racing. Who were they talking about? And what?

"This better not backfire on us," Lawrence said. "This is my life we're talking about. I'm taking a huge risk here."

"We all are."

The two men fell silent, leaving me to contemplate what to do. It was obvious they were meeting someone, but who? As far as I knew, Brad was the only other person who knew about Chuck's investment, and he was definitely not a she. Could he be the *he* they referenced, though? The one they didn't want to find out about the secret meeting?

A creeping dread oozed into me then. Hadn't I asked Trisha about whether or not she knew about an investment opportunity? She'd denied it, but what if that wasn't the case? She'd known Brad since they were in school together. Could he have let something slip to her about the investment, and she killed Chuck, deciding to go to Lawrence and Randy about it instead? Now, with me poking around and asking about it, I was a problem and perhaps they were afraid I'd tell Brad about what I'd learned.

I mentally went back over everything I knew about Trisha, which was admittedly little. She was dating Robert. She didn't believe he killed Chuck, stating the two of them were together at the time, a story Robert had corroborated.

But what if they'd both lied to protect themselves. I doubted Robert knew anything about the investment, or Chuck's murder for that matter. Trisha could have left him for a few minutes, claiming she needed to go to the bathroom, killed Chuck, and then led Robert to the body. She might not have realized how panicked he'd get, thinking he'd call for help. She decided to go with the flow, figuring that if Robert was accused of the murder, then no one would look at her as anything more than lucky to be alive.

But if she *was* involved, why not bring Brad into the fold? Was it because of their past? Or did she not trust him to follow through with it?

I shook my head and frowned. I was finding it hard to believe Trisha could have anything to do with the murder. Not only was the evidence flimsy and circumstantial, but she didn't seem the type. I mean, she'd come to me to look into the case to help Robert. She had to know that I would discover *something*.

A sound downstairs brought my attention back to the here and now. The door clicked and groaned as it opened.

Panic flared through me then. If I stayed where I
was, Trisha, or whoever was coming in, would surely
see me. If it was the killer, then I would be in some
serious trouble. If it wasn't, I'd still have a lot of ex-
plaining to do, such as why I was lurking outside
where Randy and Lawrence were waiting. They'd
quickly realize I'd followed them and I was sure they
wouldn't take too kindly to my actions.

I spun and quickly, but quietly, opened the door
across the hall. I slipped inside, careful to close the
door behind me so it wouldn't make any noise. I was
in a small conference room; the same room, in fact,
that Chief Patricia Dalton had pulled me into when I'd
first come to town so she could give me her son's
phone number.

Now, *that* had been an uncomfortable conversation.

I pressed my ear to the door, determined not to let
memories derail me from the task at hand. I listened,
breath held, hoping that this secret meeting would be
the break I needed in solving Chuck's murder. My
phone was in my purse, which was in my car, back at
the theatre, so I couldn't call Paul right away if it was.

The stairs creaked loudly as the newcomer as-
cended them. He or she reached the top of the stairs
and stamped both feet on the floor, as if just now trying
to shake away the snow instead of doing it downstairs
where there was a mat.

"Well, my Lordy Lou, it's coming down hard out
there!"

I sucked in a breath. *Rita?* What was *she* doing here?

I opened the door a crack and peeked out, not sure
I believed what my ears were telling me. Sure enough,
Rita Jablonski was heading for the meeting room.
Her head and shoulders were covered in snow. Did

she know what she was walking in on? There was no way she could be a part of any of this.

Could she?

"Ms. Jablonski," Lawrence said, voice tight. "We're here as you requested. I do hope you make it quick."

Wait. *Rita* had asked them there? Had she buried the hatchet with Lawrence, just like he had with Randy? I mean, these three people, together, in a secret meeting. It made no sense.

All three moved deeper into the room, so all I could hear was Rita's muffled voice. I couldn't make out what she was saying, though I could imagine it had a lot to do with how inconvenienced she was and so on.

But there was one thing I was sure of—this had nothing to do with Chuck's murder.

Discarding stealth, I pushed open the door and marched for the meeting room. Rita was standing with Randy and Lawrence in a loose circle. She was babbling about the cold, much to both men's annoyance. She saw me as I entered, and while surprised, she didn't seem upset by my appearance.

"Krissy?" she asked. "What on earth are you doing here this late? The meeting isn't until Tuesday."

"I could ask you the same thing," I said, crossing my arms and tapping my foot.

Both Randy and Lawrence spun to face me. Both were red in the face, though Randy's made him look more like Santa, while Lawrence simply looked angry.

"Why, I was meeting with these two gentlemen about an investment opportunity," she said.

I sucked in a shocked breath. "You knew?" I said. I couldn't believe Rita might actually be involved in a murder plot, all for some extra cash.

"It's not what you think," Lawrence said.

"Oh, really?" I asked. "And what do I think?"

"How about, it's none of your business," Randy said, stepping forward.

"She's probably heard everything already," Lawrence said. "Probably followed us here."

"I've heard enough," I said, though in reality, I had no idea what was really going on here. "But I think it best if you explain yourselves now before the cops get here." And if they thought I'd already called them, then maybe it would forestall them from coming at me with a knife.

"The cops?" Rita asked. "Why on earth would you do such a thing?"

Randy smiled. He seemed genuinely amused. "She thinks we're up to something illegal." He laughed.

"I . . ." Rita looked confused for a moment before shaking her head. "I don't know what you're thinking, dear, but we're just having a nice little chat about the possibility of opening up a new, improved community theatre."

Both Randy and Lawrence nodded.

I looked at them in confusion. "A new theatre?"

"What else would we be talking about?" Rita asked with a laugh.

"I tire of the same old problems," Lawrence said, seeming resigned to the fact I'd found out. "I've been pushing for a new rigging system for years, and you saw the sound board. It's a mess. It only works half the time, and don't get me started on the lighting." He sighed. "I've asked Kenneth to put some funds toward repairs, but it always ends up in his pocket instead." His jaw grew tight. "If you want to know about something illegal, look into Kenneth Purdy."

I was dumbfounded. *A new theatre?* It kept going through my head, as if it was the strangest thing I'd ever heard. "But . . . but you two hate each other," I said, indicating Lawrence and Rita.

"Pah!" She waved a dismissive hand. "That's water under the bridge."

Lawrence snorted and muttered something under his breath that sounded a lot like, "Sewage water, maybe."

"Okay," I said. "Will someone please explain this to me?" I was having trouble understanding why they'd met in the church, instead of just doing it in the theatre or at a restaurant somewhere. "Why did you come here?"

"I asked them to meet me here," Rita said.

"Kenneth had been hanging around lately," Lawrence added. "You saw him. He's been coming around after hours as well. I think he knows something is up."

"The church seemed like a perfectly good place to talk financials," Rita said.

"Financials? Are you . . . ?"

"Ms. Jablonski has agreed to help fund a new theatre," Randy put in. "I inherited an empty lot a few years ago, but couldn't afford to build anything on it. When Lawrence started talking about opening his own theatre, I started making calls. Things looked like they were going to fall through when, well . . ." He blushed.

"But why all the secrecy?" I asked. This whole thing felt like they were making a mountain out of a molehill. I mean, I commended them for wanting a better theatre and taking steps to make it happen, but all the cloak and dagger for *this?*

"I told you," Lawrence said. "Kenneth Purdy would make a move to block us from moving forward with the project if he knew. He has friends in the city council who would back him. It's already going to be a challenge to get approval without someone finding out."

"We figured if we went about it quietly, we'd get the ball rolling before he and his friends were any the wiser," Randy added. "By then, it would be too late."

"It's really simple, dear," Rita said.

I was at a loss for words. They were wanting to open a new and improved theatre? "Did Chuck find out about your plans?" I asked, trying to fit the murder in somehow.

"Chuck?" Lawrence made a disgusted sound. "Casting him as Santa was the biggest mistake I've ever made in my theatre career. The man was untrustworthy at the best of times. I never would have told him of my plans."

"So . . . ?" I stared at them, hoping someone would say something that would make more sense.

"No one here killed him," Randy said. "While I'm happy to resume my duties as Santa"—he puffed his chest out at this—"Chuck's death has made everything far more difficult. With all the snooping and questions floating around, we've had to be more careful with what we say and where we say it."

"It makes us seem callous to abandon the theatre now," Lawrence said. "But much like the play itself, the show must go on."

"That call at the bar," I said, looking to Randy.

"It was from the bank. They're willing to give me

a loan, but it wasn't going to be enough to pay for the building, as well as all the equipment we'd need."

"To which I'm happy to be a contributor," Rita said with a smile.

"I'll be backing most of it myself," Lawrence said. "But we were a few thousand short. I couldn't get a loan for the rest." He flashed a bitter look Rita's way.

"But you kicked her out of the theatre!" I said, still unable to believe these three people had managed to come to an understanding after all the hard feelings.

"I did," Lawrence said. "But desperate times."

"I brought her on board today," Randy said. "Much to Lawrence's chagrin, I might add."

"We do hope you'll keep this to yourself," Rita said. "It would be a shame if all our hard work comes to naught because you let details of our endeavor slip."

I made a cross over my heart. "Not a word." I wouldn't even know where to begin.

Lawrence and Randy didn't look convinced, but Rita beamed. "That's great, dear. Now, if you're interested in donating to the cause, I'm sure no one here would complain."

"I'll think about it," I said, though it was unlikely I'd be able to. While it would be great to have a shiny new theatre in town, I didn't have the spare money to give them. If I did, it would have gone toward a new parking lot for Death by Coffee by now. "I'll let you get back to your meeting," I said.

"It was good to see you," Rita said, unfazed by my interference.

Needless to say, Lawrence and Randy didn't echo the sentiment.

I turned and hurried out of the church. The snow

was really coming down now and I had to squint against it as I walked back to the theatre and my car. I'd made progress today on my investigation, but it wasn't the kind of progress I'd been hoping for. First, I find out Brad had been working with Chuck on an investment. Chuck's death had ruined a chance for him to get rich, which made me doubt Brad's guilt.

And now, I've learned Lawrence and Randy knew nothing of the investment and were only guilty of abandoning their current theatre in order to build one of their own. Once again, that was hardly a reason to commit murder.

I reached the theatre parking lot, got into my car, and started it up. I held my hands over the vents in an effort to de-ice them before I made the long drive home. Now that my three main suspects were presumably cleared, I had to start from square one yet again.

It looked like I was going to have to pay Robert another visit tomorrow. I was running out of suspects, and unless he could give me something that would help clear him, it was starting to look more and more like Robert Dunhill was going down for murder.

22

Misfit sat atop the island counter, watching me pace back and forth. I'd spent all night wondering if Robert had somehow tricked me into believing he hadn't killed Chuck when he actually did. All the evidence pointed toward him, and that wasn't something I could ignore any longer. Trisha might have said they were together at the time of Chuck's death, but I was starting to wonder if she was in on it, too.

Could my ex-boyfriend, Robert Dunhill, actually be a murderer?

To say the question put me in a dour mood was an understatement. I'd sludged my way through my morning shower and breakfast, stewing on it.

But while the Robert conundrum made for a rough night and frustrated morning, it wasn't the reason I was pacing my living room, wrapped gift in hand.

"Do you think I should give it to him?" I asked Misfit. "I mean, on one hand, he *is* a friend. If I don't give him a gift of some sort, he might think I don't care anymore." I paced from the couch, toward the counter. "Then again, what if he takes it the wrong way? What if *Will* does? Maybe I should just leave it here. What do you think?"

Misfit eyed me a moment, and then closed his eyes to settle in for a nap.

"A lot of help you are," I grumbled, resuming my pacing.

I knew I was making a big deal out of nothing, yet I couldn't help but be paranoid. If I was going to give Paul his silly little gift, I was going to do it today when I went in to see Robert again. There was a chance I wouldn't see him until after Christmas if I waited, and I never liked giving gifts late, fearing it would seem as if I'd forgotten. I know it's the thought that counts, but doing everything early, or on time, made me feel good about myself.

The snowfall last night made me question whether or not I even wanted to leave today at all. The weatherman was calling for another inch on top of what we already had, which was going to make driving—especially mine—dangerous. From what I've been hearing, Pine Hills never got this much snow before New Year's. We usually only got an occasional dusting of wet snow here or there, and saved the big stuff for late January.

But if I wanted to help Robert, I was quickly running out of time. Worrying about whether or not Paul would like his gift wasn't going to help anyone.

I stuffed the gift into my purse and headed out the door, already bundled for a blizzard. With the snow, the temperature had continued to drop. My breath plumed in front of me and I swear I saw ice crystals form in it before it was blown away by the bitterly cold wind.

Blinking away my freezing tears, I got into my car

and turned the key. The Focus complained, coughing a few times before turning over. I jacked the heat to full blast, wondering if I was going to have to look for a new vehicle soon. The poor thing was struggling in the bad weather and I definitely didn't want to end up broken down at the side of the road, turning into a Popsicle while I waited for a good Samaritan to stop and take me in.

On the way to the police station, I mentally went over everything I needed to ask Robert. I was positive he was hiding something from me; it's in his nature to be deceptive. I didn't know if it had anything to do with Chuck's murder or not, but I was going to force him to tell me everything. Even the smallest, seemingly insignificant detail could be important.

Thankfully, the roads had been plowed early that morning. While there was some ice on the roads, it wasn't all that bad. Smoke curled from nearly every fireplace, and I imagined most everyone was sitting around their crackling fires, hot chocolate in hand, enjoying the wintery morning. It was where I wanted to be—minus the fire due to a lack of fireplace, of course—yet here I was, freezing my butt off for a guy who usually annoyed me to death. How ironic was that?

I reached the station, parked, and all but ran to the door. I stepped inside, moaning in relief as the hot blast of air hit me. It felt like every ounce of water in my body had turned to ice, and we weren't even to the worst of the weather yet.

"What are you doing here?" Officer Buchannan said, coming around the front desk to scowl at me.

"I'm here to see Robert," I said, lifting my chin

defiantly. Buchannan wasn't going to scowl me into submission this time.

"That's not a good idea," he said, glancing back to the desk in which Officer Garrison was sitting, typing away at a keyboard.

"There's no reason not to let me see him," I said. "He might talk to me, you know."

"From what I've heard, you've already tried." Buchannan's jaw worked a moment as if stewing over the fact he hadn't been there for it. "Nothing he gave us before has panned out, so what makes you think this time will be any different?"

"I don't know," I admitted. "But I feel like I have to try."

"No," he said. "You don't. This is my arrest. He's going to be charged with Mr. Sanders's murder."

I almost asked him who he was talking about before I realized he meant Chuck. I felt bad for not knowing what his last name was until now.

"I need more time!" I pleaded. "I'll get something out of Robert, I promise."

Buchannan's eyes narrowed. "More time for what?"

"For, uh . . ." I scrambled to come up with something to say that wouldn't tell him I was investigating the murder. I mean, I was pretty sure he already knew, so it wasn't like I was fooling anyone.

I was saved from having to come up with an answer when the door opened and Paul Dalton walked in. "Krissy? What are you doing here?"

"Ms. Hancock wishes to speak to her boyfriend," Buchannan said.

"He's not my boyfriend!"

"You've talked to him already," Paul said.

I shot Buchannan a dirty look before focusing on

Paul. "There've been . . . developments." I flushed,
knowing how that had to sound. "I'm positive Robert
is hiding something. I don't know if it will clear him
of Chuck's murder or prove him guilty, but don't you
want to know what it is?"

"How do you know he's hiding anything?" Buchannan asked.

"I don't know for sure, but I *do* know Robert.
There's something he isn't telling us. Please," I all but
begged. "I only need a few minutes. And then I'll be
out of your hair. Promise."

Paul sighed. "What can it hurt to let her talk to him
for a few minutes?" he asked Buchannan. "Maybe
she'll get something out of him we couldn't."

Buchannan glared a moment longer before huff-
ing. "Fine. But if she interferes in my investigation,
she's going to spend some time in a neighboring cell."

"Of course," Paul said as Buchannan turned and
stalked away.

"Thank you," I said. "I really wish I could figure
out how to make him like me."

"I'm not sure you can." Paul smiled, causing his
cheeks to dimple. The temperature seemed to rise a
few degrees at the same time. Funny how that works.
"Let me get him for you."

"Wait," I said, stopping him before he could walk
away. "I have something for you." Before I could reconsider, I reached into my purse and removed the
wrapped mug. I handed it over, half afraid he'd end up
laughing in my face.

He didn't.

"You don't need to give me anything," he said, turning the gift over in his hand.

"It's nothing," I said. "You can open it now if you want."

Paul hesitated, glancing around the room. A few police officers were watching us, though Buchannan and Garrison were talking amongst themselves. Garrison glanced at me, and I hoped she was telling him to give me a chance. It would be nice to have everyone on my side for once.

Paul carefully removed the wrapping paper and smiled when he saw the mug. "Thank you."

"You can see the police station," I said, embarrassed. What was I thinking getting him such a silly gift? "It seemed appropriate."

"I'll use it every day." He paused, and then gave me an awkward hug before stepping back. "I don't have anything for you here with me," he said, looking distraught.

"That's okay," I said. "You didn't know I was coming."

He nodded, but I could tell he felt bad. "I do have something for you," he said, like he was worried I might think he'd forgotten me. "It's at home. I could go and get it." He turned to the door like he was going to do just that.

"No, you don't need to do that," I said, stopping him. "If you get Robert, that'll be enough for me today."

Paul paused, then nodded, an embarrassed look on his face. "You're right. I'm being stupid." He cleared his throat, adjusted his hat, and smiled. "I'll get him and bring him to interrogation room one. You know the way."

"I'll wait there."

Paul left to pluck Robert from his jail cell. I hurried

to the interrogation room and slipped inside, feeling eyes on me. Everyone had seen me give Paul the gift. I could almost hear the questions radiating off of them, the judgment. Even I was making more of it than what was there.

I took a seat at the table and drummed my fingers atop it as I waited. Who cared what everyone thought? Paul and I knew where we stood. And when it came to Robert and me, so what if Buchannan thought there might be something still between us? I knew there wasn't, and that was all that mattered.

Besides, it was silly to be thinking about my relationships with any of the men. Robert's life was on the line. Another man's life had ended. If Robert was innocent, then finding the real killer was the most important thing. That's where my head needed to be, and I was determined not to let these other distractions get in the way of finding out the truth.

The door opened and Robert came in, hands cuffed. He looked a thousand times worse than when I'd last seen him. His hair was a mess, face long and drawn. Dark circles surrounded eyes that were bloodshot, as if he hadn't slept in days. Even his fingernails were dirty. I wondered if he'd gotten the insane idea of digging his way out of his cell, or if that was just something that happened when you were locked up for more than a few hours.

"You look terrible," I said as Paul led him to the chair opposite me. Robert plopped down heavily, as if his legs could barely support him.

"Thanks," he grumbled, slouching.

"Are they feeding you?" I glanced at Paul, who'd taken up position by the door, much like the last time.

"I guess." Robert shrugged one shoulder. "But the food is awful. They won't let me go home. They still think I'm going to run if they let me." He snorted as if he thought the idea preposterous, but I wasn't so sure. He had run when he'd found the body. "I haven't slept, don't want to. I'm afraid if I do, I'll wake up in prison."

"That's not going to happen," I said. "Not if you come clean with me now."

"What do you mean? I've told you everything I know."

"Have you?" I asked. "The last time we talked, you seemed pretty sure Brad was the one who killed Chuck, but I've learned that's unlikely."

Robert didn't look surprised. He didn't look anything other than dejected. "So you're saying I'm screwed."

"No. I'm saying you need to tell me everything. You're hiding something, Robert Dunhill, and you are going to spill the beans, right now."

He looked up and actually managed a smile. "You sound like my mom."

"Good." I knew for a fact he was scared of his mom. I don't think he'd ever lied to her in his entire life. "Spill it."

Robert picked at his crusty fingernails. "It's nothing," he said. "Well, it has nothing to do with Chuck and there's no way it could have gotten him killed."

I crossed my arms on the table in front of me and leaned forward. "Tell me."

His eyes flickered to my hands, which were only a couple of feet from his own. He stared for a long couple of seconds, and I wondered if he was thinking of reaching out and grabbing my wrists. Why he would, I have no clue, but I was pretty sure the thought flittered through that brain of his.

"It's complicated," he said, sagging back. "Trisha and I were still in the early phases and all that. And well . . ." He shrugged. "I made a mistake."

"You cheated on her," I said, flatly. Why wasn't I surprised?

"Only once. And it technically wasn't cheating. We didn't go on a date or anything. We sort of kissed a couple of times and that was that. I realized how much Trisha meant to me, so I told Asia it was over. Haven't looked at her twice since."

"Asia? As in, elf Asia?"

Robert winced. "I know, it was stupid. Even Chuck didn't want to have anything to do with her. But I've changed since then!" He leaned forward, looked pleadingly into my eye. "I swear I have."

I was seriously beginning to wonder if it was even possible for a man like Robert to change. Sure, he seemed to be doing okay with Trisha, but it had only been a few months and he'd already strayed. How much longer before he made another mistake? And then another?

Then again, why did I care? It wasn't my life he was ruining.

And if I was being honest, I wasn't sure how this information would help in the investigation. If anything, it made him look like an even worse person, which couldn't be good when it came to judging his character.

"Think, Robert," I said, wanting to get back to something that mattered. "Who could have wanted to hurt Chuck? Brad was partnering with him. Lawrence and Randy had no real reason to kill him. So, who?"

"I don't know." He slumped back, frustrated. "It wasn't like anyone liked the guy all that much. He was always breaking things, knocking stuff over and blaming it on other people. He thought it was hilarious."

An idea started to churn. "Wait, he was breaking things?"

Robert nodded. "He'd wait until Lawrence wasn't looking and would knock over a set piece or hide something so the crew couldn't find it. That Ken guy who's in charge of the place blamed Lawrence every time something came up missing, which was why the D-man was always so grumpy with us."

Excited now, I leaned forward. "Did he have a problem with anyone specifically?" I asked. "Like, did Chuck go out of his way to get someone in particular in trouble? A favorite target?"

Another shrug. "I don't know. He got a kick out of making everyone miserable. There's no shortage of people who wanted him gone."

I remembered my first day of practice. Dean had been claiming he hadn't done something to Lawrence and Chuck had been grinning up a storm. And then, later, Dean said he believed things would be better without Chuck around.

Chuck was like the high school bully who picked on the kid with the tape holding his glasses together. He found a target, someone he thought he could torment without repercussions, and hounded them until they snapped. Of course, it's all fun and games until you learn the nerdy kid you were picking on took judo lessons on the weekend.

I tried to remember if I'd seen Dean before the body was discovered, and couldn't. He might have killed Chuck to make the bigger man stop picking on him. Heck, it could have been any one of the cast and crew who'd been a target of Chuck's mean pranks.

My phone rang, causing me to jump. I gave Paul and Robert an apologetic smile, and pulled it from my purse to reject the call, but paused when I saw it was from Death by Coffee.

"One sec," I said, bringing the phone to my ear. Robert looked disgusted, Paul mildly annoyed, at the interruption.

"Krissy!" Vicki's voice was frantic. "Can you come in? I know it's short notice and I only need you for a couple of hours, but I'm not sure I can handle this on my own." Then muffled, "Welcome to Death by Coffee. It'll be just one moment." Then she was back. "If you can't make it, I'll manage on my own, but I'm on my last leg here."

"No, I'll be right in," I said, standing. "Give me fifteen minutes."

"Thank you! I'm so sorry about this, but didn't know what else to do. Gotta go!" She clicked off.

"I'm sorry," I said, gathering my purse and heading for the door. "Something came up at work and I've got to go in."

Robert grunted and refused to look at me as Paul opened the door.

"Is everything all right?" Paul asked, following me out.

"I don't know. Vicki sounded busy and said she was by herself. I'm guessing someone called in sick and she tried to do it all alone and got overwhelmed." At least I was hoping that was the case.

"Okay," Paul said. "Let me know if there's more to it than that and if I can do anything."

"Will do." I hurried away, hoping Paul would get Buchannan to follow up on the tiny little lead I'd pried from Robert.

It wasn't until I was in my car and halfway to Death by Coffee that I realized I hadn't actually said Dean's— or anyone else's name that mattered—out loud. I only hoped that when I'd left, Buchannan or Paul had continued questioning Robert and would come to the same conclusion that I had and would try to figure out who in the cast and crew had been bullied to the point of snapping before that same person snapped again.

23

"Thank you for coming on such short notice," Vicki said, hurriedly filling an order as I threw on an apron and took over the register. There were only a handful people in Death by Coffee thanks to the snowy weather, but even a handful could be a lot when you are alone. A couple waited at the counter upstairs, books in hand, waiting for one of us to get a chance to go up to ring them up. Two more were browsing the books while another three people were waiting in line for coffee.

"It's no biggie," I said. "I'm glad you called." I turned to the next person in line. "Welcome to Death by Coffee, what can I get you today?"

Most of the tables were dirty, which wasn't much of a surprise. While most customers typically carried their trash to the trash cans, there were always a few who didn't bother. And then you had the inevitable spills and the crumbs left by the cookies. It didn't take long before the place looked a disaster.

Vicki handed over a pair of eggnog cappuccinos

and then rushed upstairs to ring up the book orders, leaving me to handle the downstairs duties.

We worked like that for another twenty minutes. Every chance I got, I snuck out to wipe down a table. By the time everyone was served, including a party of five that came through the door just when I thought I was done, I was sweating, but feeling good about myself.

"Where is everyone?" I asked as I filled two coffee pots—one decaf, the other regular. Everyone was served and happy, allowing Vicki and me a breather. "Where's Lena and Jeff?"

"Jeff's coming," Vicki said, brushing a stray hair out of her face. For the first time since I'd known her, she looked out of sorts. It was actually pretty refreshing to see her like that since I was usually the one who looked a mess. "He had a dentist appointment or he'd be here already."

"And Lena?"

"Broke her arm."

I gasped. "Oh no! What happened?"

Vicki leaned back against the counter as I moved from the coffeemakers to the cookie display, which was depressingly empty. "Apparently, she decided to do some snowboarding before coming in this morning. The hills are good for it, I guess, but I'm not sure it's the right kind of snow. She took a spill and must have landed wrong."

"Ouch."

"Ouch is right," Vicki said. "She called while driving herself to the emergency room. She said she'd come into work as soon as they set it, if you can believe that."

"You're not going to let her work, are you?" Lena

was a tough, scrappy young lady, but a broken arm would slow anyone down.

"Of course not," Vicki said, groaning as she moved upright. "We'd better clean up."

Vicki went into the dining area to wipe down the tables I hadn't gotten to, while I went about refilling the cookie display. It felt good to be back at work, even if it wasn't a planned workday. I was surprised by how much I missed it. Sure, I was busy dealing with Robert's current predicament, and the play took up quite a lot of my time, but spending some time at Death by Coffee felt like a welcome break. Strange? Probably, but it's true.

I whipped up a few batches of cookies, set them to baking, and then did a few dishes while I waited for the timer to go off. Vicki had done the best she could, but alone, there was only so much she could do. She should have called me the moment she'd found out Lena wasn't coming in and Jeff wouldn't be able to fill in right away. Instead, she'd tried to handle it herself, and ended up having to call me. I knew she didn't want to interrupt my vacation, but this was our business we were talking about. I would have come in for any reason.

The cookies finished just as I cleaned the last pan. I pulled them out, stuck a toothpick in one to make sure it was done, and then carried them out to the front where I deposited them into the display. I checked to make sure nothing else needed to be refilled, and then joined Vicki, who was back behind the counter.

"You can go if you want," she said, fixing her apron, which had become askew. "I can handle things until Jeff gets here."

"Not on your life," I told her. "You should have called earlier."

She blushed. "I thought I could handle it. I guess an entire store on my own is a little much, especially since I got hit with a rush just before I called you."

"Well, next time you'll know."

She smiled. "I suppose so. I just didn't want to bother you." She fiddled with a damp rag before tossing it beneath the counter. "How is the play going?"

"Okay, I suppose." I shrugged, uncomfortable at the switch in topics. "I still don't know half the words to the songs and I can't dance to save my life, but I think I'll make it through it."

"How's everyone taken the . . . You know?"

"It's been tough," I said in the understatement of the year. "The director, Lawrence, doesn't want anyone to talk about it. A few of the cast are obliging him, but there are others who aren't so willing to let it go." Me included.

"I can't imagine continuing after someone died." Vicki shuddered. "It's hard enough to keep your focus sometimes. To think that someone you work with could be a murderer . . ." She shook her head and grimaced.

"Do you think Robert could have done it?" I asked.

Vicki made a face. "He's a moron, but I don't think he's that big of a moron."

"I agree. I don't think he did it, but Officer Buchannan says he's going to be charged later today. I'm not sure I'll be able to convince him of Robert's innocence. I mean, even *I'm* not totally convinced."

"Had any luck with finding out who else could have killed the guy?" Vicki asked, knowing there was no way I wouldn't be looking into it.

"Some, I guess." I considered stopping there. Vicki didn't need to be dragged into it. But since she did know some of the people at the theatre, and might have to work with them someday if ever she got back into it regularly, she deserved to know. She also might already have some input on some of my suspects. "Do you know a man named Dean? He's one of the crew."

She frowned and tapped her chin with a manicured nail that had survived the rush unbroken. "I think I remember someone by that name. Younger guy? Kind of angry?"

"He's been pretty nice to me so far," I said. "From what Robert told me, Chuck was making Dean's life miserable. I was wondering if you knew him and thought him capable of murder."

"I wish I could tell you," Vicki said. "I haven't spent as much time with the local theatre as I'd like. If Dean is the guy I'm thinking of, he hasn't been there very long. I didn't think he cared all that much about the play I was in, to be honest." She shrugged. "Then again, I could be thinking about someone else entirely."

"That's fine, thanks." I wondered if Dean was the man she remembered or not. The guy I knew didn't seem to be angry, but who knows? Maybe he'd gotten good at hiding it recently, at least until he snapped and killed Chuck.

The door opened and Jeff walked in, eyes lowered, as if he felt guilty about not being able to come in right away. He was already shy and withdrawn. He didn't need yet another reason to avoid eye contact.

"Sorry," he mumbled. It came out muffled as he pulled cotton from his mouth. He gave me an embarrassed smile before heading for the counter.

"Don't worry about it," Vicki said. "You're here now." She turned to me. "And you are leaving."

"What? I can stay longer. Practice is still a few hours away. I can keep working until then."

"No, you can't." She untied my apron for me. "I have help now. You are no longer required."

"But . . ."

"No buts!" Vicki was grinning as she said it. "I expect you to be back and working after Christmas. Not until then."

I grumbled as I removed my apron and balled it up.

"Besides," Vicki said. "You could use a shower before you head to practice."

"Hey!" I sniffed. "I don't smell bad."

"No, but you look like you've spent a couple of hours working your butt off."

"You do look pretty icky, Ms. Hancock," Jeff said with a bashful smile.

"Thanks a lot," I grumped. But they were right. It got hot in the kitchen. I might have only spent a short time working today, but it was enough that my forehead was damp, my hair limp. I didn't even want to think about what my makeup looked like. "I guess I'll go home then."

"Good!" Vicki beamed. "Now shoo."

I took my apron to the back and hung it up. I gathered my purse and then made my way out front just as the door opened and a chagrined Lena came in. Her arm was in a sling, forearm in a cast.

"I'm so sorry," she said to Vicki before noticing me. "Oh no! I didn't want you to have to come in. Let me clock in." She tried to move past me to the back, but I barred her way.

"You're not working today," I said.

"I can do register! I only need one arm for that."
She winced when she tried to motion toward the
counter.

"Sorry," Vicki said. "Your shift is covered."

"Get some rest," I put in. "You look like you're
hurting."

Lena nodded, resting her good hand on the cast on
her bad arm. "They gave me something at the emergency room, but I think it's starting to wear off." She
grit her teeth together. "Okay, scratch that; it's definitely wearing off." She groaned and backed up until
she could sag down into a chair.

"Need me to get you anything?" I asked. "Maybe
a coffee or a cookie to go?"

"A cookie would be great," she said, hopefully.

"A cookie it is."

Vicki had it out and waiting before I reached the
counter. She handed it over with a mouthed, "Thank
you."

I carried the cookie over to where Lena sat and
handed it to her. She took a bite and grimaced.

"Too hot?" I asked, surprised.

"No." She swallowed and forced a smile. "Even
chewing hurts."

"Tell me about it," Jeff muttered, rubbing at his
cheek.

"Well, you go home and get some rest," I said. "If
you feel better tomorrow, I'm sure Vicki will let you
come in to work register for a few hours."

"If you don't feel up to it, call me," Vicki said. "I'll
get someone else to come in." She glanced at Jeff,
who nodded. "It's no big deal."

Lena smiled, though I could tell it pained her to do
so, and I didn't mean just physically. "I guess you're

right. I think I need a nap." She stood with a wince. "Thanks for the cookie." A look of devious defiance came into her eye as she glanced at Vicki. "I'll see you tomorrow."

I followed Lena outside as a small group of customers came in. She waved to me, wincing as she did, and got into her car, which was thankfully parked close by. She drove off slowly. Every bump probably hurt like crazy, but I thought she'd manage. As I said, she's a tough girl.

I got into my own car a moment later and made for home. As much as I would have liked to stay and help out, taking a shower and getting my thoughts in order seemed like a good idea. If I was going to confront Dean about how Chuck treated him, I'd want to be at my best, not exhausted from a long day at work.

My mind was stuck on how I could possibly broach the subject of Chuck's behavior toward Dean as I pulled into my driveway, so I didn't see the two people standing on my stoop, talking to one another, until I was out of my car and almost on top of them. Both Jules and Jane were smiling at me, amused.

"What are you two doing here?" I asked, startled.

"I came to give you these," Jules said, holding out a wrapped box I instantly recognized.

"Cookies!" I exclaimed, snatching them. I loved the cookies we baked at Death by Coffee, but Jules had a way with baking. His cookies were probably the best thing I'd ever put in my mouth.

It was all I could do to keep from digging in right then and there, but I managed. "Thank you," I told him. "Do you want to come in for a minute? I'd be willing to share."

"I can't," he said. "Maestro is waiting for me back

home. He'll want some cuddles before I go. Lance and I are going to see a movie tonight and he hates it when we leave him alone."

"What about you?" I asked, turning to Jane, who'd stepped aside to let us talk.

"I'm only here for a minute," she said with a smile.

"I'll let you two alone," Jules said. "It was nice meeting you." He clasped Jane's arm before giving me a wave and then crossing the yard, back to his house. I could hear Maestro yapping, as if he knew Daddy was on the way back home.

"Is everything all right with Eleanor?" I asked, worried. The curtain hadn't moved since we'd been standing there, which was unlike the older woman.

"She's fine," Jane said. "In fact, she's better than ever. Having you over did her some good."

"I'm glad," I said. "I never wanted things to be bad between us. It just sort of happened."

"I understand. Here." She held out a slip of paper. "It's my number. I'm leaving in a few days and since you're so busy, I wasn't sure I'd get a chance to give it to you before I had to go."

"Thank you," I said, taking the number, though I was perplexed as to why she was giving it to me. We'd hit it off well enough, but I didn't think we'd be trading Christmas cards or calling one another for birthdays.

"Mother wanted me to tell you she's going to try not to give you such a hard time." Jane glanced toward Eleanor's house, a wistful smile on her face. "We moved her chair so she wouldn't be tempted to stare out the window all day."

"She's no bother," I said, though internally, I was relieved. It was hard living next to someone who was constantly spying on you, watching your every move, including when you were in your bedroom and had forgotten to close the blinds.

"I know how big of a pain she can be," Jane said. "And I appreciate you not coming down hard on her. I'd like to think that everything will be good between the two of you from now on. Mother needs a neighbor she can count on." There was more to it than she was saying, but I think I got the gist. Eleanor was old, lonely, and needed a friend.

"I'll do my best," I said.

"If ever you need anything, please call. And if . . ." She bit her lower lip and shook her head.

"If I think she needs you, I'll let you know," I said in understanding. They might not have had the closest of relationships, but I could tell Jane truly did care about her mother.

"Thank you." Jane held out a hand. "It was great meeting you, Krissy Hancock."

"You too, Jane Winthrow." We shook.

With a grateful nod, Jane returned back to Eleanor's house, head down, hands shoved deep into her pockets. I waited until she went inside before unlocking my own door and heading in for my shower.

And a cookie or two, of course.

24

Showered, and feeling surprisingly good, I headed for practice. My brief time at work had made me realize I was focusing on the wrong thing. While Chuck's murder *was* important, it wasn't my responsibility. Christmas was coming and I should be looking forward to that, not worrying myself to death over Robert's predicament.

Now, that didn't mean I was abandoning him to the mercy of the legal system. I still planned on having a chat with Dean about his possible beef with Chuck in the hopes he might shed some light on who actually killed Santa. I'd see what he had to say, then pass on the information to Buchannan or Garrison. There was no need for me to dwell on it any more than that. After practice, I fully intended to come home, sit down with a mug of hot chocolate, and watch Christmas movies until I fell asleep with Misfit curled up in my lap.

Somewhere in the back of my mind, a voice snickered. Okay, maybe I might not be able to drop it that easily, but darn it, I was going to try. If I kept going the way I was, I was going to end up with high blood pressure, if I didn't have it already. It *had* been a few months since I'd last visited my doctor.

I pulled into the parking lot and got out of my car, shivering against the cold. My hair was still slightly damp from the shower, which made it that much worse. I hurried through the side door, hoping I didn't have ice crystals forming, and went straight to the back to get changed into my costume.

"You seem to be in a good mood," Prudence said. She was already changed and was on her way out the door.

"I am," I said. "I'm hoping tonight's practice will go smoothly." And that I'd be done with the investigation for good—having found the real murderer, of course.

Prudence didn't appear convinced. "I saw Randy on the way in. He looked half-drunk already." She sighed. "Something must have happened because I thought he was doing pretty good. Lawrence is going to bust a gasket tonight, you wait and see."

I hoped his drinking wasn't due to my interferences in his plans to start a new theatre with Lawrence. "I'm sure he just had a little too much spiked eggnog," I said, unconvincingly.

Prudence snorted a laugh.

Asia slipped in then, paying Prudence a disgusted look before giving me a little halfhearted wave. She moved to her corner, turned on her speaker, and started playing a pop song that sounded as if it was only half English. Prudence rolled her eyes, gave me a "what can you do?" gesture, and then walked out of the dressing room.

"Krissy," Brad said from the men's side. He was

seated on a metal chair, beside a glowering Greg, looking glum. Was I the only one who'd come to practice in a good mood tonight? It would put a serious damper on me leaving here in high spirits.

"Brad," I replied.

He nodded as if that was all that needed to be said, so I headed to the women's section to get changed. The music was a smidge too loud this close to the speaker, but I ignored it. Asia wasn't smiling, nor was she flanked by the female of her two friends, Prairie. A falling out? Or was the other woman simply late?

Honestly, I didn't care.

A few more members of the cast came in as I pulled on my elf outfit. No one looked happy and it was casting a pall over my own good mood. Everyone was acting gloomier than they had when Chuck died. Maybe the worsening weather had something to do with it. Or maybe they gleaned that things weren't all roses within the theatre. They might not know exactly what was going on, but I bet they could feel it.

In costume, I left the dressing room and went in search of Dean.

I didn't have far to look. He was heading straight for me, having come from the stage. He looked annoyed, which probably meant Lawrence had already gotten on him about something. He made as if to walk around me, but I stepped in front of him, a wide, friendly smile on my face.

"Hi, Dean."

He sighed. "Hey." He glanced past me, to the storage room. "I need to grab a hammer real quick." He stepped around me before I could stop him and pushed his way inside. With a shrug, and maybe a little trepidation, I followed after.

"I was curious about something."

Dean jumped a good foot in the air, knocking over a crate full of tools as he spun, hammer in hand. The rest of the tools crashed to the floor, screwdrivers and wrenches going everywhere.

"Don't sneak up on me like that!" he said, lowering the hammer from its half-cocked state. He sucked in a deep breath, free hand pressed over his heart.

"Sorry." My own heart had leapt into my throat at his reaction and I had to swallow it back. "You seem jumpy."

"I wasn't expecting you to follow me in," he said. He knelt and started picking up the tools. I bent over and helped him.

"Is something wrong?" I asked, picking up something that looked like a cross between a socket wrench and a hammer. I gave it a once over, unsure what it was for, and then dropped it into the crate.

"A nail worked its way loose on the stage. Lawrence is freaking out because he's afraid someone's going to hurt themselves on it despite the fact it's in the front left corner. No one even goes over there during the entire play, so how someone's supposed to hurt themselves . . ." He gave an exaggerated roll of his eyes.

I immediately thought of Kenneth Purdy's refusal to fix up the theatre. The whole place seemed as if it was falling down on our heads. No wonder Lawrence was so keen on moving on and starting up his own. He might be abrasive, but I bet he'd make a good building manager.

"No, I mean, is there something else wrong?" I straightened and wiped my hands on my pants, leaving dirty streaks. Great. Something else for Lawrence to complain about. "You seem tense. Everyone does."

Dean picked up the crate and set it back on its shelf. "I'm fine. We're getting closer to opening night and it always gets hectic. If something were to go wrong now, it could jeopardize the entire play."

He started for the door, but I slid to move in front of it, earning me a huff of annoyance. "So, I heard an interesting rumor recently." All innocence.

Dean looked at me expectantly, clearly impatient to get back to the stage.

"I heard you had a problem with Chuck. He used to knock things over, hide things, and then blame them on other people. You, namely."

"Good old Chuck was a real prankster," Dean said, forcing a smile that never reached his eyes.

"That had to annoy you, especially since Lawrence was already so hard on you."

He shrugged, hand tightening on the hammer. I suddenly questioned the wisdom of asking him these questions while he was carrying a weapon, especially where no one else could step in and stop him if he decided to put an end to my prying.

"So?" he said. "I wasn't the only one he got into trouble with his pranks. You should have seen what he did to Greg. He put thumbtacks in his shoes. It very nearly made Greg quit right then and there. If Asia hadn't talked him out of it, I'm sure he would have."

I winced in sympathy. "Did he pick on everyone like that?" I asked. "Or did he have a couple of favorite targets?"

"Ask around," Dean said. "I'm sure nearly every-one here had a reason to knock Chuck off. The guy was a jerk to all of us. He tormented the guys with pranks, trying to get us into trouble. With the girls, he took a different tact."

I didn't have to ask him what he meant by that, having seen it myself.

"Now, if you'll excuse me, I'd like to get this nail hammered in before Lawrence comes looking for me."

I stepped aside and let Dean pass. He paused at the door, glanced back at me, eyes narrowing, before he pushed his way out.

"As if that wasn't suspicious," I muttered with a shudder. Sooner or later, I'd learn not to question suspects without backup. He could have clunked me on the head with that hammer and been out the door before anyone realized what happened. No one had seen me follow him in, so it wasn't like anyone would know to look for me in here.

I hurried out of the storage room, my mood now completely shot. Dean was hammering away at the stage, hitting the nail much harder than he needed. Prudence caught my eye, frowned as if she knew I was responsible for his sour mood, and then turned her back on me.

"Making friends, I see," Randy said, startling me. He'd come from the back somewhere, likely the cast restrooms.

"I don't know what you're talking about."

He smiled, knowingly. "You're starting to upset the locals by asking so many questions. If we didn't know better, we'd start to wonder if you're poking around, looking for trouble."

"I'm not asking questions," I said, sounding about as believable as a kid who'd been caught sneaking a peek at his Christmas presents.

He laughed and patted my shoulder. "Sure you're

not. Dean comes out of the storage room, looking ready to crack skulls, and you sneak out a few seconds later? I'm pretty sure you two don't have anything going on between you, so I'm guessing you followed him in to ask questions, right?"

"We were just talking," I said, face reddening.

"Uh huh." Randy leaned in close, lowered his voice. "I'd be careful with Dean there. Rumor has it, he has a temper that's gotten him into trouble on more than one occasion."

"Does rumor also think he killed Chuck?" I asked, both because I was curious, and a little annoyed. Why did it matter to him if I was asking questions about Chuck's death, not unless he had something to do with it.

Randy stepped back and shrugged. I noticed he had melting snow in his beard, telling me he'd just recently come back inside. His breath also smelled heavily of mints, warning me he indeed might have been at the bottle before coming in tonight. "I'm not saying anything, but you'd be wise to be more careful with yourself." He walked away.

I headed for the stage, thoughtful. Maybe I'd been too hasty in dismissing Randy as a suspect after our little impromptu meeting at the church. Just because he was working with Lawrence, didn't mean he didn't have a reason to want to be rid of Chuck.

But dismissing Dean just because I kind of liked the guy would be a mistake as well. He'd finished hammering his nail and had vanished back toward the storage room again. He hadn't looked at me when he went, but I could feel the anger radiating off him as he passed. I'd gotten to him big time. Did that make him guilty? Or was he just mad that I was asking questions that insinuated he might be guilty of murder?

"Places!" Lawrence called. His eyes met mine and I could see a warning there not to talk about what I'd learned about him. Randy was right; I wasn't doing a very good job of making friends here. Even Prudence wouldn't hold my gaze for more than an instant.

We all scrambled to take our places and noted we were missing another elf. It took me a moment to realize Greg wasn't in place next to Asia, who looked worried as she scanned the cast, presumably to find him. She didn't need to be, however, because he came bounding up on stage a moment later smiling, having finally seemed to have gotten over what had been bothering him in the dressing room.

"Sorry," he said, absorbing a patented Lawrence stare without flinching.

Finally, Lawrence took a deep breath to calm himself and said, "I want practice to go flawlessly tonight. We have only a couple of evenings left before opening night. Tech rehearsal starts in two days. We will be starting two hours earlier and I expect everyone to be there each night, until the end. No exceptions."

There was general moaning and groaning from the cast, me included.

"Cue up the music!" Lawrence spun and raised a hand toward the booth. The lights dimmed, the music started, and we began.

To say my mind was elsewhere would be an understatement. I kept shooting glances at Brad and Randy, wondering if they'd led me astray on purpose, or if they were truly innocent of Chuck's murder. Dean was behind the curtain somewhere, presumably getting things ready for the next act, so I didn't see him anywhere, but I was sure he'd be looking at me with as much disdain as everyone else.

"Watch it," Prudence muttered when I stepped right when I was supposed to hop left. She gave me a light shove to get me into the right spot, smile painted onto her face.

"Sorry," I whispered, promptly missing my next mark, which was a spin that would take me back two steps.

"Ms. Hancock!" Lawrence shouted in warning and pointed.

I hurried to my mark, dipped, and then rushed forward to pick up my prop present. I was a good five seconds behind everyone else.

A sound came from above. My eyes flickered upward just before bending to pick up the gift. Someone screamed a warning, but I was already moving, falling backward to avoid the sandbag. It crashed into my gift, crushing the empty box flat, and missing my splayed legs by scant millimeters.

Okay, maybe it was by a foot or so, but it felt closer.

"Are you all right?" Brad said, rushing over to where I lay, too afraid to move. My eyes were wide, affixed to the half dozen other sandbags hanging overhead. "Krissy?"

"I'm fine," I said, pushing away from my near-death experience. "I'm okay." Though my heart was telling a different story.

"Dean!" Lawrence shrieked. "What happened?"

Dean came running from the back, eyes wide. "The rope must have frayed," he said. "I tried to stop it." He opened his hand to show a red welt forming on his palm where he must have tried to grab the rope as it snapped.

Or did he? If he'd been holding it and cut it, he very well might have sustained those injuries when he didn't let go quick enough.

"Why must something always go wrong?" Lawrence threw down his script and then stormed up onto the stage. The sandbag hadn't busted, but had left a mess anyway. My poor box was nothing but flattened cardboard and torn paper now. "Clean this up," he told Dean before looking at me. "Go to the back and take a few minutes to compose yourself. Get some fresh air if need be." He raised his eyes. "Everyone take ten. Then meet back here." He walked away, muttering to himself.

Brad helped me to my feet. My legs wobbled a bit and I leaned on his shoulder for support. "Thanks," I said.

"Don't mention it. That was close." His eyes rose to the hanging sandbags and he guided me away from them.

"Too close," I admitted. I'd felt the wind rush past. A half-second more and my head would have been the one to have taken the brunt of the impact. I mean, I spent most of my night on that very spot, twirling and dancing around. It was my bad timing that kept me from being there when it happened.

Prudence hurried to my side, Asia right behind her. "You okay?" they both asked in unison.

"I'm fine. It missed me." I rubbed at my butt, which was starting to throb. "The landing was a bit rough, though."

"I can't believe it broke like that," Asia said, eyes going skyward before she looked back to where Greg was standing. He was staring at me as if the break was somehow my fault. So much for his good mood.

"The whole place is falling apart," Prudence put in. "I'm afraid I'm going to fall through the stage one of these nights." She tsked. "The entire building is in serious need of an overhaul."

I held my tongue, not wanting to spill what I knew about Lawrence's plan. "I want to see the rope," I said.

"You sure?" Brad asked.

"I'm sure."

With a nervous look around, he nodded, and then led me off the stage, to the back where the sandbags were tied down.

There was a pulley system next to the wall. I'd never paid it any mind before, but now, it was all I could look at. The ropes *did* look a bit worse for wear, but in no danger of breaking. I wasn't sure why they were even hooked up since we weren't using them for anything. I supposed the sandbags and pulley system were used in other productions, but why not take it down when they weren't in use?

"It looks frayed," Brad said, examining the remains of the broken rope. It hadn't come undone, but appeared to have done just as Dean had said and broken.

It did bring up an interesting question, however. If the rope *had* simply broken, and we weren't using the system in the play, why was Dean over here in the first place? He had to have been standing right there when it happened, not across the room or else he wouldn't have gotten to it in time to grab hold.

"I guess it could have been an accident," I said, not believing it, but not wanting anyone else to think otherwise. If Dean was trying to kill me, letting on that I knew would only make him try that much harder.

"You don't think . . . ?" Brad frowned, eyes following the ropes, up past the catwalk.

I shrugged and forced a shaky smile. "I think it simply broke."

Brad looked skeptical, but nodded. "You going to be okay?"

"Yeah." I took a deep breath and let it out. I'd stopped shaking and my heart had resumed its normal beat. "We should get back. I'm okay now."

With a nod, Brad led the way back to the stage. Everyone was huddled around the crushed gift. The sandbag was gone, as was Dean, who was likely disposing of it. I received a few more well-wishes, and then Lawrence was back, shouting at everyone to take their places.

As we got started with practice again—me carrying my crushed gift, if you can believe it—I couldn't help but look up and wonder. Had it truly been an accident?

Or had I been targeted for murder?

25

If practice was stilted and a mess before the accident, it was a complete disaster afterward. Every time I moved, I found myself glancing up to make sure nothing else was going to fall from the sky to crush me. I stumbled from step to step, forgot most of the words to every song, and in general, made a fool out of myself, and the play.

But, thankfully, I wasn't the only one.

Brad, who'd I'd originally taken as a jerk, actually seemed concerned about my well-being. He kept an eye on me throughout the practice and whenever I tripped, he was there to make sure I didn't fall. It didn't totally make up for how he'd treated Trisha, but it was a step in the right direction.

Prudence was likewise rattled, though I think her discomfort came from the fact she spent most of the play dancing and singing beside me, which put her in the direct line of fire if something *did* happen. She kept herself a few steps farther to my right than she was supposed to, but I didn't hold it against her. I didn't want anyone to get hurt; me included.

Practice ended with a sad whimper. The nervous cast moved off the stage, eyes darting every which way as if they expected the entire building to come crashing down on their heads. Asia left without bothering to change. I was headed in the same direction, just wanting to be safe at home with that cup of hot chocolate I'd been craving, when Lawrence called me over.

Great, I thought, thinking he was going to lay into me for my role in the mess that was practice. I figured he'd had enough and I wouldn't be coming back. How he'd find another elf to fill my shoes, I didn't know. Maybe he'd go one short. Or maybe he'd call Rita in—taking out the seams of my costume in the process. It wasn't like I was an integral part of the show, so anything could happen.

I took the stairs at the side of the stage and joined Lawrence in the aisle. Above us, in the booth, Violet and Zander were shutting down the lights and whatever else they managed from there. Someone else—Dean, I believe, but I couldn't see him to be sure—was resetting the stage so we could begin fresh tomorrow.

"How are you holding up?" Lawrence asked, resting a hand on my shoulder and squeezing. He actually looked concerned, which was a surprise considering he hadn't seemed to care about anything but the quality of the play during practice. "You look rattled."

"I am," I admitted. "But I'm okay now. Sorry I messed up so badly."

"No, I understand." He sighed. "I realize I can be a bear when it comes to practices sometimes. Directing a play like this is stressful, and I let it get to me. Everyone wants it to be perfect. I need to keep my reputation sterling so when I . . ." He glanced past me before giving me a meaningful look. "I can't put on a dud if I want people to follow me."

"If you want me to step aside, I will," I said. I was surprised to find I didn't want to be cut from the play. Going in, I was sure I'd hate every minute of it, but practice wasn't as bad as I thought it would be. I liked most of the people, even if many of them weren't all that fond of me. And while singing and dancing wasn't exactly my forte, I was slowly getting the hang of it and enjoying myself.

"No, nothing like that," Lawrence said with yet another reassuring squeeze. "Keep practicing at home, and I'm sure you'll have the hang of things by opening night." I could almost hear the "I hope" in his voice.

"I'll do my best," I promised him.

He smiled as the lights overhead dimmed. "You'd better get changed before we lock up for the night. Get some rest. I'll see you tomorrow."

"Thank you."

Lawrence patted my shoulder once more and then turned to head up into the booth to finish the shutdown.

Feeling marginally better, I headed for the back. Most everyone was already gone, having rushed through changing to get out of there. I didn't mind since I wasn't a big fan of the dressing room arrangements. I preferred having the room to myself, though it made for a somewhat creepy experience, especially after what had happened. Behind me, I could hear the lights shutting off and the occasional thump as something was moved on the stage. Otherwise, it was a quiet walk back toward the hall leading to the dressing rooms.

What am I going to do about Robert? I wondered

as I paused at the men's side. The police tape was loose, torn on one side, as if someone had been sneaking a look recently. I rested my hand on the door, wishing I could just divine what had happened by touch and put it all behind me. Buchannan had likely charged Robert with Chuck's murder by now. I wished I had more proof that he wasn't the doer, but I had nothing but speculation.

I started to turn away when the storage room door opened and Dean stepped out, a long, pointed screwdriver in hand. He saw me and froze.

Panic zinged through me. We were alone together back here. Even if I screamed, there was no certainty Lawrence would hear me from the booth. Chances were good he'd already sent Violet and Zander home.

"Hi," I said, eyeing the screwdriver. "I thought everyone was gone."

Dean's lips pressed together in a firm white line. I could almost see the calculation behind his eyes, the anger. Even his knuckles were popping white on the screwdriver. All it would take is one quick motion, and he could jam it through my eye.

I took a nervous step back.

"Wait," he said, all the anger draining out of him at once. "I'm sorry." He closed his eyes. "Please, just wait."

I hesitated. This was the perfect chance to run, very well might be my *only* chance.

But what if he was about to confess? The pressure could be getting to him, making his life miserable. If I stayed, he might let it all out, just to be done with it.

"Did you kill him?" I asked, knowing the smart thing to do would have been to remain silent, but needing to know anyway.

"No," Dean said, opening his eyes. "A part of me wanted to, but I couldn't. I'm getting better at controlling it, you know? The anger."

I glanced at the screwdriver again, not so sure he did.

He looked down at it and smiled. "A screw came loose on one of the flats. I was going to tighten it before I left." He tossed the screwdriver aside. It clanked on the floor and rolled to a stop against the men's dressing room door.

"Okay," I said, breathing a sigh of relief. I didn't stoop to pick up the screwdriver, but I edged a little closer to it just in case he came at me. "Do you know what happened?"

He shook his head. "I wish I did." He looked at his palm, at the red welt there. "Chuck was always pushing me, trying to make me snap. He found out about . . ." He trailed off, frowned.

"About what, Dean?"

He sighed, seemed to cave in on himself. "He saw me go to my doctor one day." A slight pause. "My therapist."

"You have a therapist?"

Dean nodded, refused to meet my eye. "I used to get into fights over stupid things all the time. Someone would bump into me on a busy street and I'd retaliate as if they'd done it on purpose. I lashed out constantly, couldn't help myself. It eventually landed me in jail and a judge decided I needed to talk it out, I guess." He smiled, sadly. "My therapist told me to try out for a part in the play, saying it would give me something to focus my mind on, a sort of outlet for my anger. I thought she was crazy, but tried out anyway. I didn't get a part, but was asked to do crew.

I liked it enough, I stayed on for the last couple of productions. It can be stressful, sure, but it keeps my mind busy."

"And then Chuck started harassing you."

He nodded. "He wanted to see how far he could push me. Let me tell you, I wanted to . . ." He balled his hand into a fist a moment before relaxing. "But I held off. I'm getting better. I sometimes have to fight to keep from screaming, but I haven't lashed out at anyone for months now."

I considered him a long minute while he fidgeted with his hands. He looked genuine, and honestly, I wanted him to be innocent. I liked the guy when he wasn't getting angry at me. And he was taking steps to improve himself, which was something you couldn't say for a lot of people.

"Do you think Chuck was killed because of how he treated people?" I asked.

"I wish I could tell you," he said. "I saw him go to the back, but was so busy making sure everything was set up right, I didn't pay attention to who else might have gone in after him." He paused. "Well, I'm pretty sure I saw one of the elves hurrying by at one point, but I can't be sure who it was. I didn't look up; only heard the bells."

That fit with Robert, aside from the fact he'd taken off his elf shoes and had left before the body was found. So, who else was there? Trisha? Brad? Or did someone else have a reason to off Chuck, one I had yet to discover.

"Look, I'm sorry if I scared you. I was upset you were asking me questions like you thought I was guilty.

I've tried really hard to be a good person and to have my integrity questioned, it got to me."

"I understand," I said. "I didn't mean to upset you. I just want to know who killed Chuck, and I'll do whatever it takes to find out before someone else gets hurt."

"I hope you figure it out," Dean said. "I'm going to go. I'll see you tomorrow, okay?"

"Okay."

He slid past me and headed for the door, leaving the screwdriver, and the loose screw, behind.

I waited until I heard the sound of the cast door closing before I moved to the women's dressing room. I slipped inside, mind whirling. With Dean's admission, I found I was down yet another suspect, leaving very few options. I was starting to think Robert very well might be the killer.

The dressing room was empty, as expected. I moved to the women's side and sagged down into a chair. Asia's speaker was sitting there, silent, and I kind of wished she was here to play music. My mood was down in the dumps, a stark contrast to how the evening had started.

I quickly got changed and put on my coat. The more I thought about it, the more I realized I should have taken a closer look at Trisha. Could the easiest of explanations be the most likely? I mean, Chuck had just hit on her mere minutes before his death. She could have snapped and Robert could be covering for her. It looked like I might have to start poking into her life.

I wasn't looking forward to the prospects. It would make me look like a jaded ex, snooping around, looking for a reason to get the current fling into trouble.

I started for the dressing room door, just as it opened. I paused, thinking Lawrence was coming back to make sure the lights were off, but it wasn't Lawrence who stepped inside.

"Oh, hi, Greg. I thought everyone was already gone. Asia left a little bit ago."

Greg stood there, motionless, for a good couple of seconds before closing the door behind him. He didn't move out of the way.

"I'm not here for Asia," he said.

It was then I noticed the screwdriver in his hand.

"Um, Greg?" I asked, taking a step back. "What's going on?"

"You had to keep pushing, didn't you?" he said. "I heard you talking to that *crewman*." He said it like a curse. "You're still poking around, getting into everyone's business."

"I'm not sure what you mean," I said, knowing playing dumb wasn't going to get me anywhere.

"Don't you?" Greg smiled. "You are a lot like Chuck in many ways, you know that, right? He couldn't keep his hands to himself, and you can't keep your mouth closed."

I would have been offended if I wasn't so scared. "You killed him," I said.

"He deserved to die for what he did."

"For putting tacks in your shoes?" I guessed.

Greg laughed. It sounded half-crazed. "That was nothing compared to what he did to Asia."

"He wouldn't keep his hands off her."

A sneer contorted his smile. "I could have dealt with it if he would have done that, but no, he wouldn't even touch her! He picked on me, chased after all the women but the only one who mattered." His face reddened.

"You love her," I said, realizing it almost immediately.

"She's the moon and stars." Greg's eyes moved heavenward for an instant before settling back on me. "And he didn't see that. He pretended like she didn't even exist."

"So you killed him." It seemed like a pretty weak excuse for murder. I mean, I'd be angrier if some other woman was chasing after the man of my dreams, not if she left him alone.

"I didn't mean to." For an instant, he looked embarrassed by his actions. "But when I went to confront him about how he was treating Asia, he said she wasn't worth his time! He put her down, said she couldn't act. I couldn't let that slide."

"So you snapped."

"It was impulse." He looked at the screwdriver in his hand, fingers tightening. "He turned his back on me like I didn't matter. The knife was sitting there. I don't even know whose it was, or why it was there. I grabbed it and before I could think about what I was doing . . ."

"You stabbed him."

"It should have ended there," Greg said. "Chuck wasn't a good person. No one misses him. Randy is a better Santa anyway. I've *helped* this production."

Sounded like rationalization to me, but I didn't say that. "You did what you thought was right," I said. "If you let me go, I won't say anything. You're right, everyone is happier now." I forced a smile. My heart was beating so hard, I could feel it pulsing in my lips.

"I wish I could believe you," he said. "But you can't be trusted."

"Greg, think about what you are doing. Would Asia want this?"

"I have thought about it," he said. "She would be heartbroken if you were to turn me in to the cops. I can't let that happen."

His shoulders squared and he looked me dead in the eye.

"I'm sorry about this, Krissy," he said. "But you are going to have to die."

26

Greg advanced on me, screwdriver in his hand looking as menacing as a butcher knife. I scuttled back, but there was nowhere for me to go.

"Please," I begged. "You don't want to do this."

"I don't," he admitted. "But I have to."

I feigned to the right, hoping Greg would leap that way, but he held his ground. He was between me and the door, though he had yet to charge me. There was still some resistance to murder going on in his head somewhere. I could see it in his eyes.

But I doubted the sane, reasonable side would win out. Letting me go now would end up putting him in prison since I would go straight to the police. He knew that, just as much as I did.

Greg stopped a yard away. His shoulders were hunched, his breathing quick. I could almost hear him ramping himself up to stab me. When he'd killed Chuck, he'd already been worked up, and if what he said was true, it had been an impulse. This, however, wasn't.

"Think about what you're doing," I said, in a vain

attempt to get him to see reason. "It's only going to make things worse."

"I'm sorry," he said, raising the hand with the screwdriver up over his head.

The door opened then, causing Greg's head to swivel that way.

"Sorry," Brad said, hurrying inside. "I forgot my . . ." He trailed off as he took in the scene. His eyes widened as they moved from me to Greg and the screwdriver. "What's going on?" He licked his lips, took a step back. "I, um . . ."

"Help me," I whispered, afraid to speak normally out of fear it would draw Greg's attention back my way.

Brad stood there, seemingly frozen in indecision. On one hand, he wanted to be the hero who saved the girl from the crazy man. On the other hand, the screwdriver did look pretty pointy poised as it was. If he charged Greg now, it could very well end up jammed through *his* chest instead of mine.

I could almost see the thoughts working through his head. Instead of waiting for him to make up his mind, I used the distraction he provided me to take a quick look around at my surroundings. There was a roll of duct tape in the corner and a hairbrush on a chair nearby, which would be of little help. The costumes weren't going to shield me either. I supposed I could try to use one to grab Greg's arm and tangle him up like they do in the movies, but I had no idea how to do that. More likely, I'd end up getting wrapped in it myself.

And then I noted the small, cylindrical black shape sitting right where it's been for the last couple of days.

Asia's speaker. I took a quick step to the side, which drew Greg's gaze briefly before he turned to face Brad once more.

"I'm sorry," Brad said, raising both hands. "I've got to go." And like a coward, he ripped open the door and fled. So much for his tough guy image.

But his flight did have one advantage; Greg's attention was on him, not me.

I ducked down, snatched up Asia's speaker, and as Greg's head started to turn back my way, I reared back and swung it at his head with all my might. The speaker, while high quality, cracked on impact, but it did the job. Greg staggered backward and tripped over his own two feet. I didn't wait to see if he was unconscious or not, however. I leapt over his legs and ran for the door, calling after Brad as I went.

Brad had just reached the cast entrance as I burst through the door. I called his name, but he didn't so much as glance back as he vanished outside.

"Thanks a lot!" I shouted after him as the theatre fell dark. Greg was already moving behind me, making a weird growling sound as he scrambled to his feet. I hesitated, vaguely noting the men's room door was open, before making a move to the cast door, hoping Lawrence might still be around—which, of course, he wasn't. The delay cost me.

"Come back here!" Greg shouted, bursting out of the dressing room, red-faced and angry.

I ran for the cast door then, but I was too slow. Greg came roaring at my heels. If I continued straight on, he'd catch me before I ever opened the door. The floor was damp with melted snow from Brad's return. I used it to my advantage and took a hard left, just as Greg reached for me. His feet skidded out from beneath him and he went down hard.

Of course, now I wasn't headed for the exit.

I rushed up the stage, paused a heartbeat to take stock of the dark room, and then, hearing Greg's thundering footsteps, I leapt down and ducked behind the seats.

Greg's shoes squeaked as he came to a stop on the stage. I was too afraid to peek out to see what he was doing, but I was pretty sure he was standing there, squinting into the gloom. There were gaps between the seats, and there was something sticky on the floor where I knelt. I was counting on the darkness to keep me hidden, but for how long?

"I know you're still there," Greg said, jumping from the stage. "Lawrence keeps the doors locked at night. You can't escape."

I bit my lip to keep from speaking up. Greg had to know it was over. Brad might have run, leaving me to face a killer on my own, but I doubted he'd be such a coward as not to go to the police. Paul could be on his way even now. If I could stay hidden until then, I'd be saved.

But what if Brad didn't have a cell phone? It could be twenty minutes before the police got here. By then, Greg could check down every aisle, peer beneath every seat. I couldn't just sit here and wait to be saved.

"Come on out," Greg said, moving to the first aisle. "We can talk about it."

Yeah right, I thought. The moment I popped my head up over the seats would be the moment he tried to pierce my skull with his screwdriver.

Greg's shoes creaked as he moved to the next aisle,

putting him one away from where I hid. Slowly, I slid toward the far end. My hands stuck to the floor and made a peeling sound that sounded as loud as a scream to my ears.

Greg went completely still, as did I. I held my breath, afraid to so much as breathe lest I draw his attention.

"I can hear you," Greg said in a sing-song voice.

And then the room went utterly silent. My chest was starting to burn from lack of air, but I was afraid if I sucked in a breath, Greg would hear and would leap over the seats at me. I imagined him doing the same, standing there, breath trapped in his chest. It would be a contest to see who could hold out the longest.

Of course, I wasn't in the best shape of my life, and panic was making the need to breathe paramount, so our competition was short lived.

I sucked in a gasping breath.

"Got ya!" Greg appeared at the end of the aisle, screwdriver poised and ready.

I scrambled back, thankful I wasn't hiding near the first seat. Greg rushed forward, just as I managed to get to my feet.

"Wait!" I shouted on impulse.

Strangely, Greg hesitated. He recovered almost instantly, but it was all the time I needed.

Using skills I hadn't used since I was in high school gym, I vaulted over the seat in front of me and bolted down the aisle. Greg shouted after me, but I ignored him, mind squarely on getting out of the theatre in one piece. My chest was burning by the time I reached the stage. Instead of taking the stairs, I jumped up and pulled myself onto the stage, scrambling back to my feet, just as Greg grabbed for my foot, fingers brushing my ankle, but not quite grasping hold.

I yelped at the close call and used every last ounce of energy I had—which by this time, was mostly adrenaline—and made for the back and the cast exit. My legs were tired, and I was out of breath, but if play practice did one thing for me, it increased my usually pathetic endurance.

I reached the door a good dozen strides ahead of Greg. I burst outside, into the snowy parking lot, immediately sliding on the ice outside the door. I glanced toward the parking lot, praying Brad had hung around to make his call to the police, but his car was gone.

Jerk, I thought. I mean, who leaves a girl alone to fend for her life against a maniac? I took back every nice thing I ever said about him, limited as they may be.

A thump told me Greg had hit the door sliding. I yanked my phone from my pocket, figuring I'd need to take matters into my own hands, as I made my way to my car. Footing was iffier than ever, which meant I kept having to look away from my phone to make sure I wasn't going to hit a patch of ice.

The cast door opened, and I glanced back to see Greg lumber outside. Blood ran down the side of his head where I'd hit him, and his lower lip was busted. He snarled at me as our eyes met, and then he came forward.

I quickened my pace and found Paul's number. I was just about to press it when disaster struck.

The parking lot had been plowed, but whoever had

done it did a pretty poor job of it. The wet, tightly packed snow had frozen solid in the dozens of tire tracks that made up the parking lot. My foot landed solidly in one of the tracks and when I moved to take another step, eyes on my phone, I stepped right in a solid patch of white ice.

I screamed as I went down, phone flying from my hand to land in a snowbank. My butt hit the ice hard, feet flying straight up into the air, but I managed to keep my head from cracking the pavement somehow. Then again, with Greg bearing down on me, it might have been better if I was knocked unconscious.

Somewhat dazed, and a whole lot sore, I scrambled to all fours, glancing back to see Greg still advancing, eyes alight in victory.

"Wait!" I said, hoping it would cause him to stop again as I pushed my way to my feet. "Brad knows you're the killer. You don't have to do this."

He only snarled at me, bloody foam bubbling from his lips. He'd gone from angry to rabid, apparently.

I took a step back, my foot sliding on the ice. My car was only a few yards away, yet it felt like a million miles. If I tried to run, I'd surely end up facedown on the ice. And while Greg was having footing issues as well, I wasn't counting on him having bad balance issues.

"Think about what you're doing," I said, near tears. It was late and the weather was bad, so there were hardly any cars on the road. If this had been any other time of the year, someone would have driven past by now.

"Give it up," Greg said, spitting blood. "Don't make this harder than it has to be. You ruined everything! I can't let that slide."

And then, without waiting for me to respond, he made his move.

Greg launched himself forward with a scream, blood and spittle flying from his mouth. He no longer had his screwdriver, apparently having lost it somewhere in the chase, but his hands were curled in talonlike claws, as if he would be content on ripping me apart piece by piece with his bare hands. It looked like this guy needed anger management about as much as Dean.

No, check that; this guy needed a straightjacket and some mind-altering drugs, if you asked me.

I tried to back away, but the ice had other things in mind. I put a heel down, and immediately lost my footing again. I hit hard on my back, my feet once again flying up into the air like a comedian slipping on a banana peel.

It was probably the only thing that saved me.

Greg hit the ice at the same instant as I did. He pitched forward, his momentum carrying him, just as I went over backward. His already battered face came hurtling down just as my feet came flying up.

They met about thigh-high.

There was a sickening crunch as I inadvertently kicked him square in the mouth. My head thunked against the sheet of ice covering the parking lot, causing stars to bloom.

For an instant, I was afraid I was going to pass out and Greg would crawl over to me and strangle me while I lay there, unconscious. I had an insane thought that I should have bought winter shoes with better traction before my senses came roaring back. I pushed backward, using my heels to dig into the ice, away from Greg, who wasn't moving. I didn't stop until I bumped up against my car.

Blinking snow from my eyes, I used the side of my car to work my way to my feet. "Greg?" I asked, quietly, not sure I wanted him to hear me, but needing to know if anyone was home.

He didn't so much as twitch.

Okay, that wasn't true. His back was moving as he breathed, but he appeared to be out cold.

I glanced wildly around. A chance turn of light caught my phone's screen and I moved slowly to the snowbank to retrieve it. Paul's number was still up, so I hit call, eyes never leaving Greg.

"Hello? Krissy?"

"Paul!" I nearly sobbed in relief. "You need to come down to the community theatre. I've caught the killer."

"Are you okay?" he asked, sounding frantic himself. "We're already on the way."

"I'm fine." I crept back to my car, got behind the wheel, and started it up. "I'm going to keep an eye on him. He's taking an impromptu nap." I had an insane urge to giggle, but suppressed it. "Hurry."

And then I hung up, unable to keep watch over Greg's inert body and talk at the same time. My head was pounding, my butt hurt, and I was frozen to the bone.

Jacking up the heat, I clutched at the wheel and watched the slow rise and fall of Greg's back. He wasn't dead, which I supposed was a good thing. But I had no idea how long he'd be out, hence starting my car. If he so much as shifted, I was out of there, even if it meant he would get away.

I'd had enough near death experiences for one

lifetime, thank you very much. I wasn't about to tempt fate again.

As the skies opened up, sending down a cascade of beautiful, white snow, I settled in to wait for the police to arrive.

27

"Come in. Merry Christmas!" Mason stepped aside, allowing both Will and me to pass. "Vicki's still getting ready. She'll be down in a few minutes."

"Merry Christmas," I said, carrying my gifts into the dining room. "Where do you want me to put these?"

"The counter is fine," Mason turned to Will and both men shook. "Glad you could make it."

I set the packages down with some relief. I was bruised and sore all over, and figured I would be for a week or more. Thankfully, nothing was broken and no visits to the doctor were in order. Will had fussed over me when he'd seen me, of course, but there was nothing he could do but order me to take some aspirin and cuddle.

I was happy to do both.

Trouble was sitting in the next room, ears pinned back. He was wearing a red sweater with bells, and looked about as annoyed as you'd expect. Since we were in Mason's house, it did make me wonder if

Vicki had brought him along today, or if she was staying here with Mason more than she let on.

"How are you feeling?" Mason asked, joining me. "I heard they canceled the play?"

"They did." I sighed in disappointment. All that work for naught. "Too much happened too fast. Lawrence didn't think an elf with a black eye who could barely walk, let alone dance, would give the right impression." I didn't even remember hitting my face on anything, but in the excitement, I must have.

"At least that whole mess is over with." Mason shook his head. "I can't believe how this sort of thing always seems to happen to you. You must be cursed."

"Tell me about it," Will muttered with a good-natured smile.

"Everything worked out," I said, a smidge defensively. "Robert's out of jail and acting like I walk on water. I think he's still dating Trisha, but I hear things have gotten tense between them because she's now working closely with Brad. Hard to believe Robert can be jealous of anyone."

From what I understood, Trisha had decided to go all in with Brad on the investment he'd originally planned to do with Chuck. As far as I was aware, they weren't getting too cozy with one another, but who knows? Sometimes getting to know someone better is all it takes for love to bloom.

Of course, that would mean Robert would become single yet again, and I doubted he would leave me out of it. While I was glad he didn't go to jail for a murder he didn't commit, I wasn't looking forward to his unwanted advances and arrogant attitude.

"How's your dad doing?" Mason asked, picking up the box with his name on it and giving it a quick shake. I slapped his hand, which only caused him to smile.

"He's doing good. He's heading home with Laura in a couple of days." When he'd called, he'd sounded so happy, it made *me* happy. Any reservations I'd had about him spending time with Laura had fled right then and there. "It sounds like he had a lot of fun and is planning on making it an annual event."

"That's great!" Mason sounded genuinely pleased. "The Alps are always lovely." He glanced at Will, a mischievous look coming into his eye. "Maybe you should take her there next year."

Will's eyes widened for a heartbeat before he smiled. "I might have to think about it."

I eyed him and wondered if his hesitation was because Mason had caught him by surprise, or if there was more to it. He'd been reserved as of late. I couldn't tell if it was something I did or if it was work. He'd been spending a lot more late nights at the hospital in Levington, so chances were good he was simply tired.

Still, it made me worry.

My phone rang then. I excused myself and answered, thinking it might be Dad.

It wasn't.

"Merry Christmas," Robert said, sounding as shy as I'd ever heard him.

"Merry Christmas to you, too." I gave Mason and Will a bewildered look and shrug.

There was a long pause before he spoke again. "Just wanted to thank you again, I guess." He cleared his throat. "And I hope we can, I don't know, be friends or something."

"Friends?" My initial reaction was to laugh, but after thinking about it, I realized it might not be so far-fetched after all. "I think I might like that, Robert," I said. "As long as you can behave." I made sure my words were light, even if my meaning wasn't.

"I'll try." He laughed, then coughed as if his nerves really were getting to him. "I'll let you go. Trisha will be here any minute."

"Okay. Have a good Christmas."

"You, too." He hung up.

I shook my head and returned to the conversation. Will gave me a curious look, but I shook my head. I'd tell him later. I didn't want to confuse things by talking about Robert's strange behavior. I get that I saved him from prison, but he was acting awfully contrite, something I didn't think was possible with him.

"Did you hear the community theatre is closing down?" I asked, hoping it would keep them from asking about the call. I noticed a tray of Christmas cookies and snatched one.

"Vicki said something about that," Mason said. "She was pretty upset about it. I think she was planning on trying out for the next play." He went to the fridge and took out a carton. "Eggnog?"

I nodded. "Thank you."

"It's a shame," he said, removing three glasses from a cabinet and filling them. He handed one to Will, another to me. "I used to go there all the time when I was little."

"The place is falling apart," I said. "The guy who ran the place refused to pay for maintenance. The plays are almost always packed, yet they never seem to have any money. Apparently, after the play was canceled, someone came in and found some faulty wiring that had code enforcement up in arms." I had a feeling Lawrence had something to do with that.

"Not very good business practices," Will said.

"No, but it's going to work out." I took a sip of eggnog, followed by a bite of my cookie. Heaven. "Lawrence—the director of the Christmas play—is opening up his own theatre. It won't be ready for another year or two, but he's announced it to the public and everything is moving forward. He's invited the entire cast to be a part of his grand opening when it happens, and I'm sure if she's interested, Vicki could join as well."

"She'd like that." Mason leaned back against the counter, eyes drifting toward the stairs. "And there she is."

We all turned. Vicki was coming down the stairs wearing a red dress with a pair of candy canes crossed over her heart. On me, it would have looked corny. On her, it looked fabulous.

"You look great," I told her, hurrying over to give her a hug.

She carefully returned the gesture and beamed at me. "You do, too," she said, though I knew she was just being nice. Thanks to my recent beating, I was wearing a loose-fitting sweater with Rudolf prominently displayed on the chest. His nose used to light up if you pressed a button on the sleeve, but the battery had died years ago and I had never bothered to replace it.

"Dinner smells terrific," Will said, taking a deep breath. The room smelled of turkey and all the fixings. "You the cook?" he asked Vicki.

"Mason's handling dinner tonight," Vicki said with a grin. Her hands were behind her back and she went up onto her tiptoes as she said Mason's name, as if just speaking of him was enough to send her floating through the roof. "He gets all the credit."

Mason waved the compliment away and then moved to join Vicki. He put an arm around her waist and their eyes met.

Something passed between them, something I could feel in the air. It was like a zing of electricity, a spark that everyone wished they could have, but few rarely accomplished.

"Now that you're here," Vicki said, practically beaming, "we have something to say."

My eyes immediately dropped to her belly. It was as smooth and flat as ever, though it would be far too early for her to be showing anyway if she'd just found out.

She must have seen my eyes because she laughed. "No, I'm not pregnant." She looked at Mason again and then her hand came out from behind her back. It was adorned with the largest trio of diamonds I think I'd ever seen. "We're getting married!"

I hate to admit it, but both of us squealed like little girls and jumped around, arms clasped, for a few minutes, before gushing over the ring. Mason stood with Will during our display, looking embarrassed, but happy. Will, however, had one of those strange smiles you see when someone isn't quite sure how to act. He knew Mason and Vicki, of course, but hadn't been around either enough to really get to know them.

After we calmed down, congratulations went all around, and for a short time, everything seemed perfect. Dinner was served, gifts were exchanged. All in all, it was probably one of the best Christmases I'd ever had. My best friend was getting married!

"You know you'll have to be my maid of honor," Vicki said a short time later. "That is, if you want to be."

"Of course!" I said, touched, despite myself. This was the sort of thing we'd both dreamed about since we were interested in boys. Neither of us would have it any other way.

We hugged once more as Mason went to a cupboard, returning with a bottle and four glasses. "I think it's time we properly celebrate."

I grinned, accepting a glass. I couldn't agree more.

The holidays might have started out on an auspicious note, and I wasn't sure what the New Year would bring, but for now, life was exactly how I wanted it to be.

Please turn the page for an
exciting sneak peek of the next
Bookstore Café mystery

DEATH BY ESPRESSO

coming soon wherever print
and e-books are sold!

1

The Levington airport was a cacophony of sound, yet somehow, there were people sleeping in chairs as they awaited their flights. Seemingly unattended children screamed and pointed as planes took off and as others landed. A few cranky adults stood at counters, yelling at anyone in a nametag, demanding flight changes or upgrades. It was utter chaos.

I stayed out of the way, impatiently glancing at the large clock on the wall every couple of minutes. I wasn't big on crowds in the best of times, and today, I was not at my best. The last week had been a flurry of activity as I helped prep for my best friend, Vicki Patterson's, wedding to Mason Lawyer. The stress was really getting to me. I was the maid of honor, after all.

I should be home in Pine Hills even now. It wasn't necessary I meet anyone at the airport. The coming guests all had rental cars waiting for them, so my drive back home would be a lonely one. Still, there was something I wanted to do, and I'd much rather do it here than at home where everyone would be focused on the wedding.

Vicki would have come with me, but with the wedding and work, she was already feeling overwhelmed. And while I probably should have stayed with her to make sure she didn't pull her hair out, it was nice to get away from the madness for a little while.

Well, the wedding madness, anyway.

A kid shrieked by, arms flailing, as he ran toward an older couple who were waiting on him with dopey grins on their faces. A heavily burdened woman carrying both her luggage, as well as her son's, trailed after. She flashed me an apologetic smile before joining the happy reunion.

I watched them a moment longer before glancing at the clock yet again. I doubted my reunion would be full of shrieking and crying, but who knew?

A voice came over the loudspeaker then, announcing that the flight I'd been waiting on had arrived.

A rush of nervousness nearly had me sinking down into the nearest chair. My mouth was dry and my hands were shaking bad enough, I ended up clutching them behind my back so no one would see. I suddenly wished I would have taken more time to get ready. I'd settled on shorts and a nice blouse, going with my usual limited makeup. I was beginning to wonder if I should have gone with a skirt instead. Or maybe a dress. What if I gave everyone the wrong impression, that I didn't think them worthy of my time and effort?

A mental slap forced the thoughts from my head. I had a good reason to be nervous, but that was no excuse to start freaking out.

Tapping my foot, I waited, watching the gate. It seemed to take forever before the first passenger exited. And then it was another lifetime before the main reason for my coming appeared.

The man was bald, bearded, and looked much fitter than when I'd last seen him. His gut was gone, replaced by a flat stomach I hadn't seen in years. He was wearing glasses now, something I wasn't used to, and when he glanced my way, the eyes behind the lenses lit up.

"Krissy!" he called in his raspy voice, waving.

I waved back, unable to stop the grin from spreading across my face. "Dad!"

He took the hand of the woman next to him and I did a quick appraisal of her as he led her my way. She had a full head of ultra-curly brown hair that looked entirely natural. She was dressed casually, which I appreciated. She was younger than I'd expected, but not so much that I thought it strange she was dating my dad.

"Hi, Buttercup." Dad gave me a quick hug. "I want you to meet Laura Dresden. Laura, this is my daughter, Kristina."

"You can call me Krissy."

"Krissy," Laura beamed. "I've heard so much about you." She hesitated a moment before stepping forward for a quick, semi-uncomfortable hug.

We parted and I glanced at my dad, who had a goofy grin on his face. James Hancock had never been one to act the part of a lovesick teenager, at least not since I'd known him. By the time I came along, he and Mom were well into the comfortable years where that sort of thing was uncommon. It was odd to see him look so dopey. Honestly, it was kind of cute.

"Was Vicki able to make it?" Dad asked, glancing around as if looking for her. More people piled off the plane, filling up the too small space. The Levington airport wasn't all that big, so it didn't take much.

"She had some things to take care of." I looked past him. "Have you seen Gina and Frederick?" Vicki's parents were due on the same flight as Dad, but I'd been so wrapped up in meeting him and Laura, I hadn't been watching for them.

A look passed over Dad's face, causing me to grow nervous.

"They're coming, right?" I asked. It would be just like them to cancel at the last minute.

"They are," Dad assured me. "They're around here somewhere, but . . ." He trailed off and frowned.

It took me a moment of scanning the crowd before I saw Gina's blond curls. Frederick stood next to her, his hair dyed a dark brown. They were talking to a rather large group of people in a way that seemed awfully familiar considering they were supposed to have come alone.

Dad sighed when he followed my gaze and noticed them. "I told them they should call first."

"Who are they talking to?" I asked. I was expecting to greet four people, not a dozen.

"Friends of theirs, apparently. I think one of them might be family, but they weren't keen on introducing me." Dad put an arm around Laura's shoulder, seemed to remember I was standing there, and dropped it. He was acting as nervous as I'd been the first time I'd brought a boy home to meet my parents.

"Why are they here?" I wondered out loud. Vicki had been pretty adamant about having a small wedding. When I'd suggested she contact her entire family, as well as everyone she'd known when she'd lived in California, she'd balked.

"I hardly know anyone there anymore," she'd said.

"And I don't want to. I don't think I could handle all the drama."

And yet, here we were.

Gina happened to glance my way and her smile faltered. She nudged Frederick, who followed her gaze before closing his eyes, as if counting to ten, before he nodded. They said something to the group, and then headed over my way.

"Here we go," I muttered. Laura snorted a laugh, and I instantly liked her for it. If you knew anything about Gina and Frederick Patterson, you knew how difficult they could be.

I plastered on a smile, one I'd mastered while working in retail nearly all my life. I hoped it didn't look too fake, but I could already feel it start to falter.

"Kristina," Gina said, coming to a stop. She was dressed to kill, of course, head held high as if she expected everyone in the airport to worship her. She was still stunning, even at her age, and she knew it.

Unfortunately, her looks could only carry her so far. She was an actress who thought she deserved better roles than what she ever landed. If you'd seen her act, you'd understand why she never got anything more than a bit part.

Frederick was likewise handsome, though years of the good life had apparently started to play havoc with his figure. Like his wife, his acting skills weren't quite up to par, meaning he often played fourth of fifth fiddle to people who might not look as good as he did.

"Where's Vicki?" he asked. "I thought she'd be here."

"She was busy," I said, not wanting to tell them the real reason why she hadn't come. She didn't get along with her parents all that much, mostly because of how they treated her. She still loved them, of course, but she could only take so much. They thought she'd made the biggest mistake in the world by not following in their footsteps. I used to wonder if they might be right, but no longer. "She'll be waiting for us in Pine Hills."

"I see." The disapproval was heavy in Gina's voice. "Why are you here?"

My smile grew strained. "I thought I'd make sure everyone got here okay."

"Did you now?" Gina sniffed, sighed.

"I'll get our things," Laura said, clearly uncomfortable around the haughty actors.

"I'll come with you," Dad put in.

I gave him a betrayed look, to which he only smiled and winked. I couldn't believe he was going to leave me alone with these people. I often wondered if Gina and Frederick lived for insulting me. They rarely outright called me names, so that was a plus, I supposed. It was obvious they thought I was the reason their daughter had turned away from acting.

"Who are all those people?" I asked, nodding toward the men and women the Pattersons had been talking to.

"They're here for the wedding," Frederick said as if it was obvious. "Why else would they come to a place like this?" His nose crinkled as if the mere thought of flying all this way offended him. Neither he nor his wife had bothered to come to Pine Hills before, not even in support of their daughter, let alone Levington.

"Vicki wanted to keep the wedding small," I said, knowing it was no use to point it out, but feeling the need to say it anyway.

Gina sniffed. She did that a lot when talking to people she felt beneath her, which was to say, to nearly everyone. "She clearly forgot a few invitations. She would never have left such important people out."

I wondered. I'd lived in California with Vicki and I didn't know any of these people. If they were so important, especially to the family, then I was pretty sure I would have met one of them during one of the many parties the couple would throw celebrating themselves and their movies. I didn't recognize a single face, not even a little.

A woman approached the group as I watched. Two of the group, a man and woman, turned away and acted as if they didn't see her. She didn't seem to mind, choosing instead to approach one of the men, who pointed toward Gina. The woman nodded and then hurried over to where we stood with a decided bounce in her step.

"There you are," Gina said, giving the woman a brief hug. "I can't believe they put you in coach. We missed you in first class."

The woman reached into a bag she was holding and popped a chocolate ball into her mouth. She chewed a moment before answering. "It was uncomfortable, but I managed." She spoke in a hurried tone, as if she was afraid someone would cut her off before she finished. She was a tall woman, makeup dark and severe, as was her short haircut.

"Still, you should complain," Gina said. "Just because they lost your information, doesn't mean you should be punished."

"I'd sue," Frederick added.

"It's no bother." The woman waved her hand dismissively. "I'll be sure to file a complaint and make sure they understand I'll accept no further screwups lest I stop flying with them." She glanced around the airport. "Awfully small, isn't it?"

"It's no wonder," Gina said. "Can you imagine trying to live out here? I looked out the window on the way in and thought we'd somehow been transported to a Third World country!"

"Or somewhere in Idaho," Frederick said with a superior smile.

"And this town, Pine Hilltop, it's supposed to be smaller?"

"Pine Hills," I said, drawing all their eyes. I think they'd forgotten about me.

"And you are?" the woman asked, clearly miffed at being interrupted.

"Krissy Hancock," I said. "Vicki's best friend."

"Oh." She glanced at Gina as if for confirmation.

I could almost see the "unfortunately" in her nod.

I waited for someone to introduce the woman, but it didn't appear as if either of the Pattersons were willing, so I asked her myself. "You are . . . ?"

The woman popped a few more chocolates into her mouth. She shifted the bag and I noted she was eating chocolate covered espresso beans. My mouth watered.

"Cathy Carr." She said it like she couldn't believe I didn't know her by sight alone.

Having never heard her name before, I looked to Gina.

She heaved a put-upon sigh. "You don't know Cathy Carr, do you?"

I shrugged, feeling stupid. The Pattersons had a way of doing that to me.

"She's only the most important wedding planner in all of the United States," Gina said.

"The world, actually," Cathy said.

"Some call her the planner to the stars," Frederick added.

"Okay," I said, drawing out the word as I looked from one to the other. "So, why is she here?"

The Pattersons shared a look. It was Cathy who answered.

"I'm a wedding planner." She spoke like she was talking to someone who was hard of hearing. "I'm here to plan the wedding."

I looked to Gina. "But Vicki's wedding is already planned."

Gina flashed me a smile. "She doesn't have a Cathy Carr planned wedding, now does she?"

"Well, no." And as far as I knew, she didn't want one.

"Of course she doesn't," Gina said, throwing her hands in the air. "That's why we brought her along."

"Vicki deserves the best," Frederick said. "Cathy will look over what Vicki has planned already and improve upon it. It's our gift to her."

Another couple of chocolate covered beans entered Cathy's mouth as she looked around the airport. "Is there a coffee shop around here somewhere?" she asked. "I desperately need a triple shot after that flight."

"I don't readily know," Gina said, before turning to me. "Kristina?"

"Over there." I pointed. "Take a left. You can't miss it."

Cathy nodded and hurried away, long legs flashing as she just about ran for the coffee. I was someone who loved her coffee, yet it appeared Cathy Carr had my addiction beat.

"Okay, Buttercup," Dad said, rejoining us. "We have

our bags and nothing is lost." He held up a pair of suitcases as if in victory. Laura had a bag of her own.

"Perfect," I said, turning to the Pattersons. "Does everyone have everything?"

Gina smiled. "Of course we do."

"Then we should probably get going. The drive isn't too long, but it's quiet. It's mostly trees and farms."

Frederick looked appalled, while Gina visibly cringed.

"Does everyone know the way?" I asked, not wanting to lose someone along the way, though I doubted Vicki would mind if a few of the uninvited guests were to find somewhere else to be.

"We have GPS," Gina said. She looked to her husband and I quite clearly saw her roll her eyes.

Keeping my smile firmly in place, I went on. "Vicki will be waiting for us at Death by Coffee. Once we're in Pine Hills, we'll meet there." I was about to ask if they needed an address, but realized I'd only get a snooty response. I did feel the need to ask, "Does everyone have a ride?"

Gina only sighed and walked back to her group. Frederick hesitated and said, "We all have rentals." He didn't smile, but at least it came out somewhat civil. Of the two, I'd always liked him the best.

"Good. I'll see you in Pine Hills."

He nodded, and then went to join his wife. Cathy Carr appeared a moment later, carrying a large coffee, likely her triple shot espresso. She was still chewing away on the chocolate covered espresso beans.

It'll be a wonder if she doesn't explode before we get there. I loved caffeine, but this was ridiculous.

"Are you going to be okay driving alone?" Dad asked as we started for the rental car park.

"I'll be fine," I said. "I could use the time to figure out how I'm going to tell Vicki about all of them." I nodded back toward the group who were just now starting to head for their cars.

He laughed. "I'm sure you'll figure it out." He paused, glancing back at Laura, who was walking a few feet behind us as if not wanting to interrupt father and daughter time. "I hope you like her," he said, keeping his voice down.

"I'm sure I will," I said, and I meant it. We hadn't had chance to talk all that much as of yet, but from what I'd seen of her so far, I had a feeling we were going to get along just fine.

Dad put an arm around me and squeezed. "This is going to be a great week." He breathed in deep, let it out in a happy sigh, and then released me. He held out a hand and Laura stepped forward to take it.

As I watched them walk together, I realized that despite the strain the Pattersons were putting on their daughter by bringing so many extras, it would all work out in the end. Happiness was contagious, and Dad and Laura were the epitome of happiness. Nothing could ruin Vicki's wedding, not even a gaggle of annoying actors and actresses.

I would stop anyone who tried.